16

WELCOME TO NOWHERE

*Books by Elizabeth Laird published
by Macmillan Children's Books*

Welcome to Nowhere
Dindy and the Elephant
The Fastest Boy in the World
The Prince Who Walked with Lions
The Witching Hour
Lost Riders
Crusade
Oranges in No Man's Land
Paradise End
Secrets of the Fearless
A Little Piece of Ground
The Garbage King
Jake's Tower
Red Sky in the Morning
Kiss the Dust

WELCOME TO NOWHERE

ELIZABETH LAIRD

ILLUSTRATED BY LUCY ELDRIDGE

MACMILLAN CHILDREN'S BOOKS

First published 2017 by Macmillan Children's Books
an imprint of Pan Macmillan
20 New Wharf Road, London N1 9RR
Associated companies throughout the world
www.panmacmillan.com

ISBN 978-1-5098-4049-6

Text copyright © Elizabeth Laird 2017
Illustrations copyright © Lucy Eldridge 2017

The right of Elizabeth Laird and Lucy Eldridge to be identified as the
author and illustrator of this work has been asserted by them
in accordance with the Copyright, Designs and Patents Act 1988.

1 3 5 7 9 8 6 4 2

A CIP catalogue record for this book is available from
the British Library.

Printed and bound by CPI Group (UK) Ltd, Croydon CR0 4YY

*For my grandsons: Fergus,
Ilias, George and Iskander*

Georgia

Armenia

Turkey

Iran

Cyprus

Syria

Lebanon

Daraa

Iraq

Israel and Palestine

Jordan

Saudi Arabia

Kuwait

FOREWORD

The civil war in Syria, which has brought destruction to all parts of that ancient and beautiful country, began in March 2011, when a few schoolboys in the southern city of Daraa wrote a slogan on the wall of their school. It read: *The people want the regime to change.*

The authorities were nervous because of the revolutions which had taken place in other parts of the Middle East, and they reacted with extreme severity. The boys were arrested and tortured in prison. This harsh response enraged many people, who were already angry with their brutal government. They went on marches and demonstrations. The government responded with bullets and arrests. People began to die. Trouble spread to other cities and soon the whole country was engulfed in a civil war.

One of the results of the unrest was the rise of a new movement inspired by an extreme and fanatical version of Islam. Known as ISIS in the West, and Daesh in the Middle East, the fighters of ISIS conquered parts of northern Syria and Iraq and have encouraged and inspired acts of terrorism all over the world.

ISIS did not appear on the scene in Syria until after the events described in *Welcome to Nowhere*, and their cruel ideology would have appalled Musa, Omar and their friends in this book.

Another result of the turmoil in Syria has been that millions of people have been forced to leave their homes. Half the entire population of Syria has had to find shelter in other parts of their homeland, or outside Syria in neighbouring countries. In Jordan, for example, one in six of its population is now a refugee from Syria.

Some people have undertaken the long and dangerous journey to find peace and safety in Europe. Some have been successful and are now trying to make better lives for their families and children. Others have sadly died on the way, or have been turned back by increasingly anxious European countries.

Two generations ago, by the end of the Second World War, countless millions of Europeans had been forced to flee from their homes. We honour the memory of those who helped them to escape from the misery of war and settle in new places. How will history view us, and our treatment of today's refugees?

Elizabeth Laird

PART ONE

PART ONE

CHAPTER ONE

My hometown is a brilliant place. *Was* a brilliant place, I suppose I ought to say. It's called Bosra and it's in Syria. It's not too big, so you can't get lost, and in the middle of the town there's a huge tumbledown city of Roman ruins – whole streets, temples, a theatre, you name it. Tourists used to come from all over the world to see Bosra. Personally, if I'd had all their money, I'd have gone somewhere cool, like Dubai, or New York, or London, but then I'm not that crazy about history.

Looking back now, those days in Bosra seem like a sort of dream. Everything was ordinary and peaceful. My father worked in the tourism office (a sort of government job) and Ma did everything at home. What with school and my two jobs, I was busy all day long, running to keep up.

My early job (five to seven in the morning) was in Uncle Ali's hardware store. Baba, my father made me do that one. Then there was school till 1 p.m., home to gobble down my lunch, and I was off to work at the ruins with my cousin Rasoul.

Being with Rasoul was the best part of the day. He had a shop selling souvenirs right beside the old Roman theatre. Rasoul was the most amazing person in the world to me. He was twenty years old, funny, handsome, knew everything about sport, had the latest stuff – he was the person I wanted to be when I grew up.

My job was to try to get the tourists to choose our shop instead of one of the others that lined the route to the ruins. Tourists notice kids more than grown-ups, so it made good sense. And I was brilliant at selling. I'd got this excellent technique.

'Antiques, nice and cheap! Lovely rugs, in a heap!' I'd chant in English, doing a sort of hopping dance. 'Camel bells, No bad smells! Come and see! Buy from me!'

That was just about all I could say in English, except for 'Hello, what is your name?' and 'My name is Omar', which we'd learned in school. A young man with long blond hair had made up my rhyme for me. I think he was American. He'd spent a whole afternoon sitting in front of Rasoul's shop, watching me trying to get the tourists to come in, and then he'd scribbled down the rhyme and taught me to say it. The tourists always looked round and smiled at me when they heard it, and some of them did actually come and buy things.

Rasoul was proud of me for being such a good salesman and he got me on to selling postcards. He gave them to me for 20 cents a strip. Each strip had ten cards that you could drop open dramatically in front of the tourists' eyes. He let me keep nearly all the profits too, and I was building up a secret hoard in a plastic bag stuffed under my mattress.

When there were no tourists around, and Rasoul was busy chatting to the other souvenir sellers, I used to lose myself in my favourite daydream. One day, when the stash of postcard money under my mattress was big enough, I'd buy a donkey and rent it out to the guys who gave rides to the tourists. With the money I'd get another, and then another, till I had a whole string of hee-hawing trotters. With all the money I'd make, I'd get my own shop. It would be even better than Rasoul's. I'd arrange everything in a really interesting way and put up notices in English. My sister Eman would tell me what to write. She loved school, and was brilliant at English. Soon I'd be so rich I'd buy a car, a big white one with darkened windows, and I'd get a gold necklace for Ma, who'd start loving me more than my annoying brother Musa. Then . . .

But what's the point of going on about those old dreams? How could I know what was going to happen? Nobody saw the disaster coming, especially not me. I wasn't quite thirteen, after all.

I can remember the day when I realized that everything was going to change. My dad shook me awake as usual just after half past four in the morning.

'Going to lie there all day, are you? Come on, Omar. Get up.'

It was dark, of course, but a shaft of light shone out from the kitchen across the corridor and I could see Ma standing by the stove, heating water for tea, with steam coiling round her head.

'You push him too hard,' she called out to my father. 'Let him get his rest. He ought to be fresh and ready for school, not going out to work at this time of day.'

'School!' scoffed Baba. 'Have you seen his latest marks? He's lazy. He should learn to work, pay his own way, like I did at his age.' Then he went into the kitchen for his tea.

A cough came from the bed opposite mine. My older brother Musa was awake. I could see his open eyes glittering in the dim light.

'It's all very well for you,' I said nastily, making a face at him. 'Lazybones. You haven't got to do slave labour in what is practically the middle of the night. Stay there all day. Go on. Enjoy yourself.'

And then I felt bad because Musa would have had to come with me if he'd been able to. He's got cerebral palsy and he can only walk slowly. His hands jerk about too. To show that I was a bit sorry I shot a sort of play-kick at him. He aimed a feeble punch at me but missed, as I knew he would. He can't control his muscles at all first thing in the morning.

'Nearly had me there,' I said.

He grunted as if I'd annoyed him.

What's the matter with you? I thought. *I was only trying to be kind.*

I'd got one arm in the sleeve of my school shirt and was struggling to pull it down over my head (I'd grown out of it really and the sleeves were too tight) when I thought I heard Ma say, 'When are you going to tell the children?'

And Baba answered, 'In my own good time. No need to rush things.'

I yanked hard, got my head through, and looked at Musa. He was struggling to sit up.

'Did you hear that?' I whispered. 'Tell the children what?'

'I don't know,' he croaked. 'You'd better go. I'll get it out of Ma. Tell you later.'

At least, I think that's what he said. Musa doesn't speak clearly. He sounds as if his tongue is too big or something. I'm used to it but even I don't always understand him first time. I hesitated but I knew Musa was right. He can get Ma to tell him anything. He's her favourite out of all of us. I really mind about that sometimes, especially when he's in one of his mean moods.

Anyway, I put it out of my mind, ran into the kitchen, grabbed the flap of bread and lump of cheese that my sister Eman was holding out to me (she's three years older than me, and one and a half years older than Musa) and was halfway out of the door when she screeched, 'Come back here and comb your hair! Do you want everyone to think you're a homeless tramp?'

I made a face at her, muttered something rude about bossy sisters, ran my hand over my hair to smooth it down, and was out of the flat at last. It was already after five and I'd have to run all the way to Uncle Ali's hardware shop. It was February and freezing cold, with ice frosting up the car windscreens, but at least the run would warm me up.

Uncle Ali was old and grouchy but I liked him, even though I hated getting up so early to work in his shop. He always had a glass of hot tea ready for me when I arrived. We didn't say much to each other first thing, because I knew what to do anyway. The stands had to be wheeled out on to the pavement, then the shop had to be swept out, and all the pots and pans and plastic bowls arranged outside. He paid my wages directly to Baba, but he sometimes gave me extra tips. He didn't tell Baba about those, and neither did I.

That day Uncle Ali was grumpier than usual. He was always crusty on top, but I knew he had a soft heart, and that he actually liked me a lot, so I didn't mind his sharpness. That morning, though, I couldn't do anything right.

'Mind what you're doing!' he snapped, as I accidentally bashed the side of the stand against the door frame. 'Do you want to ruin me? Is that it?'

Then, when I started sweeping out the shop, he barked,

'Careful! You're raising the dust! You'll get everything filthy!' And he grabbed the broom from my hands and began to swish it about so violently that he raised billows of dust himself.

I didn't know what to do next, so I went outside to brush down the stands, and nearly bumped into the nosy man who owned the electrical goods shop further along the street. He started when he saw me, then he pushed me out of the way, went to the door of our shop and called out, 'Are you there, Uncle?' (Everyone calls Uncle Ali 'Uncle' for some reason.) 'How's your family? Is everyone well?'

Uncle Ali took his time answering.

'Yes, thank God,' he said at last, then slowly came out of the shop.

'You can't take anything for granted.' Mr Nosy's sharp eyes were darting round the shop, as if he was looking for someone. 'There's trouble everywhere. Tunisia, Egypt – terrorists trying to stir things up. At least we have a strong government in Syria. Law and order's what we need. Round up the troublemakers and shoot them, that's what I say.'

'If you say so,' said Uncle Ali distantly.

Mr Nosy took a step towards him.

'Your son's at university, isn't he?' His eyes had settled on the door at the back of the shop, as if he suspected that Uncle Ali's son might be hiding behind it.

He waited, but Uncle Ali only nodded.

'I hear he's been hanging around with the wrong sort.' Mr Nosy's voice had hardened. 'You'd better warn him, Uncle. Tell him to steer clear of politics. Young hotheads. They need to be taught a lesson.' He stared at Uncle Ali for a long moment, then swivelled round to look at me. There was something in his look that made me shiver.

'Omar helps me out in the mornings before school,' Uncle Ali said hastily. 'In fact, it's time he got going. Where's your school bag, Omar? Go on. Off you go. Don't want to be late, do you?'

My mouth fell open. It was much too early to leave. I went to pick up my bag, but before I could fish it out from where I'd left it behind the counter, someone out in the street called to Mr Nosy, and he hurried off without a backwards glance.

A grey look had come over Uncle Ali's face and I saw that his hands were trembling.

'Are you all right, Uncle?' I asked. 'Do you want me to get you some tea or something?'

He shook his head.

'I'm all right, son. Got a word of advice for you, though. Keep away from people like him. And never talk about politics at all, to anyone. *Ever.*'

I nodded. I was bored with being told, quite honestly. Baba was always droning on about it.

Don't get involved in things you don't understand, he'd say to us kids, over and over again. *Keep your thoughts to yourself. If you get reported for saying the wrong thing, you'll get all of us into trouble. There are government informers everywhere, and you can't tell who they are. You don't want to end up in prison, do you? You don't want me to lose my job? Then keep your mouths shut.*

I stood there uncertainly. I wasn't sure what to do.

'Shall I go back to work now, Uncle Ali?' I asked. 'You didn't mean it, about going to school, did you? I haven't finished the stands yet.'

'Yes, yes, off you go,' he said. 'I'm shutting the shop anyway. I'll go out of town for a bit. Visit my daughter in her village. Everything will turn out all right, *inshallah*.'

He reached into his pocket, pulled out some notes and stuffed them into my hands.

'You're a good boy, Omar. You've earned this. I've got another bit of advice for you too. Work hard at school. Get a qualification. Doesn't matter what it is. Bad times may be coming to Syria. You'll need all the opportunities you can get.'

I didn't like to count the money right there in front of him, but I could tell it was a lot. I just took it, mumbled some words of thanks, and left. I wish I'd said goodbye to him properly. I didn't know, of course, that I'd never see Uncle Ali again.

CHAPTER TWO

It wasn't far to my school from Uncle Ali's shop, and I was early for once, so I didn't have to hurry. I hated school. I was useless at all the lessons. None of them would help me become the big-shot businessman I was going to be.

What made things worse was that both Eman and Musa were brilliant. Eman was the teacher's pet at her girls' school, her books neat and tidy, getting top marks for everything. She wanted to be a teacher. Baba frowned when she said that, but Ma gave her encouraging smiles behind his back. She'd wanted to be a teacher herself when she was young, but her dad had married her off to Baba when she was fifteen, so she didn't have the chance.

Musa and I went to the boys' school. The teachers had written him off for years and said he was stupid. They never even tried to understand what he said, so after a while he just gave up talking. It was true that his handwriting was rubbish, because he couldn't stop his hands jerking, but that didn't mean he couldn't learn anything.

If I'd been laughed at and bullied as much as Musa had always been, I think I'd have given up going to school altogether, but Musa had guts. He stuck with school – bruises, torn-up notebooks, insults and all. By the time he was twelve, he'd earned a sort of grudging respect and most of the school bullies left him alone.

He had a lucky break in seventh grade. His teacher, Mr Ibrahim, wasn't like the others. He discovered what our family had known all along: Musa was a total brainbox. He could do difficult equations in his head as easily as blinking. He actually liked reading books, too, which was more than anyone else I knew. If you could be bothered to sit and listen to Musa's mangled-up speech, he could tell you the most amazing things about whales, human DNA, the Ottoman Empire, snakes and the atmosphere of the planet Jupiter. Once Mr Ibrahim had cracked Musa's code, he became a bit of a legend. He made a couple of friends, too. They were real geeks, quite frankly. The three of them went around together talking non-stop about no one knew what. It was social death to be seen around Musa's nerdy friends, so no one went near them.

It was annoying being a couple of years behind Musa at school because everyone expected me to be a genius, too. It was Musa who helped me out, actually. In the evenings when he could be bothered, he'd more or less dictate my homework to me. He only did it to feel superior for once. And he owed it to me, I reckoned, because of all the times I'd had to haul the bullies off him (though, if I'm honest, I had sometimes sneaked off in the opposite direction when I'd seen trouble looming).

While I'm going on about my family, I might as well mention the little ones. There was a big gap between them and me. My little brother Fuad was only five, and was quite irritating most of the time. Nadia was just one and a half so she was only a baby. She was sweet, and I really liked picking her up and playing with her.

That day at school was just as useless as any other and when it was over at last I waited for Musa by the gates. He always went boringly slowly, and I sometimes got impatient and dashed on ahead, but today I wanted to talk to him, so I didn't mind.

'Go on, then,' I said, as soon as we were on the road. 'Did you get Ma to tell you what this great secret is?'

'Yes.'

He shifted his school bag from one shoulder to the other, and didn't say anything more.

'Well then?'

'You're not going to like it, Omar.'

He loved spinning things out. He did it deliberately, just to drive me crazy.

I gave him a whack with my school bag, then had to grab his shoulder to pull him upright again as I'd nearly overbalanced him.

'Don't *do* that!' he said indignantly. 'I won't tell you now.'

But I could see that he was dying to. I swallowed my irritation.

'I'll carry your bag if you'll tell me,' I said, offering him a way out.

He passed it over. It was full of books, and was much heavier than mine.

'First you've got to swear that you won't let on,' he said. 'Ma said I wasn't to tell anyone.'

'I swear.'

'No. You've got to *mean* it.'

'I *swear*! What do you want me to do? Get down and grovel?'

'OK, then. Here it is. We're moving to Daraa. Baba's been transferred to the Ministry of Agriculture. Now, what do you think of that?'

I stopped dead, right there, in the middle of the road. The shock had sent tingles all the way through me.

'You're joking, Musa. You've got to be.'

'I said you wouldn't like it. We're going to live with Granny.'

'What? We can't. Auntie Majda lives there. With Uncle Feisal and all their kids.'

'They're moving out. Come on, Omar. You can't just stand there, blocking up the street all day.'

Somehow I got my legs moving again.

'Does Eman know?'

'I expect so. Ma tells her everything.'

'I suppose Fuad and baby Nadia and half the street know as well. Everyone except me.'

'Don't be like that. I only found out because you overheard Baba and got me to ask Ma, remember?'

'She'd have told you anyway,' I said bitterly.

Musa was walking faster than me for once. I actually had to catch up with him.

'When's all this going to happen?'

'End of the month.'

'What? But that's only four – no, three weeks away! It's practically tomorrow! What about my job with Rasoul, and my postcards?'

'Who cares about your postcards?' It was Musa's turn to sound jealous. 'You told me yourself, the tourists have nearly stopped coming anyway. "Middle" and "East" are dirty words as far as they're concerned.'

I bit my lip. I had to agree that he was right. The tourists were staying away because they were scared. I hadn't sold a single strip of cards for weeks.

I walked on in silence, trying to take in the news. Musa's feelings must have been boiling around too, because he burst out at last, 'It's all very well for you! What about me? It'll start all over again. "Thicko, dumbhead, cripple. Take that plum out of your mouth, Musa boy! Go on, Musa, run! Hey, guys, look at that! Freak show, freak show!" And the beatings. Remember that time they broke my arm? You and your postcards!'

He stopped, and I could tell he was choked up.

'Sorry,' I mumbled. 'I wasn't thinking.'

'And that's just the kids! The teachers will be worse. They'll ignore me, call me stupid, ask Baba if I can count up to ten, make me sit with the babies . . .'

He couldn't go on.

'I'll stick up for you,' I said, sounding lame even to myself. 'I promise. I won't let anyone—'

'Yeah. Thanks,' Musa interrupted. 'Like it's cool getting your little brother to fight your battles for you.'

We'd almost reached home.

'Take my bag in for me,' I said, thrusting it at him. 'I don't want to face them yet.' And I sprinted off towards the Roman theatre, desperate to see Rasoul, desperate to keep my dreams alive.

On ordinary days, the old city of Bosra was busy. There'd be coaches coming in full of tourists. The drivers would drop them off in the car park, and then everyone would head off into the ruins. There wasn't much point trying to sell things to people when they first arrived. It was after they'd tired themselves out wandering for miles up and down the dusty old streets and taking millions of photographs of each other in the theatre, that they might be up for buying things.

There was a nice, shady place with chairs under trees and stalls selling cold drinks, and that was where Rasoul had his souvenir shop. His wasn't the only one. There was a whole cluster of them. They looked pretty, with displays of rugs and painted china, strings of camel bells, old brass trays and woven scarves and bags.

That day, though, things were even quieter than usual. There wasn't even a single car in the car park. Half the stalls were closed, and the drinks place was shut up. The few shopkeepers who had opened were clustered round Rasoul, whose mobile phone was clamped to his ear. He was listening to something intently and repeating what he was hearing to the others. I could tell by the way they were standing that the news was bad.

'Egypt,' I heard him say. '*Wallah!* Demonstrators shot? That's bad.'

One man's shoulders were all hunched up. Another was half turned away, as if he didn't want to look anyone in the eye.

Even the postcard boys looked subdued. Usually, when no tourists were around, they set up targets and threw stones at them until the adults yelled at them for chipping bits off the Roman columns. Now they were looking from one serious face to another, trying to understand what was going on.

Rasoul nodded to me to come over. He finished his call and slid his phone into his pocket.

'Tunisia, Egypt, Libya – trouble blowing up everywhere.'

'It won't happen here,' one of the men said. 'This government . . .' He looked quickly round at the group and went quiet, as if he was afraid he'd said too much. One by one the men mumbled goodbye, and a little later, all you could hear was the rattle of metal shutters coming down.

Rasoul went to the back of his own shop and started rooting through the drawer where he kept papers and money. I followed him inside.

'*Tell* me,' I begged. 'What's happening?'

Rasoul looked grim.

'Bad stuff, little cousin. All over the Middle East.' He dropped his voice. 'Security here's tight, but people are angry.' He put his finger to his lips. 'Pretend I didn't say that. You don't want to get me into trouble.'

'Baba says our government's really strong,' I said, trying to think of something comforting to say. 'He says they won't allow any nonsense from troublemakers here.'

Rasoul scowled.

'Your baba . . .' He stopped.

'What?'

'Let's just say that we don't agree on politics. He *works* for the government, after all.'

'Not really. It's just the tourist office.'

I was just about to blurt out that Baba had accepted another job in Daraa when I remembered my promise to Musa.

'The tourist office *is* government,' said Rasoul. 'Anyway, he's going to be with the Ministry of

Agriculture in Daraa soon.'

I stared at him, a red tide of anger threatening to swamp me.

'Everyone – *everyone* – knew about it before I did! I only found out just now, from Musa. It's so unfair. It's—'

Rasoul laughed. 'Don't be like that. You look like an indignant little rooster. All red and furious.'

Being laughed at, especially by my hero, was the final straw. Tears spurted into my eyes.

'Sorry, *habibi*. Look, I didn't mean to laugh at you. I know because your dad asked me to sound out someone I know in the Ministry of Agriculture. He wanted to know if it was a good place to work. I was honest with him. I said he'd make more money, but everyone hates government people in Daraa, and he'd be very unpopular. He wouldn't listen to me. I expect he didn't tell you because he didn't want to upset you too soon.'

I swallowed.

'It's all right,' I managed to say. 'It's just that I want to stay here, and . . . and work with you, selling cards and stuff.'

'You wouldn't be able to do that, anyway.' Rasoul was rifling through his drawer again. He pulled out a business card, looked at it, and put it into his pocket. 'I'm clearing out myself. Tourism's finished here. Look around you. See any buses? Chinese tour groups? German families? Not even a scruffy backpacker.' He dropped his voice. 'There's so much corruption in this country, repression, arrests – people are getting tired of it. Especially in Daraa. That's where the trouble will start. It'll be nasty, too. Anyway, I don't want any part of it. You can't run a decent business in this country. I'm getting out.'

I felt another flush of anger.

'So it's a great idea, isn't it, to move us all to Daraa, into a lot of nasty trouble.'

'You'll be all right,' he said breezily. 'Just don't—'

'I know, I know,' I interrupted him. '*Don't talk about politics, keep your thoughts to yourself*, blah, blah, blah.'

I followed him out of the shop and waited while he pulled his own metal shutter down.

'I'll walk home with you,' he said. 'I'm going that way.'

'What are you going to do, Rasoul?' I asked him. He was walking so fast I had to almost run to keep up.

'I'm getting out,' he replied quietly.

'What do you mean?' A horrible anxiety was gripping me.

He slipped his hand inside his leather jacket and pulled out the business card he'd fished out of his drawer.

'This is the passport to my future, Omar.'

'That's not a passport. I know what a passport looks like.'

He gave my arm a playful whack. 'The man whose name is on this card is going to take me to my future,' he said grandly. 'I'm heading to Germany. Or Sweden. Or England.'

'But it's dangerous!' I said anxiously. 'I've heard about those traffickers. They let you suffocate in the backs of lorries, and you get drowned in the sea, and—'

'Nah,' he said. 'This guy knows lots of ways. He's expensive, but it'll be worth it.'

There was a lump in my throat and I had to swallow hard again before I could speak.

'What are you going to do in Europe?'

'Work hard. Save money. Open my own shop. In a year or two, I'll send for you. We'll go into business together.'

I felt as if the sun had come out after a freezing shower of rain.

'Do you mean that, Rasoul?'

'Course I do. You're a natural salesman. We'll make a fortune together. Hey, *habibi*, no tears! I'm not saying goodbye just yet. It'll be weeks before I'm ready to go. I'll come and see you all before you leave for Daraa.'

CHAPTER THREE

There's this weird thing about my family. We're always in the wrong place at the wrong time. If a meteor was about to fall out of the sky, guess who'd be standing right where it landed? Yup. Me and my dad and mum and brothers and sisters. That being a scientific certainty, I suppose it wasn't surprising that we moved to Daraa exactly at the moment when the trouble started.

We'd had our last day at the Bosra school. I was glad to see the back of it but I thought Musa was going to cry as we went out through the school gates. I was all set to walk home with him, even though it always took ages, but his two nerd friends caught up with him.

'I'll see you at home,' I said with relief. He didn't bother to answer.

I'd only gone a few steps when I heard Musa almost shout, '*What?* Are they *crazy*? Spraying slogans on the school walls? That's – that's awesome!'

I stopped and bent down, pretending to retie my shoelace so I could listen.

'Shut up, you idiot,' one of the nerds said, looking round nervously. 'It's dangerous even to talk about it.'

My ears were practically waggling off my head as I strained to hear.

'They're fifteen. Same age as us,' the other nerd said. 'They even wrote their names up on the walls. Practically suicidal.'

I stood up and walked on slowly, careful to keep within earshot.

'They've tortured the first one they caught,' the other boy said. 'And he's given away the others.'

I shivered. What would I do if I was tortured? I tell myself that I'd be brave and not betray anyone, but I know I wouldn't. Not really. The first fingernail they pulled out would have me screaming for mercy.

I wanted to turn round and call back, 'What did they write that was so bad?'

Luckily Musa asked the question for me.

'*The people want the regime to change,*' one of the boys answered. '*Your turn is coming. Leave.*'

Spraying political slogans on walls might not seem very bad to many people, and I now know that in most countries in the world you can't get arrested, tortured and actually executed for doing things like that, but in Syria you only had to *think* about criticizing the government and you were risking your life. I shivered, remembering the grey look on Uncle Ali's face when Mr Nosy had dropped a tiny hint about his son. It had been enough to send him running out of town.

What I'd overheard was enough for me, too. I took off as if a tiger was after me, and ran home.

It wasn't really home any more. Ma and Baba had been packing, half the furniture had disappeared, and everything was in a mess. There was a row going on, too.

Before all this upset, Ma had always been ready with snacks and questions when we'd got back from school, but the thought of going to live with Granny had made her so miserable that she'd stopped noticing us at all. Up till now, she'd just been going round muttering furiously under her breath, but today she'd given way to tears. She'd collapsed on one of the cushions that lined the walls of the living room and was rocking backwards and forwards, wiping her eyes with the ends of her headscarf. Baba was watching her anxiously. He hated it when she cried.

'Don't, *habibti*,' he was saying in a soft voice. 'You'll like it in Daraa. Think of all the shops! And my mother's flat is such a big one. Three bedrooms! The schools for the boys are better too. You want them to have a good education, don't you? Then we must take this chance.'

Ma stopped crying. She took the shawl away from her face and I saw a flash of fear in her eyes.

'The "schools for the boys"?' she said anxiously. 'You did mean a school for Eman too, didn't you? She's so clever and she works so hard. Please, Hamid.'

Baba's lips tightened.

'Education's a waste of time for girls. Eman's sixteen already. It's high time she was married. I've had a very good offer . . .'

Ma gasped.

'Marriage! Not yet! You know how much she wants—'

'She'll do what she's told,' Baba said, in the kind of voice that none of us usually dared to contradict.

Angry red spots appeared on Ma's cheeks. She took a deep breath.

'If you insist on taking her out of school, I – I won't go to Daraa. You can go with the boys, and Nadia and Eman can stay here with me.'

'Don't be ridiculous,' snorted Baba. 'I've given up the lease on the flat. You can't possibly stay here.'

Neither of them had noticed me. I watched from the sitting-room door, cheering Ma on as she got to her feet.

'We'll have to take the lease on again then. I mean this, Hamid. I won't care about the scandal.' She took a deep breath. 'Eman's education is my condition for moving to Daraa.'

I was holding my breath, stunned at Ma's courage. I'd never heard her defy Baba before.

If she stays here with the girls, perhaps I can stay here too, I thought, with a rush of hope.

There was a short silence. I thought Baba would explode, but all he said was, 'Well, Leila, if you feel like that about it, I suppose you can have your way. But if Eman steps out of line once . . .'

'She won't!' Ma's voice had softened. 'You know our daughter, Hamid. She's the best girl in Bosra. We're proud of her, aren't we?'

Then I noticed that Eman was standing, rigid with tension, in the shadowy doorway to the kitchen. She was twirling around noiselessly, silently clapping her hands above her head. I watched her curiously, as if I was seeing my sister for the first time. I'd always been jealous of how well she did at school, and resentful of the way she could do no wrong with Ma. Now, for the first time, I saw that things weren't easy for Eman. I felt a rush of affection for her.

I walked round behind my parents and went into the kitchen.

'Hey, Eman,' I said quietly. 'I heard that too.'

She shut the kitchen door, covering her mouth to stop the noise of her delighted laughter. I didn't quite know what to say.

'Good for you,' I managed to bring out at last. My voice sounded gruff and deep, the way it had been doing recently, and I coughed to cover it up. We heard movements in the living room. Baba was letting himself out into the street, with Ma close behind him.

Eman took my arm and shook it. We could talk normally now.

'Omar, you've no idea,' she said. 'I've been so afraid.'

'Afraid? Why?'

She opened her eyes at me.

'Of being married off to some nasty old man! You can imagine the kind of husband Baba would pick for me. A horrible old dictator like him. No more school! No more future! Just babies and cooking.'

'But you like babies.'

'Yes, but I don't want my own. Not yet. I want to *do* something, Omar! I want to be a teacher! Have my own life!'

I felt a rush of fellow feeling.

'I know what you mean. I do, too,' I said. I'd never felt the urge to confide in Eman before, but before I could think about it, the words came out in a rush. 'I'm going to be a businessman, like Rasoul. You know he's going to Europe? He says he'll send for me when he's settled, and when I'm – you know – older. We're going to open a shop together.'

For a horrible moment I was afraid she was going to laugh. Instead, she nodded thoughtfully.

'That's a good idea, Omar. It'll suit you. You'll be the richest person in this family. You'll buy me a diamond necklace one day, eh? Go on, promise.'

We both laughed. The world suddenly seemed a lot brighter. Something had changed between us. We weren't just bossy older sister and annoying little brother now. It felt as if we'd become friends.

'I'll be on your side,' I said, trying to sound serious and

responsible. 'I won't let Baba marry you off. I'll make
sure you get to college. You can rely on me, Eman.'

And then I felt silly. There was no way that Baba
would ever take advice from me, and we both knew it.
But Eman didn't laugh.

'I'll hold you to that, Omar,' she said. 'I might really
need you one day.'

I hated leaving our flat. I'd been born in it and had never
spent even one night anywhere else. The worst thing was
on the day we left, when the man who'd bought the last
bits of our furniture came in a van to take it away. Ma
cried, and I felt like crying too.

Baba sent me outside after a while, to get me out of
the way. I was standing in the street, feeling awful, when
I suddenly remembered the secret hiding place under my
mattress where I kept my life's savings. My heart gave a
thump and I felt cold all over. Musa's mattress was already
loaded into the van. They must be starting on mine.

I dashed inside. Baba was arguing with Ma.

'No, Leila,' he was saying. 'You can't take that table.
My mother has plenty of furniture. What do you want it
for, anyway?'

I tugged desperately at Ma's arm. She tried to shake
me off.

'What is it, Omar? I told you to go outside.'

'There's something I haven't explained,' I said
awkwardly.

She didn't seem to hear me.

'I'm telling you, Hamid . . .' she began again.

To my amazement, Baba gave in.

'Keep your silly table, then,' he said crossly. 'I've got better things to think about.' And he stalked outside.

I tugged at Ma's sleeve again. She gave me a smile, as if we were secret conspirators.

'It's all right, *habibi*,' she said. 'Your money's safe. In fact, I've stitched it into the lining of your winter coat.'

I stared at her in astonishment.

'Aren't you cross with me?'

'Of course not! You've worked hard for that money. You earned it, and I'm going to make sure you keep it.'

'When did you find it?'

She laughed.

'Months ago, darling. Who do you think washes your sheets?'

'Does Baba know?' I asked anxiously.

'No, and let's keep it that way, shall we?'

I couldn't help myself. I flung my arms round her, then stepped away again when Baba came back in from outside.

'The taxi's coming in an hour. What are you doing in here, Omar? I thought I told you to wait outside.'

CHAPTER FOUR

Baba was right about one thing. There was hardly any space in Granny's flat in Daraa. It may have had more rooms than our flat in Bosra, but they were all crammed with furniture. It was on the first floor of an old block of flats with a balcony at the front, but even that was stuffed with hundreds of dusty old plants.

It was obvious that Granny wasn't pleased to see us. She seemed to really miss Auntie Majda, who was her youngest daughter, and who had been under her mother's thumb for years. Auntie Majda's children were all little girls, and they were quiet and shy. Now Granny's flat was filled with three big teenagers – Eman, Musa and me – not to mention Fuad, who, though he was only five, could make more noise than a police siren, and Nadia, who was toddling around and into everything.

Granny couldn't bear the sight of Musa.

'There have never been any deformed children on

our side of the family,' I heard her say to Baba, looking accusingly at Ma.

Nadia was the only one of us that Granny seemed to like. She kept taking her away from Ma and stuffing her with food.

It was obvious from the beginning that Granny couldn't stand Ma, and Ma couldn't stand Granny. It was horrible being around them both, especially when Ma was trying to cook something in Granny's kitchen. Granny would sit cross-legged on the window seat and say things like, 'Goodness, Leila, do you always put so much cinnamon in your stews?' or, 'What a pity you've chipped that dish. It was such a favourite of mine.' Then, when Ma served up the food, Granny would push it around on her plate and say, 'Of course, Majda is an excellent cook. I taught her myself.'

Ma never said a word, but her mouth set in a thin, straight line. And it wasn't only inside the flat where war had broken out. Things were getting serious in the world outside as well. Ever since people had heard about how the schoolboy slogan-writers had been tortured in prison, there seemed to be a march or a protest every day. It was scary, but exciting too. People seemed to have lost their fear. The military police were using water cannons and beating up everyone they caught. People were being arrested, tortured and shot. But it didn't stop the people of Daraa. They just went on demonstrating.

I couldn't really follow what was going on. I didn't

want to get involved anyway. Being political was no part of my life plan. If you want to be a businessman and get rich quick, getting up the nose of the government isn't a great way to begin.

A few days after we moved to Daraa, Musa and I had to start at our new school. I had a sick feeling in my stomach just thinking about it.

'You don't have to wait for me,' Musa said, as we walked the short distance to school on that first day. I could tell from his voice that he was as scared as me.

'Yes I do,' I said grimly. 'What sort of brother do you think I am?'

'A stupid one,' he said with a shaky smile.

It started off as badly as we'd expected. A bunch of ten-year-olds saw Musa, hooted with laughter, and began to walk alongside him, imitating the way he limped and making monkey noises. I felt the old familiar thump of fear and anger, but I knew it would only make matters worse to lose my temper. So I turned round and said, 'I bet none of you knows how many miles there are between the earth and the moon. This guy does. He's a genius.'

It was a bit feeble, but it was the best I could do on the spur of the moment. One or two looked puzzled and a bit impressed, then the biggest one said, 'He's not a genius. He's a cripple. He's weird.'

'Weird yourself,' I said with a shrug.

My brain was working overtime, trying to think of

another cool thing to say, when the most extraordinary thing happened. All round the entrance to the school building, groups of boys were standing, talking to each other. Then one of the tallest ones called out, 'Hey, is that you, Musa?' and strode over.

Out of the corner of my eye, I saw the flock of irritating kids nudge each other, eyeing the tall boy with respect.

'Hi, I'm Bassem,' he said. 'My cousin in Bosra told me you were coming. He says you're one of us. Come and meet the others.'

And then – I couldn't believe it – he linked arms with Musa and practically dragged him off to join the group of senior boys who were standing closest to the door. And did Musa say, 'Nice to meet you, Bassem, and this is my brother Omar, who's a really cool guy'? He did not. He left me stranded in the courtyard surrounded by infuriating, cheeky kids.

'That Musa, is he your friend, then?' one of them asked. 'What's wrong with his legs?'

'He's my brother. He's got cerebral palsy,' I said shortly. 'He can't help walking like that.'

'We didn't mean anything,' one of them said anxiously. 'We didn't know he was Bassem's friend.'

There was awe in his voice when he said 'Bassem'.

Typical Musa, I thought bitterly. *Day one in this snakepit and he goes and makes friends with the most important guy in the school and leaves me with all the losers.*

I hunched my shoulders, put my head down and

marched towards the entrance. I'd just have to get on with things, find the school office, and go to whichever class they'd assigned me.

That first day was better in some ways than I'd expected and worse in others. It was better because I didn't get stuck with the 'cripple's brother' label, but worse because the bad report from my old school meant that I was put in a class with all the hard nuts.

I spent most of the day doing calculations about how many days, hours and minutes I'd have to spend in this dump before I could walk out of school forever and start my real life with Rasoul. He was still in Bosra. I was desperate to see him, actually. I wanted to hear him say it again – that he'd make me his business partner once he was settled in Europe. If I couldn't keep that dream alive, I felt I'd shrivel up and die inside.

I wanted to get out of school as fast as possible when the last dreary lesson finished, but when I reached down to get my bag, one of the other boys snatched it away.

'Come and get it, Bosra Bumface,' he said with a laugh. I lunged for it, but he'd already kicked it to someone else. The five or six boys still in the classroom were watching me with that cruel eagerness I'd seen so often in the faces of Musa's tormentors. They were just looking for an excuse to attack me, hoping I'd make an idiot of myself.

My heart was thumping, but I managed to put on a bored expression, then settled back in my chair, crossed my arms, pretended to yawn, and said, 'Suit yourselves, guys. I've got all day.' And I waited.

They soon got fed up, but then the biggest one, Farid, had the bright idea of lobbing my bag at the window. I saw what he was going to do just in time. In a flash, the consequences unrolled like a film in my mind – the smashed window, my bag lying in the school courtyard in a scatter of broken glass, the accusations, the blame, the punishment . . .

A superhuman surge ran through me. As my bag sailed towards the window, I leaped from my chair, like a cheetah springing after its prey, and caught the bag just before it hit the glass. Then I crashed down on to the table, half winding myself in the process.

'Wow! Good save!' one of the boys said.

'Nice one, Omar,' said another.

I felt as if I'd passed some kind of test. I tried to smile, but it was hard with the breath knocked out of me. I made for the door, but I'd relaxed too soon. Farid was blocking my way.

'Think you're clever, don't you, Bumface?' he said, aiming a kick at my shins. 'See you tomorrow. I'm looking forward to it already.'

Musa was already at the school gate with two of the boys who'd been with Bassem that morning, a grin splitting his face in half. The other boys moved off when they saw me coming, and I heard one of them say, 'Think he'll do it?

Bassem seems sure but I can't say I'm impressed.'

'Nor me,' said the other one. 'I can hardly understand a word he says.'

I wasn't in the mood to listen to Musa raving on about his new friends, and I'd have left him to go home alone if it hadn't been for the thought of Ma. She'd skin me alive if I arrived back without him. I was meant to be his protection. It would never have crossed her mind that the one needing protection was me.

'How did it go, then?' asked Musa, breaking the silence.

'Wonderful. Never had a better day in my life,' I said bitterly.

'Bullies?'

I said nothing. There was an empty drinks can lying on the pavement. I kicked out at it savagely.

'I'm really sorry, Omar,' he said, and I was sure I detected a note of triumph under his sympathy. 'Look, I'll tell Bassem. I'm sure he . . .'

I gritted my teeth.

'I'll fight my own battles, thank you very much.'

The words hung in the air. Things were the wrong way round. I hated the thought of Musa patronizing me.

Is that what I do? Patronize him? I thought, with a flash of understanding. The idea was unsettling. I pushed it away.

'I heard what those guys were saying just now,' I told him accusingly. 'What did they mean, "Think he'll do it"?'

'I can't tell you.' He sounded revoltingly smug. 'The fewer people who know about it, the better.'

'That's fine by me,' I said with a shrug. 'Keep your little secret. I don't care.'

Musa made a sort of gurgling noise like he does when he's thrilled about something. I had to turn and look at him. His eyes were alive with excitement.

'Look, I would tell you, but it's grown-up stuff. I don't want to get you into trouble.'

I was really offended now.

'So I'm just a silly kid, am I?

I walked a little faster, enjoying the fact that he was struggling to keep up with me.

'Listen, Omar! It's just – it's dangerous, that's all.'

I was burning with curiosity now.

'What's dangerous? You fathead, what have you got yourself into?'

He was struggling with himself, I could see. At last he said, 'All right, I'll tell you, but you've got to swear . . .'

I rolled my eyes.

'Not that again! Last time, everyone in the whole world knew the secret anyway.'

'This is different.'

The grin had dropped off his face.

'All right. I swear. And before you ask, I mean it.'

He paused, as if he didn't know where to start, then he looked over his shoulder, as if he was afraid that someone had crept up behind him.

'Revolution,' he said, so quietly that I thought I hadn't heard him right.

'What?'

He pushed his face closer to mine.

'Revolution,' he hissed.

'All right. No need to spit. I heard . . .' Then I took in what he'd said. We'd slowed to a halt. I stared at him. I almost wanted to laugh. Musa, my skinny brother, shaky on his legs, his tongue stuck in his mouth – Musa was the most unlikely revolutionary I could possibly have imagined.

'Are you kidding?' was all I managed to say. 'Since when have you known a single thing about politics, or . . .'

His face was serious now. He was watching me, as if he was trying to gauge my reaction.

'It was those geek friends of yours in Bosra, wasn't it?' I said slowly. 'Everyone thought you were spending your time swapping nerdy facts about sharks or something. While in fact . . .'

My voice tailed off.

'Ismail's father has a very powerful computer,' Musa went on. 'And an unusually good broadband connection. He lets Ismail use it in the afternoons. Who's going to suspect us of doing anything subversive – two nerds and a cripple? We've been researching what our dear government has been up to. It's disgusting, Omar. Arrests, disappearances, torture – and that's only half of it. They've got to be stopped. All we want is a proper democratic government. Freedom of speech. Freedom from torture, an end to corruption . . .'

'Are you crazy?' I burst out. 'Don't you know what they do to people like you? Haven't you heard Baba say, again and again—'

'Baba works for the government.' There was a hardness in Musa's voice I'd never heard before. 'He's compromised. And when the government falls, he'll be the one in trouble, not me.'

I stared at him. I didn't know where to begin.

'How does Bassem fit into all this?' I asked at last.

He grinned.

'We've been feeding him information. Stuff he needs for the things he's writing. You know those boys who kicked all the unrest off a couple of weeks ago?'

'The idiots who sprayed "*The people want the regime to change!*" all over the school walls?' I interrupted cuttingly. 'The ones they caught and tortured?'

He ignored me.

'They were friends of Bassem's. All the marches and demonstrations – who do you think is organizing them? Schoolboys! Kids! *Us!* We'll bring this rotten government down, Omar. There's a part for me to play and I'm not going to be left out.'

He sounded as if he was spouting something he'd read in a book or seen in a cheesy film.

'You're mad,' I said, chills running up and down my

spine. 'You've got to be mad.'

He grabbed my arm and shook it.

'Don't you care about your country, Omar? Do you *like* living under a dictatorship?'

He was really annoying me now. I shook his hand off my arm.

'Stop it. You know I'm not interested in all that stuff. It's just politics.

'Politics? Politics is *life*!' he said passionately. 'It's . . .'

I lost patience completely.

'Shut up, Musa. Just shut up! You're going to get arrested and then they'll kill you and Baba will lose his job and we'll all be in the gutter. If I had any sense, I'd tell Baba and get him to lock you up.'

I enjoyed the alarm flaring in his eyes.

'You wouldn't! You promised!'

'There are circumstances which override mere promises,' I said, trying to sound dignified. 'When it's a matter of life or death.'

I knew I sounded silly, but luckily we'd arrived back at the flat. Ma was standing watching for us in the doorway.

'Well?' she said anxiously. 'How did it go?'

'It was OK,' we both said at the same time, and we pushed past her into the flat.

CHAPTER FIVE

In Bosra, my two brothers and I had always gone to Friday prayers at the mosque with Baba. I'd enjoyed it. We'd had to put on nice clothes, and Baba had usually been in a good mood. On the way there he'd sometimes told us stories about his own father and the laughs he'd had with his brothers. Those were the only times I'd really loved my father, if I'm honest.

We used to meet friends at the Bosra mosque as well as uncles and cousins. Even Fuad had his own gang of five-year-old kids. Musa and I had done years of classes at Koranic school, of course, so we knew all the prayers. I liked standing and kneeling with everyone else as we said them. It made me feel part of something good, something bigger than myself.

But I didn't look forward to Friday prayers in Daraa. The mosque would be full of people we didn't know. The thing that really bothered me, though, was the thought of running into someone from school.

After that first day, things had improved for me, even though Farid was still like a simmering volcano, apt to erupt unpredictably into violence. Most of the boys were reasonably friendly but I hated the idea of them seeing me at the mosque with Baba. What would they think of him? I was sure all the other fathers would be tall and good looking, not small and skinny, like Baba. And then his teeth were so embarrassing.

The nearest mosque to our flat was quite small. I had a good look round as I kicked off my shoes at the doorway. I had to admit that it was nice inside, high and airy, with beautiful tiles on the walls and thick carpets covering the floor. We went into the washroom and I was rolling up Fuad's sleeves ready to scrub his forearms (Baba was very particular about being thorough with the ritual wash before prayers) when I caught sight of Bassem. I felt a flutter of fear. What if he said anything dodgy in front of my father?

Bassem saw Musa and gave a tiny nod, and Musa slightly raised his hand before turning away. The fact that they were pretending not to know each other alarmed me even more.

When the prayers were over, someone came up to talk to Baba. I could tell from what he said that he worked at the Ministry of Agriculture too. Fuad was being a bit frisky, so I grabbed hold of his hand to keep him still. I certainly didn't want this smart-looking stranger to think that our family was badly behaved. I guessed he was quite important, judging by the way Baba was smiling and agreeing with every word he said.

It was quite a while before I realized that Musa wasn't with us. I looked round, and saw his unmistakable brush of sticking-up black hair at the far end of the big mosque courtyard. He was almost at the gate that led on to the street. Luckily, at that moment Baba's colleague paused to cough, and I grabbed the chance to say to Baba, 'Musa's gone on. I'd better catch him up.'

He nodded.

'Take Fuad with you.'

I pretended I hadn't heard that last bit, and hurried off after Musa. I kept my eyes fixed firmly on him, trying not to lose sight of him in the crowd, but even then I nearly missed the moment when it happened. Bassem brushed up alongside Musa, and without either of them saying a word, or even looking at each other, he slipped something into the pocket of Musa's trousers.

I felt a rush of rage and darted through the crowd after him. Then I heard Fuad call out, 'Omar! Wait for me!'

Fuad's wail made me stop and look back. My annoying little brother was worming his way between two tall men, struggling to reach me.

'Go back to Baba,' I told him sharply.

'I want to come with you,' he said, sticking out his lower lip obstinately.

'You can't, Fuad. Look, get Baba to buy you some sweets. He will if you ask him nicely.'

He looked uncertain, but I gave him a little shove, and watched until I'd made sure he was back with Baba. By that time, of course, Musa had disappeared.

The mosque courtyard was clearing quickly. People were looking anxious, clearly in a hurry to get home. Had I missed something? Had there been an announcement or some news? I hadn't bothered to listen to the sermon. I'd been too busy wondering how Rasoul was progressing on his dangerous journey to Europe. He hadn't come to say goodbye to us as he'd promised. All I'd had was a text message to say that his chance had come up and he'd got on a flight to Turkey. I was desperate to know if he'd done the crossing over the sea to Greece and arrived in Europe safely.

There was a crowd around the gate when at last I got there, and it took me a while to push through. I assumed that Musa would be on his way home and set off in that direction, and it was only luck that made me look left along a side street. Musa was turning the corner at the top, into the main road.

I had to know what he was up to! I hared down the street and caught up with him a few seconds later. He heard my running steps and looked round before I reached him, scowling furiously.

'What are you following me for? Where's Fuad? You should be looking after him.'

'Never mind Fuad. What the hell are you up to? What did Bassem gave you?'

He flushed.

'How did you—'

'I saw him slip something into your pocket. Why all the secrecy? He hasn't given you a gun, has he?'

'A gun?' Musa's eyebrows shot up till they disappeared under his heavy fringe of black hair and he burst out laughing. 'Me? With my jerky hands? I can see it, can't you? I take aim, then *whoosh*! My hand flies up in the air. "Oh, sorry, I shot my own head off instead of yours. My mistake."'

He was trying to be funny but I refused to smile.

'What is it then?'

He glared at me.

'I'm only trying to protect you, you clown.'

'Protect me from what? And how can I go home without you? Ma will—'

'Omar, I'm fifteen! I'm your *older* brother, in case you'd forgotten. Go on, get lost.'

'But Ma . . .'

'I've texted her. Told her I'm going to a friend's house to borrow a book.'

'You can't have texted Ma. You lost your mobile before we left Bosra.'

'And Bassem's been kind enough to lend me his old one. See?'

He pulled an expensive-looking smartphone out of his pocket and waved it in front of my face. I stared at it enviously.

'That's not an old phone. It's the latest model. And why the secrecy? Why didn't he just hand it to you, like a normal person?'

'Mind your own business, little brother. Now push off.'

He walked away, quite fast for him. I stood there, on that unfamiliar street with cars hooting their way down it, and watched him go, not knowing what to do.

I still didn't know my way round Daraa very well and I got a bit lost on the way home. I'd only just realized where I was when my own phone buzzed. I looked at it resentfully. It was old and the glass on the screen was cracked. There was a message from Ma:

Where are you? Come home at once.

Ma wrenched the door open as I turned the corner of the stairwell, and as soon as I got to the top step she reached out and dragged me inside. Eman was beside her, knotting her hands with worry.

'Where's Musa?' Ma almost shouted. 'Where are Fuad and your father?'

I stared at her. Ma was often anxious about us but this time she looked genuinely panic-stricken.

'Fuad's with Baba, Ma. I think they've gone to buy sweets. Musa's gone to his friend's house to—'

'Borrow a book. We know. He texted,' Eman chipped in. 'Is he crazy? Today?'

'So? What's the problem? They'll be back soon.'

Ma pushed Eman aside. '*Problem?* Don't you know what's going on? It's all over the TV. Huge anti-government demonstrations in Daraa! Criminal rioters and undesirable elements on the rampage! And the whole family out there! In the middle of it! Getting into Allah knows what . . .'

'What? Where's Granny?'

'She took Nadia to visit Majda,' Eman said, with a sideways glance at Ma. 'She's been so awful this morning. She said Ma was a—'

'That's enough, Eman,' interrupted Ma.

There were bright red spots on her cheeks. There'd obviously been another row. I could just imagine Granny scooping Nadia up and marching her off to enjoy a long moan about us all with Auntie Majda. Ma was just having one of her flaps, that was all.

I brushed past her into the flat.

'I didn't see anything in town. What's for lunch?'

Ma smacked her hands together in exasperation. 'Don't you ever listen to a word I say? There isn't going to be any lunch until this whole family's safely back and in one place. You could try to help, Omar. You really could.'

She was really upset. I felt bad.

'Sorry, Ma,' I mumbled. 'What do you want me to do?'

'You can go round to your aunt's place and fetch Nadia home. I want her back *here*. With *me*.'

'Granny won't let me take her, Ma. You know that.'

'Just go, Omar! Tell her your father sent you. I don't care what you say. Just bring her home!'

Auntie Majda's flat wasn't far but to get to it I had to cross a big main road. I walked fast up the narrow side streets, jumping over the drain holes and gaps in the paving stones. I was angry with Ma for using me in her fight with Granny. I was fed up with Musa for going off with his new friends, and with Rasoul for bunking off to Europe, and with Baba for bringing us to this dump, and with Daraa itself. I felt as if the whole world was against me.

I was so caught up in my thoughts that I nearly bumped into Baba. He was walking fast, pulling Fuad along behind him.

'Omar? Where are you going?'

'Ma sent me to Auntie Majda's to fetch Nadia. Granny took her there.'

'Oh.' I could read his thoughts as clearly as if he had spoken them out loud. He was imagining the row that must have taken place and deciding to keep well out of it. 'Well, all right,' he went on. 'But come straight back. There's going to be trouble downtown.'

I hurried on. There didn't seem to be any sign of trouble; in fact the streets were unusually quiet. As it was Friday, most of the shops were shut, of course, but still it was weird that no one was around. I started to feel uneasy.

Was everyone so scared that they'd locked themselves into their houses? And Musa! My heart skipped a beat. He was so besotted with his new friends he'd let them lead him into all kinds of trouble.

I broke into a run. Auntie Majda's flat was only two blocks away, on the far side of the main street. Normally you had to fight your way over it through streams of traffic surging along in both directions. Today the whole road was deserted.

I was about to go down the narrow street that led to Auntie Majda's flat when in the distance I heard the rumble of heavy vehicles. Yes! I could see them now – a convoy of army lorries. They crawled slowly up the road and halted a few hundred metres away from me. Soldiers started to pile out of them. They were a scary sight. I knew I ought to get away as quickly as possible, but curiosity held me to the spot. I slipped into a shop doorway and looked out cautiously, wanting to see what would happen.

Every other sound had been blocked out by the loud roar of the military engines, but as soon as they were turned off I could hear shouts approaching from the opposite direction. I poked my head out of my hiding place and looked cautiously up the street, my heart thumping with excitement and fright. A huge crowd, a vast, rolling wave of people, was running down the middle of the street towards me. The ones in front were holding banners. Bold, forbidden words were blazoned on them:

The regime must fall!

Stop the killing!

Now I could make out the shocking, thrilling words that everyone was shouting:

God, Syria, freedom! God, Syria, freedom!

Something weird happened to me then. I wanted more than anything to run up and join the mass of marching men and boys, to shout with them, to be part of something brave and great and glorious, even though I had no idea what it was.

I was so overwhelmed that I couldn't move. I just stood there stupidly and watched the troops organizing themselves, lining up to face the marchers with their guns up ready to fire while the marchers came on fast, their banners waving, their shouts getting louder and louder:

God, Syria, freedom! God, Syria, freedom!

The marchers came to a halt, facing the guns. Time seemed to pause. I thought for a strange moment that I was watching something made up, a programme on the TV. But there was nothing unreal about the ear-splitting cracks of the guns when the soldiers opened fire. The wild urge to join the marchers turned into terror. I stood as if paralysed, unable to move.

There were yells as the bullets hit their mark, and several people screamed. Some of the boys in the front line of the march jerked and toppled over on to the ground. Three or four lay still while others were trying to roll over or crawl away. I knew then that I was seeing real soldiers, real guns and real bullets.

That was when I caught sight of Musa. My brother, my idiotic brother, who had been on the outside of the march, was hobbling along the pavement towards me, holding his precious new phone up in front of his face. He was filming the whole thing.

The troops opened fire again, straight into the crowd. More men and boys were falling, bright splashes of scarlet spreading over their clothes. I knew I needed to run, to get out of the deadly range of the guns. But Musa! How could I leave him, calmly filming the mayhem, an obvious target, in the most terrible danger?

CHAPTER SIX

I learned many things that day, and one of them was that absolute fear does unexpected things to you. It gives you a massive surge of energy. It slows time down so that you can think. It stops you feeling pain. I must have bashed myself on something as I raced towards my brother, but I didn't even notice it until later when I found a big bruise turning dark blue on my arm.

Before I'd reached Musa, the troops had opened fire again. The demonstrators were scattering, running down side streets or trying to force a passage back through the hundreds of others coming on behind them. The soldiers were rushing after them, hitting out with batons, kicking those who had fallen to the ground, rounding up any they managed to catch and dragging them back to the trucks.

My eyes were darting up and down the street. There was no chance that Musa could outrun the soldiers. We would have to find a hiding place.

I saw it just in time — a narrow passageway between

two shops, half hidden by a big garbage bin. Musa hadn't noticed me, although I was practically shouting in his ear. He was steadily filming the mayhem all around.

'Stop it! You *fool*!' I yelled, and snatched the phone out of his hands.

He turned on me furiously.

'Give it back! How dare you!'

I pushed him into the passageway. It was dark and littered with rubbish. My mind was racing. If Musa was caught with the phone on him, arrest and torture would be the least he could expect. Then I saw, above my head, a small window covered with a grille. It wasn't the perfect hiding place, but it was better than nothing. I jumped up and slid the phone on to the sill.

'Give it back! Give it to me!' screamed Musa.

'Are you crazy? It's your death sentence if they find it.'

He's a quick thinker, Musa. He frowned at me, then nodded reluctantly. 'Get it down and switch it off. Someone'll find it if it rings. Then hide it up there again. We'll come back for it tomorrow. Make sure you remember where this place is.'

'I'm not taking orders from *you*,' I snapped back at him.

'For Allah's sake, Omar. Just do it.'

I hated the idea of touching the phone again, but I knew he was right. If it was found, they'd be bound to find out who owned it, and the link would be made back to Musa. I grabbed a broken chair, balanced on it, and managed to fish the thing off the sill.

'Give it here,' said Musa. He switched it off, and I got it back into its hiding place. I was only just in time. A solder appeared at the end of the passageway, standing in sinister silhouette against the bright sunlight beyond. His head looked huge and threatening in his metal helmet. He started down towards us, stumbling on the rubbish.

Musa collapsed against me, drooping his head on to my shoulder. He gave me a sharp nudge and I understood what he wanted me to do.

'Thank God you're here, brother,' I whimpered to the soldier. 'We were so frightened! Have those crazy people gone?'

'Yeah,' growled the soldier. 'Crazies like you. You were with them. You're under arrest.'

Musa started making babbling noises and let dribble come out of his mouth.

'We didn't know what was happening,' I said. 'We're from Bosra. We're visiting our auntie.'

The soldier was looking with disgust at the drool trickling on to Musa's shirt.

'It's my brother,' I said. 'I'm supposed to be looking after him. He's a cripple. Soft in the head.'

The soldier leaned down and peered closely at Musa. Then he shot out his fist. It stopped a centimetre before it hit Musa's nose. Musa automatically ducked to avoid it and lost his balance. His arms flailed wildly and he made a mewing noise. In spite of the awful danger we were in, I had to suppress a grin of admiration. There was contempt rather than suspicion in the soldier's eyes now.

'Damn loony,' he said. 'Should have been strangled at birth. Get him out of here.'

He watched us, eyes narrowed, as we stumbled out of the passageway into the daylight.

Musa kept up the pretence, hanging on to me as if he could hardly walk and flailing his arms until we were well away from the soldier.

'Don't stop!' I hissed at him. 'There are more soldiers over there. Wait till we're well away.'

It wasn't until we were a few streets away that we dared walk normally. It was much quieter here, although we could still hear the sounds of fighting from the direction of the main road – shouts, screams and the rumble of military engines.

'Soft in the head, am I?' Musa croaked at me. 'I'll make you pay for that, little brother.'

I grinned at him.

'No you won't. I've just saved your wobbly backside, or have you forgotten already?'

We'd been going as fast as Musa could walk, but he suddenly stopped and said, 'Where are we?'

'I think that's the corner of Auntie Majda's road,' I said, pointing. 'I recognize that blue sign. Let's go and wait at her place till all this is over.'

Musa hesitated.

'I'm letting Bassem down. I ought to be with the others. I can't just—'

He was interrupted by the crack of several shots and more shouts that sounded closer than before. I grabbed his arm.

'Quick! I think they're coming this way!'

He didn't go on arguing, thank goodness.

When we reached the corner of the street I grunted with relief. I'd been right. Uncle Feisal and Auntie Majda's flat was only a few metres away. The dark entrance to the building, which had seemed almost sinister on our previous visits, looked positively welcoming now.

We dived into its shelter just as the first demonstrators erupted into the far end of the street. They were running fast towards us, and behind them came the ominous roar of an army lorry.

It was so dark in the building entrance that at first I didn't see the two figures huddled on the bottom step of the steep, narrow stairway. Then I heard an excited, high-pitched voice shout, 'Musi! Omi!' And a pair of small arms wrapped themselves round my legs.

'Nadia!' I picked her up. 'What are you doing out here? Go back upstairs. Go and find Auntie Majda.'

The dark shape sitting on the stair stood up and I saw that it was Granny.

'Granny? What's happened? Go back in. It's not safe out here.'

Granny came towards us out of the shadows and I saw

her face, its pale oval framed by her close-fitting black abaya. Her eyes were sparking with anger.

'We can't go in! They've all gone out. She knew I was coming, Majda did. I left a message with Feisal. He took them away deliberately. My Majda would never do this to me! We've been sitting here for hours waiting for them! I didn't want to go home. Your mother . . .'

She sagged, suddenly looking lost and helpless. Her lips were trembling. I actually felt sorry for her.

Nadia began bouncing in my arms.

'Tickle me, Omi! Tickle Nadia!'

'Not now, *habibti*. Keep still.'

I was desperately trying to think.

Musa was looking out into the street. Boys were running past us now. Suddenly Musa shouted, 'Latif! Over here!'

I saw one of the runners swerve sideways, look over his shoulder and dart across to Musa.

'You can't stay here,' he panted. 'They're doing house-to-house searches. Arresting any man or boy not in their own home.'

'This is my aunt's place,' said Musa, speaking as slowly and clearly as he could. 'She's not here. We can't get in. Look, there's my granny and my little sister. We've got to get them home.'

Latif hesitated. I peered round him and looked down the road. I could see the army lorry now, but it had stopped moving. The soldiers were still some way away. Granny tugged at my arm.

'What's going on? I heard shooting. Who's this boy? What's Musa saying?'

I resisted the urge to shake her off.

'Musa's trying to get us home, Granny. There's been a lot of trouble downtown.'

Her face took on its usual sneer.

'Musa? What can he do? He's worse than useless.'

I ignored her. I was trying to hear what Latif was saying. I heard Musa give him the name of our street, and saw Latif pull a long face. Then another boy running past saw him and dashed over. It was Bassem.

'Musa!' he said excitedly. 'Did you get good footage?'

'I think so.' Musa nodded. 'I've planted the phone. It's safe for now. We'll pick it up tomorrow.'

'Where is it?'

Musa grinned.

'Best you don't know.'

I stepped up to join them, with Nadia in my arms and Granny clinging to my sleeve.

Bassem's eyes widened. 'What are they doing here?'

'Got stranded,' I said. 'We've got to get them home.'

'They live over beyond the fire station,' said Latif.

Bassem shook his head. 'No chance of getting over there till all this is over. Not by the streets.'

'There *is* a way,' said Latif. 'Best for us, too, Bassem. We go behind the pharmacy, round the back of the garage, through the building site, and over a few backyards. There are some walls to jump, but we'll stay off the streets.'

Bassem's eyes narrowed as he followed the route in his mind. 'Good. We'll do it.' He nodded towards Granny. 'She can manage, do you think? I don't know how we'll get her over the walls.'

Granny caught his words. 'Get me over walls? Now look here, young man . . .'

An explosion at the far end of the street made us all start.

Granny gave a little scream. 'Is that shooting? We'll all be killed!'

Blooms of white smoke were slowly coiling along the street towards us.

'Tear gas!' said Bassem. 'We've got to get out of here. Now.'

'I won't . . . I can't . . .' began Granny.

I was losing patience.

'Granny, do you want to choke to death? Do you want to be shot?' I shouted at her. 'Just do what Bassem and Latif say. They'll get us all home.'

'Here, give me the baby,' said Latif, holding his arms out to Nadia. 'Look after the old lady, Omar. Let's go.'

Bassem was looking out of from the entrance. He waved to us to follow him. 'Come on! Now!'

We were on the pavement for no more than a few seconds before Latif and Bassem plunged into a narrow alleyway that ran alongside the pharmacy beneath Auntie Majda's building. The sight of soldiers armed with guns coming up the street had made Granny momentarily freeze with shock, but then she caught a whiff of tear gas. She put the end of her abaya up to her face and with her other hand she gripped my arm so fiercely that it felt like a claw.

I think I would almost have enjoyed that mad scramble over walls, down dark alleyways and through deserted buildings, if it hadn't been for Musa and Granny. I was scared that Musa would hold us up, and afraid that Granny would fall, or scream and draw attention to us. Every wall and heap of rubble was a challenge for both of them. I must admit, though, my respect for Granny shot up that day. She followed Latif and Bassem without a word. Even when we had to lift her up and hand her over walls like a bony parcel, she did nothing more than grunt. On her feet again, she just dusted down her long black abaya and scuttled after the boys like a busy black beetle. Musa managed, somehow. I didn't see why I should help him. He'd got me into this, after all. It was nearly half an hour before we got near home. The streets in our part of town were quiet and empty.

'We know where we are now,' Musa panted as the fire station came into view. 'Thanks, guys. You really saved us. We were in trouble, back there.'

'Worked out well for us, too,' said Bassem. 'They'd have caught us if we'd gone on running.'

Latif tried to set Nadia down. She had clung to him silently all the way, her arms wrapped closely round his neck, her eyes wide with fright, and now she seemed reluctant to be prised away from him.

'Ma's waiting for you. We're nearly home,' I coaxed her.

'Ma! Ma!' She burst into wails.

Bassem pulled Musa aside. 'When will you pick it up?' he asked him.

'As soon as it's quiet. I'll need someone to help me, though.'

'I'll send Ahmed round.'

'Don't bother,' I cut in. 'I'll go.'

Musa shook his head. 'Not you, Omar. Too dangerous.'

His superior tone annoyed me.

'I said, I'll go.'

Granny, holding the wailing Nadia by the hand, was already crossing the road and heading fast towards the entrance to our building. I hurried after her. She turned a stern face towards me. 'Who are those two boys? And what's Musa got to do with them?'

'He's their classmate. They're from school. Musa's friends.'

'Friends already? He's only been at that school a few weeks. They're using him. They can see he's simple. They've taken him in.'

I felt my temper rise. 'There's nothing simple about Musa!' I was speaking too angrily and forced myself to drop my voice. 'Musa's really clever, Granny. Much cleverer than me. Or Eman.'

'He doesn't look it. Got the face of an imbecile.'

I heard a shout overhead and a head appeared through the thickets of dusty greenery on our balcony. Eman had seen us coming.

'You boys are up to something,' Granny said. 'You can't pull the wool over my eyes.'

'I'm not up to anything,' I said with a shudder. 'I just want to get home.'

'You can't have been out there in the middle of all that without a reason.'

'Ma sent us to fetch Nadia,' I told her angrily. 'We ran into the march without realizing.'

We were inside the building by now and starting up the stairs. Musa was close behind. Granny turned and gave him a sharp look.

'What did that boy Bassem mean when he said "Did you get it"?'

Musa smiled up at her innocently. 'You really don't want to know, Granny.'

She frowned at him. 'I can't understand a word the boy says,' she muttered.

There was no time for more. First Eman, then Ma, came clattering down the stairs to meet us with cries of relief and questions.

CHAPTER SEVEN

I couldn't sleep that night. Ma and Baba's raised voices kept me awake till late, and then I was tormented by frightening dreams. I woke in the middle of a nightmare and remembered at once that I'd promised to fetch Bassem's phone out of its hiding place. My stomach clenched with fright.

It was a Saturday so there was no school, but I don't think Baba would have let us go even if it had been a weekday, as the funerals of those shot the day before would be taking place. Furious crowds would be sure to gather, and since the police had shot to kill at a quiet demonstration the day before, they'd probably go murderously wild with an excited mob.

Musa was as edgy as I was, and I knew he was thinking about that stupid phone. There was nowhere in the flat where we could talk privately. Granny seemed to be sulking and hadn't come out of the room she shared with Eman. Fuad was playing a noisy game with toy cars in our bedroom, Ma was in the kitchen, and Baba was stuck in front of the TV in the sitting room, watching endless news programmes.

The only person who seemed cheerful was Eman. She had spread her books out on the little table in the corner of the sitting room and was buried in her homework. But she'd only been at it for a few minutes when Baba turned on her.

'Why aren't you in the kitchen, helping your mother?' he barked at her. 'What's the point of all this study? If things go on like this, do you think I'm going to risk letting you go out to that school every day?'

Eman looked up at him, shocked. Her face flushed with anger. She opened her mouth to say something, thought better of it and shut it again. Even if she'd dared, there was never any point in arguing with Baba. She gathered up her books and went into the kitchen.

It was Nadia who gave me my chance. She'd been grizzling all morning, and by midday she was lying listlessly on the sofa, her cheeks flushed, whimpering if anyone tried to move her.

'Feel her forehead,' Ma said to Baba, coming in from the kitchen to check on her for the hundredth time. 'She's burning up with fever. You'll have to go out and get her some medicine, Hamid.'

Before Baba could answer, I said quickly, 'It's OK, Ma. I'll go.'

'Not you.' She was still looking at Baba. 'I don't want

any of you kids going out there today.'

Baba hadn't moved his eyes from the TV screen.

'Let him go, Leila. There's no trouble at this end of town.'

'I'll go with Omar,' said Musa, struggling to get to his feet. He had been watching the TV too, his forehead scored by a deep frown. I gave my head a little shake to put him off. He subsided reluctantly on to the sofa again, frowning in frustration.

'*No.*' Ma's voice was sharp. 'It's bad enough one of you being out there. I'm not letting you both go.'

She was looking pointedly at Baba as she spoke, but he didn't seem to notice.

My heart was pounding as I hurried up to the main road. The pharmacy was only a block away. I could be there almost at once, buy Nadia's medicine and be home in a few minutes. Then I thought of the scorn I'd read in Musa's eyes. He'd find an excuse to go out himself, make a hash of getting the phone back and get caught. I forced myself to turn the other way, and keep to a steady walk. A running boy would look suspicious.

There was some traffic going up and down the main road but not as much as usual. Many of the shops were shut, their metal shutters rolled down and padlocked, but the ones that were open made the street look different from yesterday. I had a moment of panic. Where was the entrance to the passageway where I'd hidden the phone?

It was only when I saw a minaret in the distance that I realized I'd come too far. I stopped, then pretended to look in the window of a mobile-phone shop before turning back.

There! I recognized the place now. The bin that had been pulled halfway across it yesterday wasn't there any more. No wonder I hadn't seen the dark little entrance at first. I bolted into the passageway entrance and stood for a moment, waiting for my eyes to adjust to the deep shadow.

There was the window! I crunched across the rubbish underfoot. The chair that I'd used to reach the sill the day before had gone. I had to jump up and feel along it, but my fingers only scraped on loosened bits of concrete. My heart sank.

You're such an idiot, Musa! It's been found. We'll all be in trouble now, I thought.

I gathered myself for another jump. This time I caught hold with both hands and pulled my head up so that I could look along the sill. Yes! The phone was there, right in the back corner. I lunged for it, and dropped back on to my feet with it in my hands, relief singing in my ears.

I slipped it into my pocket and was at the entrance of the passageway when a massive hand clamped itself round my arm.

'Dirty kids!' said a deep voice. 'Haven't you got a toilet at home? I'm fed up with you, stinking up that passageway.'

The man was huge, with a ferocious face and a jutting belly.

'S-sorry,' I stammered. 'I was desperate. I . . .'

He gave me a shove that nearly sent me spinning into the path of an oncoming taxi.

'If I catch you again—'

'You won't! I promise!'

I righted myself and dashed off, not stopping until I was round the corner. I had to stand still for a moment and lean against a wall, until my pounding heart slowed down.

I was so pleased with myself for getting the phone back that I was almost home before I remembered Nadia's medicine. I doubled back to the pharmacy. A crowd of people were waiting impatiently to be served, so that by the time I was finally running up the stairs and banging on our front door, more than an hour had passed.

Ma wrenched the door open, with Musa close behind her.

'Where have you *been*?'

I put the packet of medicine in her hands and pushed past her.

'Sorry, Ma. I had to wait for the pharmacy to open. There was a huge crowd. I couldn't get served.'

'Everyone's stocking up, I suppose,' Ma said, calming down. 'Who knows what's going to happen, after all? You're a good boy, Omar.'

'See any trouble in the street?' Baba called out. He was still sitting in the same spot on the sofa.

'No. It was quiet. Some of the shops were open . . .'

Musa gave me a warning look and I shut my mouth. There were only a couple of shops between our flat and the pharmacy. I'd nearly given myself away.

Musa hobbled towards our tiny bedroom. I followed him. Fuad was lying on the floor, pushing a toy car around.

'Out,' we said to him together.

He sat up. His hair was sticking straight up on the top of his head. He looked like an indignant chicken.

'Why? 'S'not fair. This is my room too.'

'Out,' Musa said again.

I took pity on Fuad.

'I'll play with you later on, I promise. We'll do a superhero game. You can be Batman.'

He trailed reluctantly towards the door. I shut it behind him and stood with my back against it.

'Did you get it? Did anyone see you? Where is it?'

Musa's questions came so fast they were tying his tongue in knots.

'Here you are.'

I pulled it out of my pocket and threw it on to his bed. Behind me, the door handle rattled.

'Omar! I want my digger!'

Musa hurriedly hid the phone under his pillow.

'All right,' I said, opening the door. 'Come and get it. Then hop it, OK? Or no game.'

Fuad looked suspiciously from Musa to me.

'You've got a secret, haven't you?'

I fished his digger out from under his little bed and gave it to him.

'Musa's helping me with my homework. Now buzz off.'

He went out of the room at last.

Musa pulled the phone out from under his pillow.

'I'm calling Bassem,' he said, looking for the number. When it was ringing, he handed it to me. 'You speak to him. No one ever understands me on the phone.'

Bassem answered the call at once. Before I could speak, he said shortly, 'You got it then?'

'Yes.'

'Are you at home?'

'Yes.'

'Good.'

And the line went dead.

'Charming,' I said, throwing it back to Musa. 'No "Hello, Omar? How are you doing?" Just "Are you at home?" Then he cut me off.'

Musa raised his eyebrows.

'The government monitor calls, stupid. The less time you're on the phone the harder the call is to trace.'

'Oh. I didn't realize.'

He pulled up the good side of his face into a crooked grin.

'Welcome to the world of underground politics, little brother. You've been great. You've struck a blow for freedom.'

I shuddered. 'That's the last time, OK? Keep me out of it from now on.'

Musa was cradling the phone in his good hand. I eyed it with suspicion. 'What are you going to do with it?'

'Bassem or Latif will come and pick it up.'

'When?'

'Soon as they can, I expect.'

Now that I knew the thing was on the way out of the flat, I felt a stab of curiosity.

'I hope you pressed all the right buttons and actually filmed all that stuff,' I said.

He smirked. 'You want to look, don't you?'

'No. Why should I?'

He started to swipe the screen.

'Come on. Let's see.'

I couldn't resist, but as I moved away from the door towards his bed, it opened behind me. Eman put her head into the room.

'Ma says——' she began.

'Why can't you knock before you come in here?' I interrupted crossly, moving swiftly to block her view. 'How do you know we weren't changing or something?'

'Sorry. No need to get ratty. Ma says come and eat.'

She withdrew.

Musa had stuffed the phone back under his pillow. He shook his head at me.

'Later,' he said softly.

*

In the sitting room, Eman and Ma had laid a cloth on the floor as usual, and we sat down on Granny's plump cushions around the steaming dishes. The smell of the food was so delicious that I forgot everything except how hungry I was.

Nobody said much as we ate. I was too busy, anyway, enjoying the food. Ma had done my favourite – lamb meatballs – and there were her own home-pickled aubergines as well. She'd brought her own massive stock from Bosra.

Granny was sitting opposite me, her back against a large cushion. For once, she was eating greedily. She sat back at last and said, 'That was nice, Leila.'

We all looked at her in surprise.

'Thank you, Um Hamid,' said Ma. 'Um Hamid', meaning 'Hamid's mother', was Granny's formal name, and Ma never called her anything else. She wiped her mouth to hide her triumphant smile.

The meal over, Musa and I went back to our room.

'What's got into Granny?' I asked Musa.

He laughed.

'She was yelling down the phone at Auntie Majda half the morning. I reckon Ma's her favourite now.'

Fuad came into the room.

'You've got to play with me now, Omar. You promised.'

I don't want to admit it, but sometimes I really liked playing with Fuad. And after all the tension of the last two days it was great to behave like a five-year-old again, pretending to shoot at each other, diving on to our beds and making silly noises. I was just beginning to get tired of it when Ma called out, 'A friend's come to see you, Musa.'

Musa had been lying on his bed watching us. He shot me a look. Fuad ran out to see who was there. Musa pulled the phone out from under his pillow and levered himself off the bed. He looked quickly round the room and snatched up one of my old *Majid* comics. He slipped the phone inside it.

'Hey,' I objected. 'I haven't finished reading that yet.'

'He'll give it back,' Musa said shortly. 'You'd better hand it over. If my hands go funny the phone might drop out.'

Latif was perched on the edge of a chair opposite the sofa, listening politely to Baba. He looked smart, with his crisp white shirt and oiled black hair.

'You're right, Abu Musa,' he was saying earnestly. 'The situation is very serious. Who knows where it will end?'

'The government hasn't got any choice,' Baba said in his sharp, bossy way. 'A strong response, that's what's needed.'

Beside me, Musa was making a face, rolling his eyes and pulling down the corners of his mouth. Latif looked up and caught his eye. I could see he wanted to laugh, but he pulled himself together and nodded meekly at Baba.

Hypocrite, I thought.

Granny and Ma came out of the kitchen and Latif jumped to his feet.

'How are you, Um Hamid?' he said to Granny, in a low, caring voice. 'I hope you didn't suffer any . . .' His voice petered out.

'Are you the boy who carried Nadia all the way home?' said Ma, picking up Nadia, who had been clinging to her skirt and peeping shyly at Latif. 'I'm so grateful! And looking after Um Hamid too!' She turned round and called out over her shoulder, 'Eman! Bring coffee and the honey cakes!'

Granny hadn't said a word. She was staring inquisitively at Latif with her bird-bright eyes. My heart skipped a beat. What if she suspected something? What if she told Baba?

After a moment she smiled, and I saw with relief that Latif's respectful manner, his brushed hair and his nice clothes had reassured her. She went into the kitchen, and through the half-open door I could hear her chivvying Eman.

Latif threw a glance at Musa.

'Thank you, Um Musa, but I can't stay,' he said. 'I just wanted to find out how Nadia was, and – and . . .'

'And he's come to borrow this magazine,' interrupted Musa quickly.

He gave me a nudge in the back. So, under the eyes of half my family, I had to edge round the sofa and hand over to Latif something that might as well have been an unexploded bomb, wrapped in *my* magazine.

Latif nearly bungled it. He took hold of the bundle the wrong way, and I felt the phone slip inside the folded paper. I snatched it back.

'I'll put it in your bag for you,' I said hastily.

By the time the thing was tucked inside the bag he'd dropped by the door, my hands were clammy and I was longing for him to go.

I never got to watch Musa's film after all.

PART TWO

CHAPTER EIGHT

Would Bassem and Latif and all those other boys have done what they did in Daraa if they'd realized that they were lighting a fuse that would explode into total war? I don't know. I tried to ask Musa the other day, but he just scowled at me. Maybe one day we'll be able to talk about it.

Daraa was such an ordinary place when we first went to live there. The pavements were crowded with shoppers, the streets were full of traffic, and there were all the usual things that make up a city – shops, schools, hospitals, mosques, churches – but a few months later it was all wrecked. Ruined. Dead.

I suppose, looking back, that it happened quite quickly. Moving from those first scrawled slogans on school walls to full-scale disaster only took a few weeks. But during those weeks time crawled by.

There were demonstrations and marches by the angry people of Daraa all the time. The tickly smell of tear gas often hung over the city, and from streets away you could hear the shouts of the marchers: '*We sacrifice our blood and our souls! We are no longer afraid! God, Syria, Freedom!*'

The police and army fired on the demonstrators time after time. 'Terrorists', they called them. It's what Baba called them too. But Bassem and Latif and Musa weren't terrorists. They just wanted to live in a country where they didn't have to be afraid all the time. They wanted a government that was fair-minded and open.

The day after every march there would be funerals. Furious men and boys would tramp down the streets, carrying coffins shoulder high and shouting so loud that everyone could probably hear them over a hundred kilometres away in Damascus.

Yet it still didn't seem real until Musa got a text on his old phone. We'd finished supper, and I was playing a silly clapping game with Nadia, putting off the moment when I'd have to start my homework.

Musa made a sort of gurgling noise as he looked down at the tiny screen.

'What?' I demanded. 'You sound like a frog in a swamp.'

I was annoyed with him because he'd refused to do my homework. He'd even given me a lecture on how I'd never learn anything if I didn't do the work myself.

He looked too shocked to speak. His hand jerked violently and the phone flew out of it. I lunged for it before he could get it, then had to read the words three times before they sank in:

Latif shot in head. Died in hospital just now. Funeral tomorrow.

'It's not true,' I said, my voice going horribly wobbly. 'Bassem's having you on.'

But it was true, and we both knew it.

I think I grew up a bit after Latif died. It wasn't as if he'd been my friend. I'd only met him a couple of times. But whenever I hear of the deaths of 'resistance fighters', I think of Latif standing beside Bassem at the school entrance, Latif running through the back streets of Daraa with Nadia in his arms, Latif sitting on the edge of the chair in our flat in his crisp, white shirt listening respectfully to Baba, Latif almost dropping the mobile phone folded inside my comic.

Until Latif died, there'd been a ding-dong battle going on in my head. I'd hear Musa's voice, talking passionately about our wicked regime, our police state, the repression, corruption, and all the rest of it. And then the TV would butt in with the voice of our President, droning on about 'foreign powers', 'conspiracies', and Syria going through 'a test of unity'. And there was always Baba's harsh voice, preaching about 'law and order' and 'teaching hotheads a lesson'.

After Latif's funeral, I didn't want to listen to any of those voices any more. Maybe I'm a coward, but fighting and dying isn't for me. I'm not brave like Musa. I don't understand what's really going on, who's right, who's wrong, who's good and who's bad. I just want things to go back to the way they were before.

But I know they never will.

For a while, we all tried to go on doing normal things. Baba went to work at the Ministry, and Ma looked after Nadia, did everything round the house, and tried to put up with Granny. We all went to school, and, as usual, there was no peace for me at home, because every time I tried to do something of my own, Ma sent me out to buy something at a shop, or made me water Granny's horrible plants.

Nothing was really the same, though. Baba seemed to hate his new job and he came home every day in an awful temper. He was all knotted up inside and flared up over the slightest thing.

Eman had the worst of it. She'd bought a flowery-patterned hijab and spent hours gazing in the mirror, fixing it in place with a little pearl-headed pin. I thought it looked nice and fashionable, but when Baba saw her coming home from school in it, he went crazy.

'Are you trying to shame me?' he yelled. 'Is this a respectable family or . . .'

I won't repeat the rest.

Musa was hardly ever around. At night, when he'd crept home at last and Fuad was asleep, I'd pester him to tell me what was going on. He'd just shrug and pretend he hadn't heard.

'You don't trust me! You think I'm just a little kid!' I'd snarl at him. 'So who risked his neck to get that phone back for you? Who—?

'Give it a rest, Omar,' he'd say, brushing me off as if I was a fly buzzing round his head. 'You don't feel about things the way I do.'

'You don't know what I feel!'

'Yes, I do. Are you prepared to die to free Syria from tyranny? Are you willing to go to prison and be tortured?'

That silenced me. I wasn't at all willing, and we both knew it.

'Be a martyr,' I'd say. 'See if I care.'

I knew I sounded like a sulky kid but I'd have sounded sillier still if I'd said what I really wanted to: *I really, really don't want you to die, Musa. I think you're awesome. I actually love you, you know.*

One good thing was the change that had come over Granny. She'd never forgiven Uncle Feisal and Auntie Majda for locking her out of their flat that day. To get back at them, she'd started being really nice to Ma. After a while, I could tell that she wasn't playing a game any more. They began to spend hours together in the kitchen, gossiping.

She was as shocked as the rest of us when Latif was killed.

'That nice boy,' she kept saying. 'So respectful. These soldiers, who do they think they are, shooting innocent boys like that?'

And when Baba started with his usual tirade about strong government, and law and order, she startled everyone by saying, 'You've got your head in the clouds as usual, Hamid. That boy Musa knows what's going on. He's got more sense than you ever had, even if he is a cripple.'

It was just as well that peace had broken out at home, because outside in the city things were getting more and more scary. Rumours flew around like demented crows. Granny stood for hours on the landing outside our front door, ranting on with our ancient neighbour about the damage the government troops had done to the famous old mosque in the middle of town. Eman had her pink mobile constantly clamped to her ear as she and her new friends debated whether or not it was safe to go to school. Baba came home every evening raging about the insolence of the 'youths' who had been pulling down portraits of the President on government buildings. Even Fuad came running in from playing in the yard with garbled stories about other kids' older brothers who had disappeared.

It wasn't easy to work out what was true and what wasn't. There was no point in watching the news on TV either, unless, like Baba, you wanted to listen to a lot of hot air and lies.

Musa, of course, said nothing at all. He'd acquired another smartphone, given to him by Bassem, I assumed. He spent hours on it surfing the web and tapping out emails and texts.

And then, quite suddenly, the authorities cut off the internet. It was the weirdest thing being without it. It felt as if we were living on a desert island. Without it, there was no way of finding out what was happening in the rest of the country. There was no social media, no way to keep in touch with friends, nowhere to look for information, no *news*.

I minded less than Eman and Musa. The only person I wanted to be in touch with was Rasoul, but although I'd kept sending him messages on my beaten-up old phone, he'd hardly ever answered. He'd managed to get as far as Germany, I knew that much, and he'd decided to go on to Norway.

It's surprising how quickly you can get used to things. Demonstrations, marches, shootings and funerals – they all started to feel like a normal part of life. I'd go to school every day, and sometimes the gates would be open and I'd have to endure boring lessons and kicks from stupid Farid, but on other days the gates would be closed and we'd all drift off home again.

I didn't think about where it was all heading. Even if I had, I'd never have guessed in a million years what the government would do next.

I wasn't feeling well the day the tanks rolled into Daraa. It was the end of April, and the weather was getting hotter all the time. Eman was at home. Baba had forbidden her to go outside, and anyway, the girls' school had been closed for days. Fuad and Musa had gone off to see if the boys' schools were open, but I used my horrible cough as an excuse to stay at home.

The boys had only been gone an hour when they came hurrying home, with Baba right behind them. Ma came out of the kitchen, holding Nadia in her arms.

'What's happening? Why have you all come back?'

'It's a showdown,' Baba said shortly. 'The terrorists –' I saw Musa wince at the word – 'have taken over the old mosque and the government have sent troops in to flush them out.'

'They've sent tanks in. *Tanks*,' Musa added savagely. 'They've started shelling the mosque.'

Granny had come out of the kitchen too. She looked scandalized.

'They're shooting at the Great Mosque? With *tank shells*?' She clapped her hands to the sides of her face. '*Ya haram!* Allah will punish them for this!'

'Don't talk about things you know nothing about,' Baba said shortly. 'Eman, look after your little sister. Leila, you'll have to come out shopping with me. Bring bags. We need to stock up as much as we can on food. Omar, stop pretending to be ill and come with us. We might have a lot to carry.'

Outside in the street, you could almost smell the panic in the air. Cars crammed with people were trying to carve through the traffic, their roof-racks weighed down with mattresses and bulging bags, their drivers furiously sounding their horns.

Only some of the food shops had stayed open, and they were crammed with people desperately buying everything they could lay their hands on. Some things had sold out before we could get to them, but we still managed to fill our bags with stuff like dried lentils, flour, rice, tea, cooking oil, and cheese. I tried to sneak in a few candy bars, but Baba slapped my hands down.

I heaved a great sigh of relief when we were safely back indoors. It was hard to tell where the tanks were, but I'd kept thinking, as we'd run from one shop to another, that at any moment one would appear at the end of the street and blast us all to pieces.

I don't know if you've ever heard the rumble of tanks coming down a city street? They make an incredible noise. It's not only the deafening engines. It's the sound of their caterpillar tracks churning up the tarmac, and the crunch of metal and broken glass as they knock down street lights. And that's before their guns start to fire. When they do, the boom and crash are so frightening you stand paralysed for a moment, then dash as fast as you can to any shelter you can find.

That day, when the siege of Daraa began, was when the knots in my stomach began to tighten up. It was the day when I started to feel truly afraid. And that night, and for nights after, I couldn't get to sleep, and when I did drop off, I had terrible dreams.

Late in the afternoon, after the longest day I could

ever remember, there were shouts in the street below and loud banging sounds. Musa and I crawled out on to the balcony to peer through the jungle of plants.

'Get back in here!' shrieked Ma. 'Do you want to be shot?'

We didn't need to be told twice. Anyway, we'd seen enough. The banging sounds were rifle butts pounding on doors, and the men doing the pounding were soldiers.

'They're doing house-to-house searches,' Musa said, his face suddenly pale. 'Omar, you've got to help me.'

My heart gave a sickening thump.

'It's that phone, isn't it? That stupid phone.'

'Not just that.' He was fumbling in his trouser pocket and pulled out a little notebook with a red cover. He held it out to me.

I jumped back. I felt as if he was handing me a poisonous snake.

'No,' was all I managed to say. 'No.'

He thrust it at me. His jerky spasms always got worse when he was nervous, and now his hands were flailing all over the place. When I didn't move he turned away.

'All right. I'll hide them myself.'

The shouts and bangs below were getting closer. Musa lost control of the book, which flopped out of his grasp and on to the floor. Reluctantly, I picked it up.

'Where?' I said shortly. 'Under your mattress?'

'Too easy.'

'Flush it down the toilet?'

'Take too long.'

'I'll chuck it out of the window at the back,' I said, making for the bathroom door.

'Wait!' He clutched my arm. 'Sub-ta-fa.'

I may be the world's most brilliant expert in understanding Musa, but no one could have cracked that.

'Sub-ter-fuge.'

I was dancing with impatience.

'Stop trying to impress me with long words! There's no *time*! What does "subterfuge" mean?'

'Trick them. Only way. Stuff it into your pile of school notebooks.'

'*Your* school notebooks, you mean.'

'Yes, yes. Mine. Quick. Stick a label on the cover. They're on the shelf by my pencil case. Write "Physics Notes" on it. Hide it between the others.'

I flicked quickly through the notebook. It was filled with jottings, lists of numbers and weird words in Musa's terrible handwriting. I was pretty sure that even if the soldiers found it, they wouldn't be able to read it.

'What about the phone?'

'Leave it to me.'

I dashed into our room, and a moment later the notebook had its new label and was tucked in among Musa's other books. As I came out of our room, a deafening noise sent my hair standing up from its roots. The soldiers had reached our building and were battering on the street door downstairs. Baba hurried to our own front door and pressed the buzzer to let them in.

Musa wasn't in the sitting room. I rushed to the kitchen. Ma was handing strips of sticky tape up to Eman, who was standing on a chair by the window taping criss-cross patterns with them across the glass. Granny was by the table, feeding biscuits to Nadia with trembling fingers.

'Omar, come and help your sis—' began Ma, but I'd backed out of the kitchen before she had time to finish.

I could hear raised voices from below, then heavy footsteps running up the stairs. I stood, frozen, watching Baba, who was standing by the open front door looking out on to the landing, with a sheaf of papers in his hands.

Musa came out of Granny and Eman's bedroom.

'Have you hidden it?' I hissed at him.

He had time to nod, then the soldiers were at our door. Musa leaned against me, going floppy. He put his head on one side and smiled vacantly. I willed him not to take it too far and start dribbling.

Baba was talking calmly to a couple of soldiers, showing them his papers.

'You see, sir? Ministry of Agriculture. I'm a government employee. You wish to search our flat? Of course. You have to do your duty.' He turned and saw us standing by the kitchen door. 'Omar, Musa, show these gentlemen whatever they want to see.'

It was impossible to read the expressions in the two

soldiers' eyes, which were shaded by their heavy military helmets. They glanced quickly from Musa to me, then at Fuad, who was peeping nervously at them from behind the sofa.

'Other family?' one of them barked.

'My wife, mother and two daughters,' Baba said, with an anxious smile.

'Where?'

'In the kitchen.'

A shouted command came from the bottom of the stairwell. One of the soldiers pushed passed Baba. He hurried round the room, opening door after door and looking quickly inside. There was a muffled scream from Eman and an angry outburst from Granny when he looked into the kitchen. He shut the door again quickly and hurried back out on to the landing, pushing past Baba without another word. As their boots went clattering noisily down the concrete stairs, Baba called out after them, '*Inshallah*, you will be successful in your good work, rooting out . . .'

I could tell he was winding himself up to make one of his pompous speeches. The men didn't bother to wait, but turned the corner of the stairwell and a moment later we heard the metal street door clang shut behind them.

Musa had dropped his play-acting as soon as they were out of sight, and had slipped back into Granny's bedroom. He came out a moment later with the phone in his hand.

Ma opened the kitchen door cautiously and peered out.

'It's all right,' she said over her shoulder to the others in the kitchen. 'They've gone.'

Granny came out after her.

'Outrageous!' she croaked. 'Those men – ogling my granddaughter in her own home with her hair uncovered!'

'They didn't have time to ogle, Granny,' said Eman. 'They looked like a couple of frightened rabbits at the sight of a room full of women.'

She was the boldest of all of us in talking back to Granny, and I'd noticed that Granny seemed to like it.

'They were only doing their duty,' Baba said stiffly. 'I told them I worked for the government. They saw at once that I wasn't the kind of man to allow subversive activities in my family.'

Musa had gone into our bedroom. I hurried after him. He was looking for his little red notebook.

'Where did you hide the phone?' I asked him.

He grinned at me.

'In Granny's underwear drawer.'

'You didn't! She'll kill you if she finds out.'

'She won't. Anyway, I reckon she deserves it. Do you think I like being called a cripple all the time by my own grandmother?'

I saw it in my mind's eye – Musa's phone, that little stick of revolutionary dynamite, filled with who knew what films and photos and incriminating messages, hiding among Granny's big black knickers and armour-plated corsets. Musa and I stared each other. Then we fell on to our beds, and stuffed our pillows into our mouths to muffle our shrieks of laughter.

CHAPTER NINE

Is it right for a government to send tanks to terrorize ordinary people (like me) in our own homes? Baba used to say, 'Maybe.' I say, 'No.' What do you think about a government sending in snipers to hide on rooftops and take shots at people in the streets below? Baba doesn't say anything. I say, 'I hate them.' Is it OK for a government to send attack helicopters clattering around in the sky, and to drop huge bombs out of them on to the city below? Even Baba says, 'No.' I say, 'No, no, no.'

It took a while before we realized that a full-scale war was getting going, even after the government cut off the electricity supply to the whole city. When it first happened, it was a shock. No lights, no TV, no mobile chargers, no fridge, no freezer, no nothing. At first, I kept forgetting, and went on uselessly pressing switches and going to the fridge for a cold drink.

We got used to it quite quickly. We had to. Ma sent me rushing out to the shops to buy candles and matches before they sold out. Luckily Granny had a couple of old oil lamps, so we were sort of all right for light. The worst thing was not being able to charge our phones. There was still electricity at the Ministry, so Baba kept his and Ma's phones going, but he refused to charge ours, which I thought was mean of him. With no TV and no internet, we had to rely on gossip for news, and rumours went racing around the city – crazy, wild stories that seemed impossible to believe, until some of them turned out to be true.

Being without electricity soon became the new normal, like the bombings and shootings. We even began to forget what life had been like before all the trouble started. At least, I did.

At first, whenever I heard the rattle of gunfire, a thump of fear made my heart pound and my skin prickle. It was exciting in a way. I felt more alive, somehow. Even after Latif was killed, the fighting didn't seem quite real. There were times when it was almost as if I'd woken up in the middle of a computer game.

Very soon, though, the war didn't feel like a game any more. The blood on the pavement after a car bombing or a shooting was horribly real. The clouds of choking dust billowing up to the sky when a bomb wiped out a building were real, too.

The sense of excitement turned into a permanent, awful, gut-wrenching fear. Everyone was feeling it. Fuad began to wet his bed. Nadia cried every time Ma tried to put her down. Granny rocked on her cushions in the corner of the room, fingering her prayer beads. Eman came out in spots, and Musa sometimes woke me up when he was in the middle of a nightmare.

And then the government shut off the water supply, too. That was the worst thing. We had to listen out for the man with the water tanker sitting on a rickety old cart, pulled by a scraggy little horse. The minute Ma heard the clop of hoofs, she sent me dashing down the stairs with jerrycans and buckets, while Baba, if he was at home, hurried down behind me. It wasn't always easy, I can tell you, getting them filled up. Bigger guys than us were always shoving in front. Sometimes we only managed to buy enough to fill one small jerrycan each.

It was awful having so little water. We could still buy bottled drinking water in the shops, but Ma needed a lot for cooking and cleaning the dishes, so there was hardly any left for washing. Our clothes got dirtier and dirtier, and as we could only wash our hair occasionally, our heads were soon itchy with dust and grease.

But the worst thing of all, even more than the lack of water, was that Musa fell ill. I suppose it was my fault in a way, only I couldn't help it. I'd caught a horrible flu bug off someone at school before we broke up in June, and I passed it on to Musa.

I was better a few days later, but Musa had it really badly. It was the end of July by then, and horribly hot. I'll never forget the night Ma panicked because Musa's fever was so high. There were hardly any taxis left in town because petrol was so scarce, and Baba had to pay a fortune to get one to take him to hospital. I couldn't sleep all night, thinking he was going to die and wishing I hadn't made such a fuss about the space his books took up in our little cupboard of a bedroom.

He stayed in hospital for weeks hooked up to a drip. They said something had gone wrong with his kidneys, but I don't know what it was. He did get better, but it took months and months. Even when he came home he was as weak as a baby rabbit, and so depressed it made me feel miserable just to look at him.

I'd started hanging out with a couple of boys from school by then, and I'd slip out to play football with them whenever Ma would let me, which wasn't often. Both she and Baba were suspicious of any new friends I made. I think they were scared I'd get led astray by some fundamentalist loony with a black scarf tied round his face, who'd try to make me cut off people's heads. As if.

Ma kept me busy most of the time, fetching water, queuing in shops and taking messages to people whose mobile phones weren't working any more. I felt bad about not being able to keep Musa company, but I don't think he wanted me, quite honestly. It was Bassem and the others he was missing, but they never came to visit him.

One afternoon, I was in an especially bad mood because I'd been running round town all morning, trying to find cooking oil for Ma (all the shops seemed to have run out), and I was tired and hot and itchy with all the sweat and dust I couldn't wash off. The flat was boiling hot, and of course there was no electricity for fans. Then Musa asked me to take a note round to Bassem's house for him.

'Why should I?' I said nastily. 'Bassem's dumped you, hasn't he, him and all your clever friends? Haven't you even noticed? Not one of them has been near you since you got ill.'

'That's all you know about it,' he said, flaring up at me. 'Ever heard of keeping a low profile? Don't you know they're being watched? All of them? All the time? Want me to be arrested? Do you?'

'OK, cool it,' I said, backing away and feeling guilty. I knew I was wrong about his friends, anyway, because every now and then someone would come up to me when I was out in the street and slide a note into my hand for him. I'd shove it into my pocket with a shudder and slip it to him when I got home without reading it. So I guess they were keeping in touch with him, after all.

Term was supposed to start up again in September, but it never really got going. Even when the schools were open, a lot of the teachers didn't bother to turn up. *Probably gone to Germany or Britain*, I thought jealously. And then I'd think about Rasoul, and wonder for the hundredth time how he was getting on in Norway. I was actually quite happy when the schools were shut. I was fed up with sitting on a hard bench hour after hour, while someone droned on about stuff I didn't care about.

Summers are blisteringly hot in Daraa, but the winters are bitingly cold. I'd liked it in Bosra when it had snowed. It was good fun having snowball fights and sliding around on the ice. It wasn't the same in Daraa, stuck upstairs in a flat. Baba said he couldn't afford the kerosene for the heaters, except for an hour or two first thing in the morning, so we went around all day shivering and piling on all the clothes we could find.

You have to get used to all kinds of things when you're living in a war. You forget what it's like to eat fresh stuff. You stop noticing the burned-out shops, set on fire by the authorities for daring to go on strike. You step over piles of rubble and smashed paving stones without thinking about it. You ignore your dirty clothes and greasy hair. You don't even flinch when you hear gunfire or an explosion, as long as it's not too near.

There was nothing normal, though, on the day the heavy shelling started. It was February by now, and we'd been in Daraa for nearly a whole year. Musa, who was completely better at last, had gone off on his own. He'd given Ma the same old lies about going to 'borrow a book from a friend', but he didn't fool me. I knew he was back plotting with Bassem and the others.

There'd been rumours for a while about troops bringing big guns up outside the city. They'd made Baba fiddle nervously with the buttons on his jacket, the way he always did when he was upset. For days Ma had sent me out to queue at every shop in the neighbourhood trying to build up stocks of food, but my bags were nearly always half empty when I came home.

'You didn't give me enough money, Ma,' I'd say. 'I got the rice, like you said, but there wasn't enough for tea.'

She'd go on at Baba when he got home from work.

'What do you want to me do?' she'd say, her voice rising. 'Feed your family on air? I can't work miracles.'

The first weird thing that day was that Baba was at home. He'd gone out to work first thing, but he'd come back soon after, saying that the Ministry of Agriculture was closed. Ma had a fright when she saw him come through the door.

'*Wallah!* What's happened? Has somebody died?'

Without answering, Baba sat down heavily on the sofa. A few months ago, he'd have started on one of his lectures about how the President was working day and night for the good of the country and the terrorists were being defeated and so on. All he said now was, 'There's going to be trouble today.'

Ma clasped her hands to her chest.

'I knew it. I felt it suddenly half an hour ago. I shouldn't have let Musa go out.'

Baba turned on her.

'Musa's out? You let him go out?'

Ma looked guilty.

'He said he wanted to borrow a book from a friend. You know how depressed he gets. I couldn't—'

Baba whacked his fist down on the arm of the sofa.

'Today of all days! Are you mad?'

'I'm sorry, *habibi*. I didn't know—'

'I'll have to fetch him back,' Baba said furiously. 'Where does this friend live?'

'Omar knows.'

My stomach jumped. How could I lead Baba, a government employee, to Bassem's house? If anything happened, I'd be accused of betraying the cause, and Musa would never forgive me.

'Tell me where this fellow lives,' Baba said impatiently.

Ma gave a little scream. 'No, Hamid! Don't leave us! What'll happen to us all if you get killed?'

'I'll go,' I said quickly, leaping to the door and shoving my feet as fast as I could into my trainers. 'I'll bring him home straight away.'

'No,' Baba said, frowning. 'It's not safe for boys out there. Musa will have to look after himself. You shouldn't have let him go, Leila. I *told* you—'

'It's not far,' I said quickly. 'It won't take long.'

I saw a struggle in Ma's face and I guessed she was weighing up whether she cared more about Musa getting home safely, or me getting my head blown off. Musa won, like he always did.

'Let him go, Hamid,' she pleaded, touching Baba's

arm. 'Musa can't run, he needs his brother.'

Baba's fingers were working so hard at his jacket buttons I thought he was about to pull them off.

'All right,' he said at last. 'Go on, Omar, but be quick. Look out for trouble and take cover if you have to. Be sensib—'

He was still talking when I was out of the flat and halfway down the stairs.

It's amazing how fast news travels in a war. Somehow everyone seemed to know that something big was on the way. The shutters over most of the shop windows had rattled down already and the last few were closing, their customers hurrying down the street clutching their precious bags.

I was nearly at Bassem's place when I almost ran into a group of gunmen, checked scarves wrapped round their heads, who were standing on a street corner, shouting to another group further down the road. I shivered at the sight of them, crossed the road and slipped past quickly, trying to make myself invisible.

I'd never been inside Bassem's family flat, but I knew where it was. I was almost there when I saw Musa himself coming out of the entrance.

He frowned when he saw me.

'What are you doing here, Omar? They're going to start shelling. There are resistance fighters everywhere. They'd shoot at a cat if they saw one.'

'Do you think this is my idea?' I snapped. 'Ma sent me to fetch you.'

'*Fetch* me?' He glared at me. 'How old does she think I am?'

'You're her darling boy,' I said bitterly. 'Always was, always will be.'

'Not that again.' He rolled his eyes in irritation. 'You always . . .'

At that moment, shouts from the end of the street made us turn, and before we had time to take in what was happening, the crack of a rifle made us flinch. It wasn't until I'd bolted into a doorway, half dragging Musa after me, that I felt the pain.

'They're not shooting at us,' he was saying scornfully. 'What are you panicking for?'

But I'd made a terrifying discovery. The pain came from my arm. There was a fresh rip in the sleeve of my jacket, and I could feel something warm trickling down the inside of my shirtsleeve.

Musa must have noticed how white my face was looking, because he said, 'Stop worrying, Omar. I told you, they're not shooting at us.'

I was starting to feel faint. I leaned against the wall and slid down it till I was sitting on the ground. The blood had reached my wrist and was seeping out over my hand.

Musa saw it, and gasped.

'I think I've been shot,' I said weakly.

I'd always thought that Musa was the cool guy, the one

who filmed demos, who plotted with the resistance and play-acted being an idiot to throw soldiers off the scent. He wasn't acting cool now.

'Omar! You're bleeding! How bad is it? I can't . . .'

Stricken with panic, his words were coming out more garbled than ever.

There were more shots from down the street, and further away came the wail of a shell and the crump of a massive explosion.

'Where are they? Are they coming this way?' I managed to say.

He looked cautiously out of our hiding place. His hands were flying about all over the place.

'They're running away, down towards the crossroads, but there might be more, up here, they might . . .'

I was so unused to Musa going to pieces that it shocked me into action. I tried moving my arm. It hurt but it wasn't agonizing. Blood was still flowing down my arm, but it was a trickle, not a flood.

'Give me your scarf,' I said.

With shaking fingers, Musa wrenched the scarf off. It was a bulky, black-and-white-checked keffiyeh with a tasselled fringe. When he'd wrapped it round his neck that morning, I'd said nastily, 'Think that thing makes you look macho, loser? Fat chance.' I felt bad remembering it now.

It's not easy, tying something round your own right arm, which is hurting like mad, when you can only use your left hand. Musa tried to help, but his hand jerked as he pulled it. It was too tight, but at least it meant I wouldn't bleed to death.

He'd stopped panicking by the time the scarf was tied.

'We've got to get out of here,' he said, peering out into the street again. 'Can you walk?'

I lurched to my feet. He put his hand under my good arm.

'Come on. Let's go.'

Stepping out into that empty street was the scariest thing I'd ever done. The gunmen seemed to have gone, but in the sky above us was the terrible shrieking of shells, followed by huge explosions which seemed to shake the air. It was impossible to tell where they were landing. We didn't know if we were running into the bombing or running away from it. I only had one idea in my head – to get home. I felt like a rat, running for my hole.

We had only one more corner to turn before our street, when a shell screamed deafeningly right over head. At that moment I was absolutely dead certain that I was going to die, right then and there. I grabbed the nearest thing to me, which was Musa, and he must have been thinking the same, because he grabbed hold of me. I was so stunned with terror that it took me a second or two (after the massive bang which made the ground shake under my feet) to realize that I wasn't dead after all.

It took another second to work out that the shell might

have landed on our building and wiped out our whole family.

I flung Musa's hand off my arm, not caring if I'd knocked him flying, and dashed round the corner yelling, 'Ma! Ma!' at the top of my voice.

I didn't recognize our street. It looked like something out of a film. A cloud of choking brown dust was rolling along towards me, like a weird sort of monster. Flames were shooting up into the sky, and blocks of masonry and panes of glass were crashing to the ground.

Musa caught up with me.

'Can you see?' he shouted. 'Is it ours?'

I didn't bother to answer because people had started running towards us through the dust and smoke. I recognized the man from next door. He was holding his little girl in his arms. Blood was running down her face. She was really pale and she looked too shocked even to cry. Her mother was running after him.

'Please,' I called out to the man. 'Was our building hit?'

He came right up close and shoved his face in mine.

'We are human beings!' he yelled, as if it was all my fault. 'We're not animals!'

His wife was behind him. Her mouth was wide open, making a sort of horrible black hole in the middle of her face, and wails were coming out of it.

'My parents!' she was crying. 'They're buried! Who's going to get them out?'

Musa had already hobbled on, into the smothering dust. I raced after him.

I only recognized our building because of the smashed plant pots lying in the street below. The blast had almost ripped the balcony off and it was dangling by one corner, looking as if it was going to crash down at any moment. The windows had been blown in, and a huge crack was running down the wall from top to bottom. The building next door, where our neighbours had lived, wasn't there at all. It had collapsed into a smoking pile of rubble.

'Omar! Musa!'

Baba suddenly appeared out of the smoke. His grey jacket was smeared with dirt and his black hair was thick and brown with dust. I ran to him. I think I was sobbing, but it felt more like choking. Baba put his arms round us. I could feel that he was trembling.

'Where's Ma? And Eman?'

'Safe. Your grandmother and the children too. Come with me. Quickly. It's not over yet.'

The next deafening wail of a shell cut him short. He grabbed my wounded arm, trying to drag me along with him. I yelped with pain but he didn't notice. There was another air-shattering bang in the next street, and I took off, running, making for the blown-in door of our building as if a tiger was after me.

'Don't go in there!' Baba yelled after me. 'Go round the side of the building! To the back!'

The narrow passageway that led to the yard was

spattered with broken glass. Baba caught me up as I reached the end.

'Over there!' he panted. 'Get into the shed!'

A door in the caretaker's small shed on the far side of the courtyard was open, and Ma was looking out.

'In here!' she shrieked. 'Quickly!'

I don't know how long we were in that shed, cowering in the dark. It felt like days, but I suppose it was just a few hours. We were crammed in like olives in a bottle, and there was only just room for Granny and Ma to sit down, with Nadia on one lap or the other.

Every time a shell landed, we huddled closer, as if we could protect each other with our own bodies. The shed was only a flimsy old thing, and if a shell had landed on it, it would have been blown to bits. But it felt safer there than being inside a building made of layers of concrete which could bury us alive at any minute.

I don't know how we managed to pass the time. Fuad went on about his digger toy, which he'd left in the flat.

Shut up! I wanted to shout at him. *You'll probably never see your digger again, but I may never see my* Majid *comics again, and Granny might have lost all her furniture!* But I managed to keep my mouth shut. In my head I tried to imagine I was a superhero (lame, I know), and when that stopped working, I pretended that the streets around Daraa were in a computer game, and I was hunting the gunman who had shot me.

It was ages before Ma noticed the 'bandage' on my arm, which didn't really surprise me. I had to nearly shove it under her nose.

'Omar! What's the matter with your arm?' she said, not sounding very interested.

'He was shot,' said Musa.

She gave a little scream.

'Oh *habibi*, oh my darling! A doctor! We need to get you to a hospital!'

Another explosion, a bit further away this time, cut her short. Eman was already beside me, untying the knot in Musa's scarf.

'Hold your arm up,' she said. 'It'll stop the blood flowing downward.'

'What are you doing, girl?' Baba said roughly. 'It's a doctor he needs. When this is over I'll take him to the hospital.'

'The hospitals will be full of badly wounded people, Baba,' Eman said calmly. 'It can't be too bad or it would still be bleeding. It's not agony, is it, Omar?'

I wanted to say 'Yes!', but I could only shake my head.

Another explosion made us all freeze, but it was further away. We let out sighs of relief, and Eman went on looking at my arm. There was a jagged rent across the arm of my jacket, and the sleeve of my sweatshirt underneath was ripped right across. I swivelled my head round to look at the wound. It wasn't as bad as I'd thought. No more than a deep scratch, really, already crusted with dried blood.

'It only needs washing and a dab of disinfectant,' Eman said briskly. 'I'll see to it when we get back inside.'

'*If* we get back inside,' Musa muttered.

'You were lucky,' Eman went on. 'A few centimetres to the left and it would have smashed the bone.'

Yes, and a few centimetres to the right and it would have gone smack through my heart, I thought, my head spinning at the very idea.

Baba was staring at Eman as if he'd never seen her before.

'Where did you learn to do that?' he demanded.

'A teacher at her school has been giving first-aid classes,' Ma said hurriedly. 'I did tell you, Hamid.'

At that moment, the loudspeaker on top of the minaret that poked up from the corner of the nearby mosque crackled into life, and right in the middle of all the mayhem that was going on outside, the *muezzin* started singing out the call to prayer.

I'd heard those words chanted five times every single day for the whole of my life, but I'd never actually listened to them before. They seemed to talk to me, as if they were sending me, Omar Hamid, a message from the real world, the good, peaceful, right world. They sounded so beautiful that I felt stupid tears sprout in my eyes. The old imam was boring and stern, and whenever he caught sight of Musa and me he glared at us as if we were a couple of alley cats, but I was glad he was standing there beside the microphone, cupping his hands round his mouth, calling out the words of the *azzan*.

Things outside quietened down soon after that. Baba made us wait until there'd been no explosions for a good long while. It was horrible in that stuffy shed, desperately thirsty, needing the toilet, and just waiting, wondering if we'd even have a home to go to and somewhere to sleep that night.

At last Baba wrenched open the door of the shed.

'Come on out,' he said.

No one said a word as we pushed open the shattered street door and ran up the glass-strewn stairs to Granny's flat. The first thing I noticed was how cold it was. The windows had all been blown in and the freezing February wind was howling straight through the building. A hole the size of a fridge had been punched through the wall as well, and along with the broken glass there was rubble and dust all over the floor and on the furniture.

'Omar, get the broom and start sweeping up the mess,' Ma said. 'We can't put Nadia down on the floor in the middle of all this.'

Then she caught sight of the little table her mother had given her, which she'd brought from Bosra. A chunk of masonry had fallen on it and it was smashed to pieces. I thought she might start crying, but she just frowned and went up to Granny, who was standing in the wreck of her sitting room, tears rolling down her cheeks. Ma put Nadia into her arms.

'Take her into your room, Mother,' she said. 'Play with her on your bed.'

Ma had been amazingly calm all through the time in the shed, but as soon as she went into the kitchen, she let out a furious shriek.

'My pickle jars! Everything smashed! My aubergines and cucumbers!'

She came storming out of the kitchen and confronted Baba, who had been picking bits of broken glass out of the curtain.

'That's *it*, Hamid. We're not staying here any longer. Look at those cracks in the wall! What if the building collapses? We'd be buried alive!'

None of us had ever heard her speak to Baba like that. We stood watching, electrified. Baba was too astonished to say a word, either.

Ma folded her arms across her chest.

'We're going back to Bosra. We're going home.'

'Leila, we can't,' said Baba. 'The flat was let to someone else months ago.'

Granny had appeared at the door of her bedroom.

'Listen to your wife, Hamid,' she said, tears rolling down her wrinkled cheeks. 'We're finished here.'

'But there'll be fighting and shelling in Bosra too,' Baba said, looking strangely helpless.

'Not in the countryside, where my sister's family lives,' Ma said firmly. 'We'll manage here tonight, but we'll have to take the children away tomorrow.' She felt Granny's hand on her arm. I could see she wanted to shake it off, but instead she put her own hand over it, and said, 'And your mother will have to come with us.'

It was getting dark by the time we'd cleared up enough to make the flat just about all right for the night. Apart from the cold and the massive amount of gritty dust that had spread over everything, the glass was the worst thing. Fuad's bed was covered with jagged spikes of it. He and I spent ages picking all the bits off and sweeping splinters of glass off the floor. He cut his finger a bit, not badly, but he cried a lot more than I thought he needed too. He was only six, after all.

Eman cleaned up my gunshot wound with a bit of water from the precious bucketful and then she helped Ma with the mess in the kitchen. Somehow they even managed to make a meal for us all. There was some lentil stew left over, which we had to eat cold, of course, some of yesterday's stale bread, a chunk of cheese, a few olives and some gherkins from one of the only pickle jars that hadn't been smashed. Miraculously, Baba had managed to buy in a whole crate of bottled mineral water two days earlier, so we had enough to drink.

It was dark by half past six. We sat huddled together on the far side of the room from the window, trying to keep warm. Fuad kept trying to push Nadia off Ma's lap so he could curl up there too, and that sent Nadia into a tantrum. Baba tried to lift him off Ma, but Fuad just clung to her more tightly. In the end, Ma managed to hold them both, one in each arm, and after a while they went all quiet and sleepy.

Without the glass in the windows, we could hear every noise coming up from the street below, and somehow being in the dark made it feel as if we were down there too, with nothing to protect us. Occasionally, a bright light would sweep across the ceiling as a car honked its way down the street, weaving round the piles of rubble brought down by the shells. We could hear the sirens of ambulances, too. Every now and then there was a crash as a building collapsed, and then there'd be shouts and screams and the sound of running feet. I started to feel really scared that our building was about to cave in too.

After an especially loud crashing noise, in among all the screams that followed, I heard someone yell, 'Bring all your tanks! Bring all your guns and shells! We won't kneel! Daraa won't kneel!'

A bit later on, there was the *tac-tac-tac* of a machine gun not far away, and the answering cracks of rifle shots. We all flinched, and Ma gasped out, 'Allah, help us! Allah, save us!'

Once Fuad and Nadia were properly asleep, Ma and Eman carried them off to bed. Then I heard Ma go into the kitchen, and a few minutes later, a glow of yellow light appeared and she came back into the sitting room holding a candle, shielding the flame from the draught with one hand. She put it down in the middle of the floor.

It was extraordinary, the difference that little fluttering spike of light made. We all sat and stared at it. I could almost imagine that I felt warmth coming off it. It was a brave little flame. It showed how dirty our faces were, and how anxious we all looked, but I could see how close we all were to each other, and somehow that made me feel stronger.

'We'll have to have transport,' Baba said suddenly. 'We'll need two taxis. I'll go out first thing in the morning and—'

The clang of the broken street door at the bottom of the stairwell below interrupted him. We all jumped and then sat frozen with fright as footsteps came running up the stairs. I held my breath as they reached the landing outside our flat.

Don't stop! I shouted in my head. *Go on up! Get the people on the second floor!*

But the footsteps did stop, and then there was a scraping noise as someone struggled in the dark to fit a key into the lock of our front door.

'Who is it? Who's there?' Baba called out, struggling to his feet. 'What do you want?'

The door opened and Uncle Feisal came in.

The gasps of relief we all let out would have blown the candle out if the draught from the open door hadn't got there first.

'Feisal! Thank God it's you,' cried Baba.

'Shut the door!' Ma called out. 'I'll light the candle again.'

'Is my Majda safe?' Granny called out. 'And the children?'

'Allah be thanked, I took them out of town to my family's village,' Uncle Feisal said.

'She's sent you to fetch me.' Granny's lips were twisted in a smile of triumph. 'I knew she wouldn't desert her own mother.'

Even in the candlelight I could read the irritation on Uncle Feisal's face.

'I beg your pardon, Um Hamid. It's not possible for you to join us. Majda sent me to tell you. She expresses the hope that you're well.'

I could see what an effort he was making to sound respectful, and at any other time I'd have nudged Musa and we'd have had to stop ourselves laughing.

The smile fell off Granny's face. She pointed a finger at Uncle Feisal and screeched, 'You monster! You've turned my daughter away from me! You forced her to abandon me. You—'

Baba waved a hand to cut her off.

'Feisal,' he said urgently. 'We can't stay here. You see how it is. No electricity, no water, and the building's not stable. You should see the cracks running up the outside.'

Uncle Feisal took him by the elbow and drew him back towards the door. I leaned forward, trying to hear what he was saying, which wasn't easy, because Granny was still going on.

'That's why I came,' Uncle Feisal said. 'How are you going to get out of Daraa?'

'That's the problem,' Baba said. 'Everyone will be trying to get hold of a taxi and there's no petrol anywhere. It's going to be difficult.'

'Not a problem for me,' said Uncle Feisal. 'I saw this coming and stockpiled. My business would run aground completely if I couldn't use my van. I'll come by first thing and get you out. Where do you plan to go? Seriously, Hamid, I'm sorry we can't accommodate you. My parents' place is small and my sister's family have moved in with them too.'

'Don't worry.' Baba was smiling with relief. 'Leila's brother-in-law has a farm outside Bosra. They'll welcome us, I know.'

Uncle Feisal nodded.

'Can you be ready by seven? Don't bring too much. The van's old and the springs won't take a lot of weight. We'll be lucky if we get there at all.'

PART THREE

CHAPTER TEN

I keep finding things out about myself, and here's what I've discovered so far:

- I'm rubbish at school work, which I may have mentioned already. Once or twice.
- I'm not as clever as Musa or Eman, but I've got a lot more common sense than Musa.
- I'm brilliant at selling things. I may have mentioned that too.
- I'm *quite* good looking, or I would be if I could only grow a bit taller. And if my nose was smaller. And my ears didn't stick out so far.
- I don't care about politics, and I never will.
- I used to think that I was a bit of a coward, but now I know that I'm really quite brave, after all that business with the phone, and no one can say I'm not because I've got a bullet wound to prove it. (Hope it leaves a scar.)

• I like living in towns and cities and I'm not a country boy. And I'll *never* be a farmer.

We got out of Daraa just in time, because the shelling started up again just as we were leaving the city. It had been a mad rush to get ready in time for seven o'clock in the morning. It's not easy to choose what to take with you when you're about to leave your whole life behind.

'One bag each,' Ma had said, as soon as the front door had closed behind Uncle Feisal. 'Clothes. Shoes. No, Eman. No school books. We'll need warm bedding and pillows. Beans, rice, flour. Get to bed now, all of you. We'll have to be up by dawn if we're to be ready in time.'

As it happened, Uncle Feisal was late.

'Traffic,' he panted, as he came in through the door. 'There are hardly any cars, but everyone's gone back to using their old carts, with horses and donkeys and even camels. And thousands of people are just walking! The whole city's on the move. Are you ready? We've got to go now. They say the shelling's going to be bad again today.'

His anxiety was like an infection. I hurtled up and down the stairs, carrying stuff out to the van and then rushing up to the flat again, without even thinking of feeling tired. I saw Eman and Musa whispering together as we left the flat for the last time, and noticed how heavy Eman's bag seemed to be.

Books, I thought with disgust. I was only too pleased at the thought of leaving schoolwork behind.

The back of Uncle Feisal's van had looked quite roomy, but by the time we'd packed it full of blankets and rugs and cushions and bundles of clothes and bags of food, there wasn't much room for us passengers. We piled in somehow, all crammed in like pickles in a jar. It was horribly stuffy, and at first there were long waits as Uncle Feisal sat, fuming, in the traffic jams. Once we were out of town, I saw what he'd meant about the van's springs. It didn't seem to have any. We were shaken about so much that we all started looking green.

When at last the van stopped, and we tumbled out on to the stony path that led up to the little courtyard outside Uncle Mahmud's farmhouse, it was as if we'd arrived in another world. It was still only the middle of the morning, and the sun was warm rather than hot. It wasn't even the beginning of springtime, but everything looked green and fresh and sort of washed and sparkling, quite different from the dirt and dust and rubble of Daraa.

'*Alhamdulillah!* Thank God!' Ma said, beaming at Uncle Feisal as he opened the doors of the van to let us out. 'You saved us, my brother. How can we ever thank you?'

'Listen! What was that?' Baba said sharply.

Boom! Bo-oom!

We scrambled out of the van and turned to look back along the way we'd come. Daraa was more than thirty

kilometres away, beyond the horizon now, but we all
knew what that sound meant. The shelling had started
again. The noise was rolling all the way across the innocent
fields and up to the quiet village on the rise behind the
farmhouse. I could almost imagine what it looked like: a
nasty, grey, miserable, choking cloud of horror.

Nobody moved. Then, up by the farmhouse, the
guard dog began barking, and Nadia, who had slept right
through the journey, woke up, looked round, and started
grizzling. Eman had been holding her, but Ma took over
and started rocking her up and down. Musa was still
staring in the direction of Daraa. He was frowning so
hard his thick black eyebrows met across the top of his
nose. I knew he was thinking of Bassem and the others,
and perhaps even wishing he was there with them.

Granny was standing beyond Musa. She was clutching
a large photograph of Grandfather in a glass-fronted
frame and was leaning against Baba, who was holding
her up with one arm. She looked smaller, somehow, as if
she'd been shrunk in the wash.

The door of the farmhouse creaked open. There was
a shriek as Auntie Fawzia caught sight of us. She came
running down the path, the edges of her black hijab
flapping, calling out, '*Ahlan wa sahlan!* You are welcome!
Come, come in!'

Behind her, I could see her two little girls, my cousins
Yasmin and Fatimah, peering shyly out from the doorway.
As she reached us, another boom from Daraa made

her stop and squeal with fright.

'All day yesterday it was going on! I said to Abu Jaber, "Leila and her family, how are they? *Inshallah*, they are still alive! We must send them a message, tell them to come", and now here you are! How can I live if my family is in danger?'

Ma threw Nadia over her shoulder and turned to Auntie Fawzia. She opened her mouth to say something, but Auntie Fawzia had pulled her into a hug, talking all the time.

'My poor sister! Bring all your things. There's always room for you, even if our house is small. This is your own home.'

She took Ma by the arm and led her towards the courtyard, shouting at the dog. I'd never had much to do with dogs, and I was a bit worried about the way it was straining on its rope, showing a couple of rows of sharp-looking teeth, but it shut up at once and sank back. It kept a close eye on us, though, and I decided I'd keep well away.

Auntie Fawzia was still talking non-stop as Uncle Feisal unloaded our things from the back of the van.

'Omar, Musa, help your uncle,' Baba called out to us. 'Feisal, you'll stop for tea?'

Uncle Feisal looked anxiously at his watch.

'No time. My parents' place is on the other side of Daraa. There'll be roadblocks everywhere by now.'

'Of course.' Baba nodded. 'I can't tell you how grateful I am.'

Uncle Feisal cut him off with a wave of his hand.

'You're Majda's brother. We're fond of you all.' He dropped the last bundle into my arms and slammed the van's back doors. He climbed into the driving seat, then leaned out of the window, looking embarrassed.

'Sorry about your mother, Hamid. Majda has had enough. She says it's your turn now. All the best!'

A moment later, the van was rattling away.

Footsteps crunched behind us. I turned to see Uncle Mahmud, coming round the side of the farmhouse. He smiled warmly when he saw us.

Uncle Mahmud's face was brown and leathery from working out of doors in the sun. He was in his working clothes, a long grey tunic hitched up with a belt to keep his legs free, and a red keffiyeh wrapped round his head. Unlike Auntie Fawzia, Uncle Mahmud never said a word more than necessary. Just as well, I suppose.

My cousin Jaber had followed him. I nodded at him and tried out a smile. He nodded back, stony faced. He had just turned fifteen so was a year older than me, and every time we'd met, we'd circled round each other like a pair of hostile dogs.

Uncle Mahmud jerked his chin towards the old building with a curved stone roof that stood at right angles to the farmhouse. Jaber bent to scoop up a bundle of our blankets. I grabbed another load, and Musa picked up a couple of cushions and tucked them under his good arm.

'Can he walk that far?' Jaber said to me.

'Why don't you ask him?' I replied shortly.

Musa flashed a smile at Jaber and pointed to the satellite dish on the flat roof of the farmhouse.

'You got broadband?' he said, as clearly as he could.

Jaber looked doubtful.

'We got TV, if that's what you mean.' He seemed uncomfortable talking to Musa and turned back to me. 'There's a mobile phone mast in the village but it doesn't always work. The electricity's off here, anyway. They cut if off weeks ago.'

Musa's face fell. Jaber didn't notice. He kept his eyes on me.

'We've got a generator,' he said proudly. 'Don't use it much in case the oil runs out. It's for the farm stuff.'

Musa's eyes brightened again.

'A generator? That's wonderful.'

Jaber ignored him.

When you pull an elastic band until it's tight, and then tweak it, it makes a twanging noise, but when you let it go, it sags and doesn't make a sound at all. Those first days in the village, I felt as if an elastic band tying up my insides had been let go, and now I was all floppy and quiet. It was hard to get used to not been scared all the time, not having your nerves vibrating like guitar strings at every unexpected sound.

Baba only stayed a couple of nights. He insisted on

going back to Daraa, even though Ma begged him not to. A colleague had offered to put him up, he said, in a quiet part of town away from the fighting. He needed to show up at the Ministry every day, even if the offices were closed, if he was to make sure that his salary would go on being paid.

Auntie Fawzia had been right about the farmhouse being small. We could have packed in there if we'd had to, but she and Uncle Mahmud had had a better idea. The old stone building at the side of the courtyard had been the main farmhouse long ago, but it was a storeroom now. It was quite long and narrow, just one room, with a curved roof, no windows and a heavy wooden door at one end.

I realized that Auntie Fawzia must have been expecting us for days, because she and Uncle Mahmud had cleared the storeroom out to make a place for us. There were still sacks of stuff and bottles and jars at the far end, and you could tell that the donkey had lived in it by the smell and the wisps of straw they hadn't quite managed to clear off the beaten earth floor.

'Your grandfather was born in this house,' Ma said, looking round fondly at the stone walls. 'We used to stay in here when I was a little girl. Our family's lived in it for hundreds of years.'

That's all very well, I'd wanted to say, *but it's poky and stuffy and I'd die if anyone from school saw me in here.*

*

The storeroom had looked like a miserable kind of place at first, but by the time we'd given it another good sweeping, and Ma and Eman had strung up a cloth across the middle to make a kind of bedroom at the far end for the two of them, as well as Granny and Nadia, it wasn't too bad. In the front section, closest to the door, Ma arranged rugs on the floor and cushions round the walls to make a sitting room and a place for us boys to sleep.

She shared the cooking for everyone with Auntie Fawzia in the farmhouse kitchen, and didn't seem to mind having her ears bent all day long as Auntie Fawzia talked on and on. Ma and Auntie Fawzia and Eman had spent ages washing all our clothes with water from the farm's well, getting the months of dirt and dust out of them. It really cheered me up to put on a clean shirt and trousers, and after scrubbing myself from head to toe, and shampooing my hair, I finally felt as if I could respect myself again.

The village school didn't take boys beyond the age of twelve, so only Fuad could go. With no school, I'd thought I'd have an easy time of it but I realized almost at once that I'd got that wrong.

'You must make use of Omar on the farm,' I overheard Baba say as he set off back to Daraa.

Great, Baba, I thought. *Ask me first perhaps?*

'Thank you, Hamid,' Uncle Mahmud replied. 'I did have a farmhand but he went back to Egypt last year. I'd be glad of the help.'

It was a long speech for him.

Jaber was standing nearby and he shot me a look of triumph. My heart sank. Jaber had only done three or four years of school, and I knew he was a bit shaky with reading and writing, but he'd run rings round me on the farm, and he'd enjoy it, too.

Uncle Mahmud let me have a couple of days to settle in, and then it was the end of the week, and we all had to go off to Friday prayers. I'd never liked the mosque in Daraa, but this little village mosque was much worse. The carpets were dusty and the water pipes red with rust. The imam was ancient and all he seemed to talk about was sin and how Allah would punish us if we did the wrong things. It was embarrassing the way everyone stared at us, too, and talked about Musa as if he wasn't there.

By Saturday evening I was getting bored, and was actually quite looking forward to doing a bit of work on the farm. It wasn't much fun being with Musa and Eman, anyway, and I stayed out of Jaber's way as much as I could.

Eman seemed to have shrunk back into herself. In Daraa, she'd managed to keep on with her schoolwork, but now that we were in the village, education was over for her. She didn't even open the books she'd smuggled into her bag. When she wasn't helping in the kitchen, or looking after the children, she spent hours unravelling an old sweater of Musa's and knitting it up again for Fuad. She was horribly moody, and bit my head off if I tried to talk to her.

I'll be on your side, I'd said to her, all those months ago in Bosra. *I'll make sure you get to college.*

There was no chance that I could keep my promise. I just kept out of her way.

Musa was lousy company too. He had nothing to do except fiddle on his mobile phone, trying to get through to his friends in Daraa, and when he couldn't, which was most of the time, he was in a really foul temper.

Uncle Mahmud had told me to be ready early on Sunday morning to start work, and I was waiting when he came to call me, feeling keen and eager to do my best. Jaber was standing behind his father as I came out of our storeroom house, looking sulky and holding the donkey on a rope. Uncle Mahmud, who worked on building sites when he wasn't needed on the farm, slapped us both on the shoulder, then turned and hurried off into the village, where I could hear a minibus revving its engine, telling everyone it was about to go.

'What are we supposed to be doing, then?' I asked Jaber, looking nervously at the donkey. It had tried to kick me a couple of times, and I didn't like going too near its teeth, either.

'You'll see,' was all Jaber said.

He started off quickly, with the donkey behind him. There was a large basket slung against each of its sides and they bounced as it trotted along. I had to hurry to keep up.

The field we were going to work in was down at the bottom of the slope below the farmhouse, beyond a fringe of olive trees. Uncle Mahmud had ploughed it the week before. The plough had turned up lots of white stones as well, some as big as melons.

'We've got to pick all the stones up,' Jaber said, 'and pile them on the edge of the field.'

I stared at him.

'You've got to be joking. There are millions of them. It'll take forever.'

'So we're not posh enough for you, is that it?' he said, flushing. 'Welcome to the real world, city boy.'

'No, I mean . . . It's fine,' I said, bending to pick up a stone.

Jaber had already scooped up three or four, and had dropped them into one of the donkey's baskets.

I couldn't believe how slowly time passed that morning. I dropped stones on my feet and yelped with pain. I broke my fingernails and bruised my hands. After half an hour of bending over, lifting and heaving, my back was aching and my arms felt as if they were strained all the way up to my shoulders. I was determined not to look weak in front of Jaber, but I could see he despised me for being feeble. He kept teasing me, too.

'Scorpion, scorpion!' he'd shout, and fling something at me, making me jump with fright. I flinched and fell over a couple of times, before I learned to ignore him.

CHAPTER ELEVEN

The first day working out in the fields with Jaber was horrible, the second day was worse, the third was worse still, the fourth was a bit better, the fifth was better still, and then it was Friday again. By the time we went back to work on Saturday, my back was feeling stronger and I'd stopped aching all over. I was developing quite good muscles in my arms, too.

I couldn't resist showing them off to Musa.

'Yeah, cool, Mr Universe,' he said, hunching a shoulder and turning away.

I saw that I'd hurt him. He wouldn't have minded a few good muscles to show off, after all.

'Sorry,' I mumbled, but that only made things worse.

After three weeks, I was picking up stones as fast as Jaber (which really annoyed him) and I could let my mind go off into its usual daydreams – the shop I would have one day, the money I would earn, the car I would buy, the look on Ma's face when I poured a gold necklace into her hands.

There was only one good thing about those early days on the farm: Ma started making a fuss of me. She even rubbed olive oil into my cracked hands every evening.

Uncle Mahmud was a good boss, I suppose. He didn't make us work more than six or seven hours a day. He paid Baba for my labour, so I never saw any of the money, but I'd expected that. Baba brought stuff back from Daraa whenever he came to visit – food, medicine, a new cardigan for Nadia and shoes for Fuad, so I suppose I was helping my family, at least.

As the summer got going and the weather got hotter, Uncle Mahmud took us off stone clearing. Auntie Fawzia had been bringing on tomato seedlings in the farm courtyard, and it was time to plant them out. Weeding, watering, weeding, watering – that was how it went from now on, but at least I didn't have to put up with Jaber on my own. Auntie Fawzia and Ma came to help in the field too, leaving Eman and Granny in charge of Fuad and the little girls.

It sounds as if it was just a hard grind on the farm, nothing but back-breaking work and my lousy cousin Jaber. But at least we weren't about to get bombed or shot at. Things were as bad now in Bosra as in Daraa, and as Bosra was closer to the village, we could hear the shelling and gunfire even more clearly.

Most of the time, while we were living on the farm,

I tried to ignore what was happening outside in the rest of Syria. The thought of it just made my stomach tighten up. It was different for Musa, though. He was itching to get back into the action, to be with his friends doing something in the 'struggle against tyranny', as he put it.

He would splutter with rage, too, about the lunatic fanatics in the north, with their black scarves hiding their faces, their habit of blowing up Syria's priceless ancient monuments, their mania for cutting off people's heads, blowing themselves up and selling people's mums and sisters into slavery.

'Do you think they might be *a bit* right?' I asked Musa one evening, partly to get him going and partly because I wasn't quite sure in my own head.

He wrinkled his nose as if I'd made a bad smell.

'Are you crazy? You think what they do is good? That it's Islamic?'

'I'm only saying. Jaber says—'

'I thought you hated Jaber.'

'I do, but we have to talk sometimes. He thinks those guys are a bit . . . well, cool.'

And then I wished I hadn't said anything, because Musa gave me a lecture that seemed to last forever, and quoted chunks of the Holy Koran at me, and then he told Ma that Jaber was turning into a fanatic, and Ma told Auntie Fawzia, and Auntie Fawzia told Uncle Mahmud, and Uncle Mahmud gave Jaber a rocket, and the next day Jaber gave me a black eye, and I had to pretend that it was the donkey who had kicked me. Which it might have been, as a matter of fact, because that animal had hated me from the very beginning.

It might sound as if I'm really shallow, but probably the thing I liked most about being on the farm was the food. Auntie Fawzia was a brilliant cook. She and Ma and Granny sat together for hours in the afternoons, on a mat outside the kitchen door, sorting through pans of dried lentils, picking out all the little stones, while Eman looked after the younger children. Then they'd get into the kitchen and the loveliest smells would come wafting out, and at dinner time we'd sit down to eat stuffed cabbage leaves with pomegranate sauce, and minced lamb with spinach and wedges of lemon, and fresh eggs, and beautiful bread, hot from the oven.

I could tell that Ma was happy. She and Auntie Fawzia had always been best friends, and now she had an ally against Granny. Every now and then, Granny would let out a screech of fury at Musa, or me, or Eman, if we broke some little rule or other, but she was outnumbered and she knew it.

It was late in July when things came to a head with Jaber. All through spring and early summer, I'd had to endure his stupid teases, tricks and insults. I don't think I'd ever hated anyone before, but I really came to hate him.

It was a Friday afternoon, the best time of the week. We'd got back from the mosque and had eaten our way through Auntie Fawzia's huge weekly feast. Now we had the afternoon to ourselves.

I was sitting in the shade outside our storeroom house, idly watching Fuad picking up wisps of grass and feeding them to the donkey. He loved the farm. He was quite happy chasing the goats and going off with Auntie Fawzia to look for the eggs the chickens had laid. Then Jaber came out of the house and saw him with the donkey.

'Do you want to ride him, Fuad?' he called out. 'I'll lift you up if you like.'

Jaber was nice to Fuad, I'll say that for him, and Fuad loved him back (which really annoyed me). A moment later, there was my little brother, sitting on the donkey's back squeaking with pleasure, and Jaber was leading him round the courtyard. Then Jaber saw me.

'Hop off now, Fuad,' he said. 'It's Omar's turn.'

I'd nearly dropped off, but I opened my eyes at that. There was something in Jaber's voice that was making me wary. Anyway, I didn't want to tangle with the donkey. He liked me as little as I liked him.

'No thanks,' I said.

'Your big brother's scared,' Jaber said mockingly to Fuad.

'You shouldn't be scared, Omar,' said Fuad, looking uncertainly at Jaber. 'He's really nice. It's fun riding him.'

'Nah, he's scared,' repeated Jaber.

At that moment, Nadia came trotting out of the house.

She was always picking up words and repeating them.

'Scared,' she said. 'Omar scared.'

That did it. I was being mocked by my own baby sister. A red mist of fury rose behind my eyes. With a roar, I jumped up, ran across to the donkey, and somehow, with a wild flailing of arms and legs, managed to get on to his back.

'You have to kick him a bit to make him go,' Fuad called helpfully.

I sensed Jaber doing something behind me, but I was too afraid of falling off to turn around and look. I gathered up the reins and steeled myself to kick the donkey's flanks. All of a sudden there was a loud bang, and the donkey bolted out of the courtyard and galloped down the lane with me clinging like a monkey to his back.

I know I said I was brave, and I know I'd dodged gunmen and been shot at and survived the shelling of our street, but those few minutes on the donkey's back were the most terrifying of my life. His ears were laid back, and he belted down towards the cistern at the bottom of the slope, swerving under trees so that I had to lie right down along his neck to avoid being whacked by the branches, while far behind me Fuad was yelling, 'Omar, make him stop! Omar!' and Jaber was laughing like a hyena.

I don't know how I clung on. In the end, I was halfway off the side of him, with my arms around his neck. He came to a sudden halt right beside the cistern, so sudden in fact that I flew right over his head, crashed down on my front against the low wall that ran round the top of the cistern, and landed with a splash in the water.

The water felt icy. The cistern was quite deep and I went right under, coming up again with my mouth and nose full of green slime. I tried to spit it out, but the blow to my stomach had winded me and I couldn't take a breath. I stood up, with only my head and shoulders out of the water, gasping and choking. Then I started seeing black spots behind my eyes and I passed out.

The next thing I knew I was lying on the ground with Jaber pummelling me on the chest and Fuad shouting, 'Omar, are you drowned? Say something, Omar!'

Another whack sent a stinking stream of stagnant water shooting out of my mouth, then I turned over on to my hands and knees and was violently sick. So much for Auntie Fawzia's Friday feast.

I looked up at last and glared at Jaber. He must have read the rage in my eyes because there was an anxious look in his own. He was wet through as well, so I suppose he must have pulled me out of the water. I wasn't about to feel grateful, though. It was still hard to breathe, but I managed to gasp out, 'You – tried to – kill – me.'

He flinched.

'I didn't! Honestly, Omar. Don't tell my father that. I didn't mean—'

'You set off a firecracker. You made the donkey bolt.'

'It was just a bit of fun! Can't you take a joke?'

'Not a joke. You tried to hurt me.'

He scowled. He was becoming his hostile self again.

I lurched to my feet, still feeling shaky, and peeled off my sodden shirt. 'Fuad,' I said. 'Lay this out to dry, then take the donkey back to the farm. I've got something to sort out with Jaber.'

'Are you going to fight him, Omar?' Fuad said anxiously. 'Baba doesn't like us fighting. He said—'

I didn't take my eyes off Jaber.

'Just take the donkey and go.'

Fuad looked from Jaber to me and back again.

'Go on, Fuad,' said Jaber. 'If he thinks I'm going to fight him, he's got another think coming.'

I waited, fuming, till Fuad was well up the path, then I spat out, 'Got another think coming, have I? You're just scared. Loser.'

He folded his arms.

'Shut it, Omar. I'm not going to fight you.'

My fists were bunched. I was dancing on my toes, horribly aware of the wet trousers slapping against my legs.

'Who's scared now?' I taunted him.

'Look at yourself,' Jaber said mockingly. 'You're smaller than me, half winded, covered in muck, and I'd beat you to a pulp. Not that I wouldn't enjoy it, but I'm not going to give myself the pleasure.'

He meant it, I could tell. I wanted to rush at him and hurl him into the cistern. But tears of humiliation were filling up my eyes. I brushed them furiously away.

'Why do you hate me so much?' I burst out. 'What did I ever do to you?'

He snorted disbelievingly.

'You're actually asking me that? You really don't get it? You come here, all of you, living off *my* family, playing at being farmers—'

'I work as hard as you do! I've never worked so—'

'No, you've never worked at all, have you? You've been to a fancy school in the city. You've got an education. When this is over, you'll go back to your granny's posh *three-bedroom* flat and go to university, while I—'

I couldn't believe what I was hearing.

'You don't know what you're talking about!' I yelled at him. 'For starters, I had two jobs when I was at school in Bosra, and I had to be out of the house every morning by half past five. Second, I'm thick, right? Not as thick as you, but thick. Never mind university, I won't even get into upper school. Third, Granny's flat in Daraa isn't there any more. The building collapsed two days after we got out, which you'd have known if you'd ever listened to anything any of us said.'

He had the grace to look ashamed.

'I didn't realize.'

'No. You didn't think, either. Did it cross your mind that we have lost everything we've ever owned, except what we managed to bring here?'

I was still feeling a bit funny in the head. I turned my back on Jaber and went to sit on a boulder above the cistern, in the shade of the old gnarled fig tree.

'Anyway,' I went on. 'Musa's the clever one, not me.'

'That cripple? He can't even walk properly.'

'Doesn't keep his brains in his legs, does he?' I snapped. 'Haven't you ever listened to him talk about stuff?'

'Why should I? He can't even speak properly.'

'More fool you. Musa's even cleverer than Eman, and she's practically a genius.'

Jaber frowned.

'So what? She's a girl.'

'Really? I hadn't noticed!' The burning sun seemed to be getting to him and he came closer, squatting down under the fig tree not far away from me. 'Eman was going to be a teacher till all this happened.'

Jaber frowned.

'She ought to be married by now. How old is she? Seventeen? Education's bad for girls, my dad says.'

'So does mine, but it doesn't mean he's right.'

But Jaber had sown an unpleasant thought in my mind. Now that Eman had had to give up her education, was Baba going to marry her off? Was he looking around for a husband for her already?

A fly landed on my bare arm. I flicked it off. Jaber, who had never seen me without my shirt before, was staring at the scar on my arm.

'What's that?' he asked.

'Bullet wound,' I said, as casually as I could.

He couldn't hide the fact that he was impressed.

'What happened?'

So I told him. I did exaggerate a bit. Well, quite a lot, actually. After all, I hadn't really dodged about between cars or felt bullets whizzing through my hair. I didn't bother to mention Musa, either. By the time I'd finished, I realized that I'd been talking to him as if he was a real human being.

'What was it like in Daraa then, being shelled and all that?'

I hadn't expected the question, and I didn't know how to answer. I still had bad dreams about bombs falling, and the man with the little girl in his arms running through the streets.

'Not much fun,' I said at last.

It had been a while since I'd thought about Granny's flat. I'd never liked it, but we'd lived in it for a year and it had become home in the end. It hit me suddenly that we didn't have a proper home of our own at all now, and I started to feel cold inside. I was afraid that if I said much more my voice would start to wobble.

To break the silence, I picked up a stone lying at the edge of the cistern and sent it plopping down into the water.

'Omar,' Jaber said quietly. 'Don't move your foot. Keep still. Just don't move.'

'What? Why?'

'There's a scorpion right there. It was under that stone.'

'Oh yeah?' I said. He'd played that trick on me too often, but there was something in his voice that chilled me. I looked down. There was a scorpion there, a vicious little black one, just ten centimetres away from my bare foot.

I let out a terrified yell and jerked my leg away as Jaber picked up a bigger stone and smashed it down on top of the scorpion, then he prodded its little black corpse with a stick to make sure it was really dead and flicked it into the cistern.

'Thanks,' I said grudgingly.

He shrugged.

'Put your shirt back on. We'd better get home.'

CHAPTER TWELVE

I can't say that Jaber and I became friends, exactly. But after that day we understood each other better, and sometimes, when the vegetables had ripened and we started picking them and boxing them up, we even had a bit of a laugh, especially when one of the aubergines had a funny shape like something rude.

Jaber didn't say any more about thinking the Islamic State nutters were cool, and I wouldn't have listened if he had. Things were getting really, really bad all over the country, especially in the north. I didn't follow it all. I left that to Musa, who was electrified by every bit of news that came his way. Occasionally he persuaded Baba to take him back into town for a couple of days. He said he wanted to meet up with his old teachers and get work for private study, but I knew he was up to more than that.

One Thursday evening in August, he came back from town with a smart new laptop.

I'd been lying on the cushions in our little house playing

a card game with Fuad, and I sat up to have a look.

'Baba bought that for you, didn't he?' I was boiling with indignation. 'That's so unfair!'

He laughed.

'Are you kidding?'

'How did you get it then. You didn't nick it?'

It was just my bad luck that Ma came in and heard me.

'Omar!' she said, shocked. 'How could you say such a thing? Musa's got some very kind friends. It's good to know that even in these bad times some people think about others who need special help.'

Musa winced. I hid a smile. Ma went back out again.

'Friends, eh?' I said. 'Don't tell me. It was Bassem, wasn't it? Don't tell me what you're going to do with it, either.'

He ignored me and started tapping the keys, frowning with frustration.

I tried again.

'Hello! It's me! Your favourite brother? Don't suppose you'd let me play games on it, would you?'

He looked up.

'Are you kidding? Seriously, Omar, don't touch this thing. It's got a built-in satellite link but that makes it easy to detect. I must never be online for more than a minute at a time. They can trace it if you're on for longer. Soldiers could come here and get me.'

I shivered.

'Musa, you can't do this. It's too dangerous! Anyway,

how's Bassem going to pick up your messages? His phone must have died weeks ago.'

He looked up at me.

'His dad's got a generator. You know how rich they are. Anyway, I can't not. Getting the word out there, telling the world what this wicked government is doing to our country – it's the only thing, *the one thing*, I can do.'

I suppose Ma thought, when she made us all come to live on the farm, that the trouble would stay in the city. She was right at first, but then things began to change.

There were shortages in the country, too. Food was getting more and more expensive. It was lucky that Uncle Mahmud's farm was a big one, and that Auntie Fawzia had pickled and stored so much of last year's harvest. The farm animals gave us eggs and milk, and meat occasionally, and she had big dry stores of lentils and flour and rice.

Nothing really bad had happened so far in our village, but there were reports all the time of army vehicles being blown up, attacks on policemen, horrible reprisals by the government forces, ambushes and arrests. And everyone knew what arrests meant. Prisoners would be starved, beaten, tortured and probably shot.

The knots in my stomach were tightening up again. I worried about Musa most of all, but I was scared that something bad would happen to Baba, too. He was

still living in Daraa, in a small room he'd rented on the
outskirts, trying to go to work. Ma kept trying to call
him on her ancient mobile. She hardly ever got through,
but when she did, she'd relay his instructions to us and
repeat our dutiful replies, which she had to make up half
the time. Once or twice, when she was on the phone to
him, I saw her eyes flick towards Eman and move away
again, then she'd go outside where we couldn't hear her.
I knew what she was up to, though.

I suppose Baba's right, I told myself uncertainly. *Eman
can't be a teacher now, so she ought to get married. She's got to
have someone to look after her.*

The thought of what would happen to my sister if
rampaging soldiers stormed the farm was so terrifying
that it kept me awake sometimes, even though I was
always worn out from the day's work.

I didn't realize it at the time, but the person who was
keeping us all together was Auntie Fawzia. She wasn't
someone you would have noticed, quite honestly, if you'd
passed her in the street. She was short and sort of round
all over. Her ankle-length dresses were old and worn,
her hijab was always on crooked, and her face and hands
were leathery and wrinkled from being in the sun. She
also had a wart on her chin with bristles sprouting from
it. Ma was only a couple of years younger, but you'd have
thought that Auntie Fawzia was her mum rather than her
sister.

Auntie Fawzia had a way of sweeping us all up in

her life and making us feel as if we belonged there. She talked so much it was easy to think she was just a silly old woman, but she never said anything unkind. She liked laughing, too, and when she did her whole body wobbled like a bowl of shaken yogurt.

By September, the fiercest heat of the summer had softened a bit. The grapes on the vine that grew over a frame in the courtyard were ripening, and Ma and Auntie Fawzia had spent days bottling, pickling, making jam, and filling shelf after shelf with jars for the winter.

Friday had come round again. Uncle Mahmud took us boys to the mosque as he always did, and when we got home we found the donkey standing in the middle of the courtyard with his two pannier baskets already filled up with plastic containers, while Auntie Fawzia was tying bundles of rugs and cushions on to his back.

'We're going on a picnic!' she announced, laughing at our faces. 'Down by the cistern where there'll be a nice cool breeze.'

Jaber and I caught each other's eye, then looked quickly away. We hadn't gone back to the cistern since the day when I'd fallen in. It had seemed like a forbidden place, somehow. Fuad had found a chicken to chase and was running after it, flapping his arms and shouting, 'Picnic! Picnic!'

Ma came out of the kitchen carrying a basket.

'Stop that, Fuad. Here, take this basket. Omar you'll have to carry the crate of drinks. It's heavy. Don't drop it. Musa *habibi*, will you manage? It's quite a long walk. Where's Eman? There she is! What are you wearing that old thing for? I told you to put on your other dress. Go and tidy yourself up. Hurry up.'

Eman opened her mouth to object, but Uncle Mahmud was fiddling with the donkey's girth and she didn't dare argue in front of him. She flounced into our house.

'It's only a stupid picnic, for heaven's sake,' Musa muttered to me. Why's she got to dress up?'

He was obviously irritated by it all, but everyone else looked happy. The little girls were darting about excitedly, Auntie Fawzia was beaming, Granny was hanging on doggedly to a walking stick that Uncle Mahmud had cut for her, and even Jaber was smiling. It felt as if we were celebrating something.

'Here, give me a handle of that stupid crate,' said Musa. 'Let's get started before some idiot tells me I can't manage it.'

The path was rough and it was easy to slip on the loose stones. I could tell when we were halfway down that Musa was struggling and that the crate really was too heavy for him, but I knew he'd die rather than show it.

'You know what you are?' I said, to wind him up.

'What?'

'Stupid.'

'Huh. That's rich, coming from you.'

We exchanged insults all the way down the rest of the slope, and by the time everyone else arrived, with the donkey trotting along behind, Musa and I were sitting under the old fig tree and I was showing him exactly where I'd found the scorpion.

'Yeah, right,' he said disbelievingly when I opened my hands to show him how big it had been. 'Scorpions that big don't exist.'

As I remember it, there was something golden about that afternoon. A light breeze stirred the still-green leaves of the grove of fig and olive trees. The cistern was nearly empty now, but frogs still plopped occasionally in the shallow water. I felt – I don't know why – a rush of love for all my family, and even a little bit fond of Jaber.

As I sat with my back against the rough, grey trunk of a fig tree, looking round at all of them, it was as if I was noticing things I'd never noticed before.

Uncle Mahmud had lit a fire and was roasting skewers of lamb over it. I saw, from the glances he sent over to Auntie Fawzia and the nods she gave in return, that they loved each other. It made me feel a bit sad, actually, because there was nothing like that between Ma and Baba. I understood, too, that Jaber was boiling inside to get away from the farm and do something big in the world. I even felt sympathetic. I watched Granny push up her loose black sleeve and lean forward to take a stuffed vine leaf from the dishes piled on the cloth laid out on the ground and noticed for the first time how her hand trembled. She looked up and caught my eye. She looked puzzled all of a sudden, as if she didn't quite know who I was.

She's really old, I thought.

Eman was tying ribbons in Yasmin's hair, laughing at something Fuad had said. For the first time, I realized that my sister was beautiful. Ma was watching her too. She was on edge for some reason and kept looking up towards the village.

I'd eaten all I could, and was wondering if I could possibly squeeze in another few grapes, when Yasmin planted herself in front of me, her eyes dancing with anticipation.

'You've got to chase us,' she said. 'Me and Nadia and Fatimah.'

I felt too lazy and full to get up.

'Grr!' I growled, making my hands into claws and pretending to be a lion. 'Be careful or I'll eat you!'

She screamed with delight and ran behind the tree.

'No! You've got to chase us properly!' she shouted.

Jaber had got up already. I wasn't going to be outdone, so I lumbered to my feet.

It was fun chasing the little girls, scaring them with our growls and snarls. Nadia got tired of it almost at once, and went to sit on Ma's knee. Then Fatimah, the smallest one, fell over, grazed her chin on a stone, burst into loud sobs, and rushed into Auntie Fawzia's lap to be comforted. Eman called her over to play cat's cradle and Yasmin followed her.

I stood there panting. I didn't feel like sitting down again.

'Want a game of football, Fuad?' Jaber called out.

Fuad had been watching us enviously. He jumped to his feet.

'Yes! But you haven't got a ball.'

Jaber went over to the donkey, who was hitched to the furthest tree, looking half asleep, and dug to the bottom of one of the baskets.

'Wa-hey!' he said triumphantly, pulling out a shapeless bundle of blue plastic bags wrapped round an old drinks can.

I tried not to let my disgust show in my face. Jaber's 'ball' was what all the poor kids in the village played with, what the postcard sellers in the old ruins in Bosra had made for themselves. But I had once had a proper ball, with black and white panels all over it. It would be flattened now, and unrecognizable, buried under tons of concrete.

Jaber was watching me suspiciously, and I could almost see the words 'Not posh enough for you?' rising up from his head in a speech bubble.

'I'll be goalie,' I said quickly. 'See those two stones over there? You've got to shoot between them.'

'Penalty shoot-out!' shouted Fuad excitedly. He kicked out wildly at the 'ball' and it landed with a splatter in a half-finished bowl of salad right in the middle of the picnic.

Auntie Fawzia only laughed, and waved us away, as if she was shooing flies.

'Go further away! Play over there!'

It was the first time I'd played football with Jaber. The ground was all rocks and stones, the ball kept unravelling and Fuad kicked in every direction but the right one. Even so, I hadn't had so much fun for ages.

'You boys look hot!' Auntie Fawzia called out, as we stopped at last, panting. 'Come and have a drink.'

Fuad rushed up to me and gave me a high five. I surprised myself by giving one to Jaber, too.

I was just gulping down the last mouthful of a long, cool drink of water, when Fuad shouted out, 'Look! Baba's coming!'

Everyone's head swivelled round. Baba, who looked out of place in his city suit and polished shoes, was picking his way down the path towards us. Someone else was walking along a few paces behind him.

The sun was low in the sky and I had to shade my eyes to see properly. And my stomach kicked, and the hairs on my arms stood up, because the man coming down the slope towards us was Mr Nosy.

You know how sometimes there's a thing at the edge of a nightmare, a sort of nameless dread? Mr Nosy was that thing for me. It had been over a year and a half since I'd watched him terrifying kind old Uncle Ali, making him shut his shop and flee from town, but I'd never forgotten the threat that oozed out of him, like poison dripping off a snake's tongue.

Uncle Mahmud had been slumped on a cushion, gently snoring, but at a nudge from Auntie Fawzia he struggled to his feet and hastily straightened the keffiyeh on his head. The little girls hid shyly behind their mothers.

'Eman,' hissed Ma. 'Pull your hijab straight. Your hair's showing.'

Musa was examining Mr Nosy with the usual watchful look he gave to strangers.

Musa! I thought, with another stab of fear. *He's come to arrest him!*

I slipped across to Musa, bent down and whispered in his ear, 'Play dumb. Be careful. He's dangerous.'

Musa cocked an eye at me.

'Doesn't look scary,' he whispered back. 'Got a face like a rat.'

I gripped his arm. He must have felt my fingers trembling.

'He's the man who threatened Uncle Ali. Secret police.'

Musa shuddered and let his head droop sideways, an inane grin spreading across his face. Mr Nosy was looking in our direction, and I tried to smile politely, willing him not to recognize me.

'Come here, boys!' Baba called out.

I helped Musa ostentatiously to his feet. He had gone floppy and it needed all my heft to lift him.

'No need to overdo it,' I growled at him. 'You weigh a ton.'

I could feel his own hand trembling under mine. He was as scared as I was. We made our way slowly, past the ruins of the picnic, to stand at the edge of the group of men. Jaber was there already.

I was in such a state by then that I could hardly follow the men's conversation. They had moved away to stand beyond the trees, respectfully ignoring the women, who were beginning to clear up the picnic. Mr Nosy's real name, it seemed, was Bilal. He had a cousin in the village, and he had brought his mother from Bosra on a family visit. They would be staying for a few days, and his mother would very much like to visit Um Musa and Um Jaber in the morning

As he spoke, I noticed that he was shooting sideways glances towards Eman, and a dreadful suspicion burst into my head. Mr Nosy, with his rat-like face and creepy eyes, thirty-five years old at least and stinking of menace, had come to marry my sister and force himself into the heart of our family.

That can't be right, I told myself. *Baba couldn't. He wouldn't.*

But then I caught sight of Eman. She was sitting bolt upright, spots of red flaring in her cheeks, her eyes round with shock. Ma was sitting next to her, patting her arm, whispering words of encouragement.

Ma knows! I thought disbelievingly. *She's in on it too!*

I couldn't bear to stay so close to The Rat, as I now called Mr Nosy in my head. I saw that Auntie Fawzia was struggling to fold up one of the big rugs we'd been sitting on, and stumbled off to help her.

'Has that man come to marry Eman?' I mouthed at her.

She waggled her head from side to side in a non-committal sort of way. I could see she knew all about it, but didn't like the idea any more than I did.

Eman suddenly made a strangled noise, got up and began to run towards the house, nearly tripping on her long skirt. Ma hurried after her. I saw Mr Nosy following them with his weaselly little eyes, and I clenched my fists, wishing I could punch him.

I wanted to run after Ma and Eman. I wanted to tell Eman that I'd never let that man take her away, but I knew there was nothing I could do. I had as much power as the wretched donkey, still dozing away in the shade of the trees.

CHAPTER THIRTEEN

I suppose I'd imagined, if I'd thought about it at all, that Baba and Ma would pick a really nice guy for Eman, someone like Rasoul, cool and good looking, a kind of ideal big brother for me and Musa.

They can't know about Mr Nosy, I told myself, as I followed everyone back from the picnic spot. *I've got to tell them. They won't go ahead if they know what he's like.*

I could hear Eman's furious shouts inside our little house while I was still only halfway up the path, and as I hurried into the courtyard there was the sound of a ringing slap. Eman squealed, then I heard Granny's rasping voice saying, 'Shut your mouth, you wicked girl. Do you want to bring shame on your family?'

After that, Ma started talking. She sounded soft and soothing. I pushed open the door and went in.

'It'll be all right, *habibti*,' Ma was saying. 'Mr Bilal's a good man. So rich! You'll have a nice house, lovely clothes, everything you could want.'

Eman was on her knees, pummelling a cushion with both her fists. Her shoulders were heaving with sobs.

'He's old and nasty and I hate him! His eyes are cruel! You can't do this to me, Ma. You can't!'

'Ma!' I burst out. 'He's not a good man! You've made a terrible mistake. He's in the secret police! He's the man who scared Uncle Ali so much he had to run away from Bosra. He's scary, Ma. You can't—'

Granny pointed a stick-like finger at me.

'Get out of here, you stupid boy. You know nothing about Majda's husband.'

'I'm not Majda! Why do you keep calling me Majda? And he's not my husband!' cried Eman. 'I won't marry him! You can't make me!'

'We'll see about that,' Granny said grimly. 'I chose him myself. I know his mother. They're a good family. And you'll do what you're told.'

Her old eyes were snapping with excitement.

'It's all wrong,' I said desperately. 'You can't do this to Eman.'

Ma had been bending over Eman, trying to cuddle her, while Eman, still sobbing, was shaking her off. Now Ma came up to me, and put her arm round my shoulders.

'Come outside, Omar. I know it's hard for you to see your sister cry. Let me talk to you.'

I couldn't resist the touch of Ma's soft arm. I let her lead me outside. She sat down on the big slab of stone that made a kind of seat outside our door and patted the space beside her.

'Come, darling. Sit down.'

I could see, on the path below the farm, Baba with Bilal the Rat and Uncle Mahmud. They were walking slowly away in the direction of the village. The rest of the family was trailing into the courtyard.

'You know it's time for Eman to get married,' Ma began.

'I don't *know* anything. She wants to be a teacher.'

'*Habibi*, you know that's not possible now. This war has ruined everything. All we can do for her now is keep her safe, and Mr Bilal—'

'I *told* you, Ma! He's a bad man! You should have seen how mean he was to Uncle Ali.'

Ma pursed her lips.

'I don't know about any of that. I never liked you working for that old man, but your father . . .'

'Uncle Ali was nice! He was kind and good and he didn't deserve to be frightened like that!'

'Look, Omar.' Ma squeezed my shoulders. 'We need you to help Eman accept this marriage. So far, thank God, we've been safe here, but at any moment there could be attacks, soldiers running riot, rebels bursting in, shells raining down.'

From inside the barn came an anguished cry from Eman.

'I'll kill myself! You can't make me!'

There was the sound of another slap.

Ma lowered her eyes.

'I know you love your sister, Omar dear,' she began again. 'We all love her. But for her own sake we've got to let her go. And we'll all become fond of Bilal, I'm sure.'

'Fond? Of that rat? He's evil, Ma!'

'Don't be silly.' She was beginning to lose patience with me. 'He's a very successful businessman. He's managed to get a lot of money out of the country.'

'So?' I said bitterly. 'You're selling Eman, is that it? For money?'

Ma stood up.

'Stop being childish, Omar. It's always a shock for a girl when her marriage is arranged. I cried for days when I was told I was going to marry your father.'

'I will!' Eman was shouting. 'I'll kill myself!'

'Go and find Musa,' Ma said briskly. 'I'm sure he'll talk some sense into you.'

There was only going to be one end to it all. Eman was going to marry The Rat, and there was nothing I could do about it. Jaber made snide remarks about Eman's headstrong behaviour until I wanted to punch him, Auntie Fawzia wouldn't look me in the eye, and even Musa refused to get involved.

I hardly saw Eman over the next few weeks. I had to go out early every day to work in the fields as usual, and

Eman was closely guarded in the house. Meetings were going on with The Rat's family, and no one could talk about anything but dowries and clothes and how much gold jewellery Eman would get.

'Traitor!' I hissed to Musa as we left the farmhouse one evening, after another tense supper during which Eman, her eyes red and swollen, had eaten almost nothing. 'You won't lift a finger to help your own sister!'

He shrugged.

'What can I do?'

'Talk to Baba! Talk to Ma! Tell them!'

'Tell them what?'

I wanted to bash my head on the stone wall of our house.

'That Eman *can't* marry that monster!'

It was dark by then, but there was a full moon, and Musa's eyes glimmered as he turned to look at me.

'Get real, Omar. Eman will be all right. He's got a lot of money. He might even let her go on studying.'

I couldn't believe my ears.

'You can't be serious.'

'Life's not perfect for anyone.' His voice was suddenly harsh. 'You get given your fate. You have to deal with it. I should know.'

There was no answer to that.

It was horrible to see the change in Eman. She'd stopped eating and had started to lose kilos of weight. Her eyes looked bruised with tears. She stood like a dummy as Ma and Granny fussed around her, trying on the new clothes the village dressmaker had run up for her.

The Rat had been generous, I had to admit. A good chunk of dowry had already been paid. Even I was impressed by the size of the gold necklace that Ma and Auntie Fawzia cooed over. They didn't seem to notice that Eman turned away from it with loathing.

A few days before the wedding, I came into the house to find her sitting listlessly, staring at the wall. I sat down on the cushion beside her.

'Eman, I'm sorry. I'm really really sorry. I wanted to help you.'

She turned her head and gave me a pale smile.

'I know, little brother. Thank you.'

Granny came into the house, a big piece of bread held in her hand like a weapon. She glared at Eman.

'I saw you!' She jabbed the piece of bread into Eman's face. 'Not eating again. What are you trying to do? Starve yourself?'

'Yes,' said Eman baldly.

Granny's face twisted with rage.

'I'll ram this down your wicked throat! I was married when I was thirteen. If I'd behaved as badly as you, my father would have beaten me unconscious.'

She lurched forward and tried to prise Eman's mouth open.

Ma had come in behind her.

'Please, Um Hamid,' she said, pulling Granny's hand away. 'Eman will understand soon that we're only thinking of her happiness.'

I felt disgusted with both of them. I snorted with anger, and barged outside to stamp around the courtyard until I'd calmed down.

Ma had been right about one thing. Trouble was spreading out into the countryside. Every day we heard stories of rebel raids and government attacks, farms set on fire and roadside bombs. The picnic by the cistern, only a few weeks ago, seemed to belong to another age.

Two days before the wedding, trouble came right to the heart of our village. It was the middle of the night and we were all asleep when the shattering sound of gunfire jerked us awake. Almost at once people started shouting, and a woman began to scream, on and on, a demented sound that sent shivers right through me.

Ma burst through the flimsy curtain behind which she slept with Granny and Eman, with Nadia wailing and thrashing about in her arms.

'God have mercy! There's shooting in the village! Oh God, who's trying to kill us now?'

Suddenly someone started banging on the door. Eman had struck a match to light the candle. It lit all our faces, staring at the door in terror.

'Leila! Open up! It's me, Fawzia!'

I was at the door before anyone else and wrenched back the heavy bolts.

Auntie Fawzia almost fell into the room.

'It's so frightening! So close! Mahmud has gone to find out what's happening. I begged him not to. "It's not safe," I told him. But he wouldn't listen.'

Cries from the farmhouse sent her rushing out again, calling out, 'Now the children have woken up! I must stay with them, but you're all alive, thank God!'

It was only a few minutes before Uncle Mahmud came running into the courtyard. We all clustered round him.

'Couldn't find out anything,' he said. 'Saw a gunman. Not safe in the village yet. Go back inside, all of you. Nothing we can do.'

Nobody obeyed him. Auntie Fawzia stood swaying on her feet, her little girls crying and holding on to her skirt.

'God have mercy on us,' moaned Ma.

Granny had come outside now.

'God will punish them!' she shrieked, shaking her fist at the sky.

At last, Uncle Mahmud shooed us all back inside.

None of us, except for Nadia, slept again that night. There was no more shooting, but we lay with our ears straining to hear what was happening in the village. There were more shouts and the sounds of a car or truck starting up and driving away. Towards dawn, there was a chorus of women wailing.

When it was light, Ma went to the door, unbolted it

and looked out cautiously. Then she ran across to the farmhouse.

'What do you think's going to happen?' I asked Musa.

'The army will come soon.' He was chewing his lip anxiously. 'Arrest any young men they find. Make them join the army.'

My heart skipped a beat.

'How young?'

'Fifteen, sixteen.'

'But Jaber's fifteen! And you're sixteen!'

'Don't need to worry about me. There's no army in the world that would take a cripple like me.'

'And what about me?'

'I'd stay out of sight if I were you.'

I looked round wildly, as if there was a hiding place to be found in that bare little barn. My eye fell on Musa's laptop, lying on the floor. The sight of it made me feel sick.

'Musa, if they find that, they'll kill you.'

'Don't think I don't know.'

He picked it up. His hands were trembling.

'What are you going to do?'

'I've been trying to think of a hiding place.'

'And have you?'

'Not yet.'

Ma came back.

'Fawzia's so wonderful!' She was half laughing, half crying. 'Never mind our troubles. Breakfast's ready in the farmhouse.'

*

It was an awful breakfast. The children were crying, Jaber, Musa and I were tense with nerves, Granny was moaning and fingering her prayer beads. Only Eman was the same. She picked at a couple of mouthfuls of bread but stared at the wall as if she didn't care what was happening.

Uncle Mahmud hadn't stayed to eat. He'd gone back to the village to get news. He came back as the awkward meal came to an end.

'They've gone,' he said. 'The rebels.'

'Who were they? What happened? Is anyone dead?' we all asked him at once. Uncle Mahmud's unwillingness to speak had never been more irritating.

'Four or five rebels only,' he said. 'Targeted killing. Two policemen. Shot lots of rounds. They hit a baby as well. Ricochet through a window.'

'Whose baby? Is it dead?'

Auntie Fawzia's eyes were wide with horror.

'Abu Karim's youngest. Not dead. They've taken him to hospital. All quiet in the village now.'

'They'll come though, the army, won't they, Uncle Mahmud?' I said.

He nodded.

'We're in God's hands now.'

'I tell you what we'll do,' Auntie Fawzia said briskly. 'We'll prepare for the worst. If soldiers or rebels or anyone like that comes, they'll take our food, as sure as anything. It's a good thing we kept those plastic sacks

with *Fertilizer* written all over them. We'll pack them full
of lentils and flour and stack them in the old wooden shed
with the donkey. And the jars of olive oil, the preserves,
the jam – as soon as the wedding's over, we'll seal the
bottles tight and put them in the cistern.'

Everyone stared at her.

'You should have been a general in the army, Auntie
Fawzia,' Musa said admiringly.

'Don't be ridiculous, *habibi*. Now, Jaber and Omar, get
off to work. There are still tomatoes and aubergines to pick.
Eman dear, you can help your mother and me to pickle as
many as we can. Off you go now, boys.'

It felt weirdly like a normal day, going off to the field
with Jaber. Baba was supposed to be arriving from Daraa
late in the afternoon, ready for the wedding the next
day. We'd just set off down the path, and it was only
half past eight in the morning, so I was surprised to see
him hurrying up the road. I could tell at once that he
was in a terrible state. He began running up towards the
farmhouse, then he caught sight of me and called out,
'Where's your mother?'

I pointed to the farmhouse.

'Come with me!' he shouted over his shoulder. 'Find
Musa. Quick!'

Uncle Mahmud had pulled the donkey to a halt
alongside me. He'd seen Baba too. I looked at him for
permission to go, and he nodded. I ran as fast as I could

towards the farm, my heart skipping with fright.

The army's on its way already, I told myself. *They're going to blow up the village, and kidnap Jaber and me, and arrest Musa, and do terrible things to Eman!*

Baba was in the courtyard talking to Ma. One hand was pressed against her cheek, and her face was white with shock.

'Leave now?' she was saying. 'Go where?'

'Out. Anywhere. Out of Syria.' Baba was still out of breath. 'Pack only what we can carry.'

'How can we leave? Did you get a taxi?'

'Mahmud's going to take us as far as he can in his truck.'

'He can't! He hasn't got any petrol.'

'Emergency store. Come *on*, Leila. Hurry!'

'Is it because of the shootings? Is the army coming?'

'What are you talking about? Will you just stop arguing, and start packing!'

'But the wedding!'

'There'll be no wedding.'

Eman had appeared at the door of the house. Her mouth had dropped open in joyful disbelief. Ma was struggling to understand.

'No wedding? Why not? Everything's ready. All the clothes, and food, and . . . Why have we got to go? Can't it wait?'

Baba's hand flew to his suit buttons. He was twisting the top one furiously.

'I've had a tip-off. A friend in the Interior Ministry called me at one o'clock this morning. You know the man I've been staying with? They arrested him last week. They threw his body out of the police station yesterday. You wouldn't believe the state of him, what they'd done to him. I don't know what he was up to. But they think *I* was in it too. "They'll be coming for you tomorrow," my friend said. "Get out *now*." Then he put the phone down. Don't argue, woman. We've got to go. Now.'

'Surely—'

'Leila, there's no *time*! Put what you can together. Take only what we can carry. And don't forget food and especially water. We may have to walk quite a long way.'

A year and half earlier, I'd thought it was hard moving away from Bosra, leaving our house and all our old furniture behind. What a baby I'd been then! It had been tougher running away from the ruined flat in Daraa, losing almost everything we had. Now we were running again, and this time we would be skinned to the bone.

Baba had filled us with such a sense of panic that we all seemed to be paralysed. Ma was helplessly sorting through a pile of clothes. Musa was clutching his laptop as if he was afraid someone was going to rip it away from him. Only Eman seemed to have a sense of purpose. She was filled with an almost joyful energy, and was systematically packing Nadia's clothes into a suitcase.

'Where's your gold necklace?' Ma called out to her.

Eman made a face.

'I don't want it. Let it go back to him.'

Ma rounded on her furiously.

'Eman, are you crazy? We have nothing now, do you hear? Nothing! That necklace could feed the whole family for months! Put it on right now, and tie your hijab over it so that it can't be seen. Musa, Omar, I know it's a warm day but you'll have to put on all your winter clothes. Fuad! *Fuad!* Leave Nadia alone. Go and find your shoes.'

I suddenly noticed Granny. She was standing with one hand pressed against the stone wall of the stable, while her other plucked at her skirt.

'Are you all right, Granny?' I called out to her.

She turned a puzzled face towards me.

'What's happening? Is it the wedding? Why isn't Majda getting dressed? Abu Hamid ought to be here. Where's Abu Hamid?'

That gave me a shock. Abu Hamid was her husband. He'd been dead for ten years. Ma stopped what she was doing, went to Granny and helped her to sit down.

'We have to leave now,' she explained slowly. 'Hamid's in trouble. We have to go.'

'To Daraa,' nodded Granny. 'Go home.'

'Not home, Mother. We have to go to Jordan.'

Baba came into the stable.

'Hurry up! What are you all doing?'

Ma signalled to him urgently with her eyes.

'Come and talk to your mother, Hamid. She's a bit . . . confused.'

Baba crossed the room and stood looking down impatiently at Granny.

'I've called Feisal, Ma. He's coming to fetch you.'

'Feisal?' she looked up at him vaguely.

'Your son-in-law!' snapped Baba.

'Hamid,' Ma said, shaking her head in a quiet warning.

Baba stared into Granny's bewildered eyes, and looked away.

'How long's this been going on?' he asked Ma quietly.

'A while. She's been strange for weeks. Completely quiet most of the time, then she gets violently angry. Especially with Eman. She seems to think she's Majda. Have you really spoken to Feisal?'

'Yes. He'll come as soon as he can. There are checkpoints everywhere and the soldiers are so trigger-happy you don't know where you are. Mahmud says Mother can stay here until Feisal gets through.'

His face softened as he looked down again at Granny. He sat down beside her and gently took her hands in his.

'I'm sorry, Ma, but we have to leave now. Fawzia's going to look after you. And Feisal will come and take you to Majda and the girls. You'll like that, won't you?'

It was as if Granny had been wandering off on a track into nowhere, but she suddenly snapped back to reality.

'Majda's got some explaining to do,' she said tartly.

'She hasn't been to see us once while we've been living in this dump.'

A horn beeped outside. Baba stood up.

'That's Mahmud. He's promised to take us to the border crossing at Tel Shihab.'

Musa had been struggling into his heavy winter jacket. He looked up sharply.

'Tel Shihab's closed, Baba. Haven't you heard? They're shooting anyone who tries to get into Jordan that way.'

Baba didn't seem to hear him. He hurried outside. I followed him.

Uncle Mahmud was sitting in the driving seat of the truck, while Jaber was taking crates out of the back.

Uncle Mahmud leaned out of the driving seat and called back, 'Leave the tools and the sacks. We haven't got time to unload everything.'

'Fuad!' Baba called out. 'Eman! Where are you?'

Auntie Fawzia came running out of the house with Nadia in her arms. She passed her to Eman, and ran to embrace Ma, tears running down her leathery cheeks.

Baba was looking anxiously down the hill at the road running towards the village between the long fields. Billows of dust in the distance showed where vehicles were approaching up the dirt road.

'Climb in, all of you! Quickly!' he called out anxiously.

With a sharp exclamation, Ma peeled herself away from Auntie Fawzia, and darted back into the stable.

'Leila! Are you crazy? Come quickly!' shouted Baba.

Ma emerged a moment later with Baba's city suit jacket in her hands.

'Our papers,' she panted. 'In the pockets. You forgot them.'

Baba turned pale, grabbed the jacket and felt in the pockets.

'All here, thank God. Now get in.'

Baba climbed into the cab beside Uncle Mahmud with Ma beside him and Nadia on Ma's lap. I was helping Musa to climb up the tail of the truck into the back when Jaber came to give him an extra heave on the other side.

'Good luck,' he said gruffly. 'I hope you make it OK.'

'Good luck to you too,' I said, and I meant it.

My last sight of the farm was of Granny, hunched over like a little black beetle, hanging on to Auntie Fawzia's arm, while Jaber led the donkey into our old home, which was once more to be his stable.

CHAPTER FOURTEEN

The main road leading out of the village gave a good view right across the plain towards Daraa. I'd expected Uncle Mahmud to drive straight down it, but he swerved suddenly to the right and headed along the bumpy farm track that led to the fields behind the village. As the truck turned I could see beyond the cab, which had blocked our view. Four military vehicles, which a short time earlier had been invisible in clouds of dust in the distance, were now frighteningly close. There was a big gun mounted on the back of one of them, and the others were packed with soldiers.

I shivered at the sight of them. Beside me, Musa too was trembling violently.

'Get down, all of you!' hissed Eman. 'Quick, Omar, help me with the plastic sheet!'

I saw at once what she meant. It was really lucky that Jaber hadn't had time to empty the back of the truck properly. Along with the tools, as well as a few sacks of fertilizer, lay a large, blue plastic sheet, loosely folded, which Uncle Mahmud used to tie over the open back of the truck when it was fully loaded. I grabbed it, and a moment later, Musa, Eman, Fuad and I, along with all our bags, were huddled underneath it. The last time it had been used was to cover a pile of donkey and goat dung, and it stank, but I hardly noticed the smell. I was too busy checking all round the edges to make sure that nothing was showing.

There was a shout from behind us and the truck juddered to a stop.

'I'm frightened, Eman,' said Fuad, in a high, piping voice.

'Shh, *habibi*.' She wrapped her arms round him. 'Pretend we're playing hide-and-seek. Keep very still and quiet.'

Footsteps were crunching over the rough stones of the track towards the truck.

Two men, I thought. *Perhaps three.*

A loud rap on the side of the truck's cab made me jump.

'Papers,' a deep voice barked.

'Good morning, brother,' came Uncle Mahmud's slow voice. There was a pause, then the sound of rustling paper.

Someone coughed and spat, then the deep voice spoke again.

'Where are you going? What's in the back of the truck?'

Footsteps came round to the tailboard, and there was a grating sound as someone tried to force the stiff bolt that held it in place.

'*Inshallah*, my brother and I are going to our field, down there,' Uncle Mahmud said. 'We're spreading fertilizer today.'

I could hardly breathe. My eyes were squeezed so tightly that my eyeballs ached.

'You're taking that little kid to the field?' the man said disbelievingly.

Uncle Mahmud coughed nervously.

'Our sons have all been called up, sir. My brother's wife has to help out. How are we to feed our nation if the fields aren't farmed? We can't leave the child at home. She's happy down there playing with a pile of stones.'

'Corporal!' the man said. 'If you can't get that tailboard down, climb up the side and take a look.'

Musa's arm jerked violently. I grabbed it and pinned it to the floorboards, praying that the movement hadn't been noticed. The truck rocked as the corporal put his foot on the wheel and prepared to heave himself up over the side.

And then, Nadia, darling little Nadia, said loudly, 'Uncle, you've got a funny bend in your nose.'

The man climbing on the wheel laughed, then the truck rocked again as he jumped down.

'There you are, Sergeant.' He said. 'The truth from

a pretty girl at last. Nothing up there. Just a load of fertilizer and manure. It stinks, too.'

There was another agonizing pause, then papers rustled again.

'Thank you, sir,' said Uncle Mahmud. '*Inshallah*, all this trouble will soon be over and we can get our Syria back again.'

'*Inshallah*,' repeated the sergeant. A hand slapped against the side of the cab again. 'Go on then, but make sure you're back well before dark. There are rebels all over the countryside. It's not safe for honest men to be out.'

Now we could hear shouts and wailing coming from the village. The policemen's funerals had already started. The sound of the soldiers' retreating feet was cut off by the truck's noisy engine, spluttering back to life.

Fuad began wriggling out of Eman's grasp, trying to push back the plastic sheet.

'Stay still,' Musa warned him. 'They might still be watching.'

It was horribly uncomfortable being jolted around in the strange blue twilight under the plastic sheet. Uncle Mahmud was usually a slow, cautious driver, but he was racing down the uneven farm track at top speed, making the truck bounce through potholes and skid round corners. It felt as if we were clinging to the back of a dragon's lashing tail.

After what felt like hours, he jerked to a halt and we heard the cab doors open.

'You can come out now, children,' Ma called out. 'Oh my darlings, thank God you had the sense to hide yourselves!'

I threw back the plastic sheet. The brilliance of the sun blinded me for a moment.

'Where are we? Is this the border?'

No one answered.

'Get out, all of you,' said Baba. 'Pass the bags down to me.'

We handed over our few bags. Eman and I helped Musa over the side and hopped down ourselves. Fuad, huddled up against the back of the cab, didn't move.

'Fuad, come on, *habibi*,' said Ma. 'It's time to get down.

Fuad shook his head.

'Fuad!' Baba commanded sharply. 'Get down here at once.'

Fuad stood up, holding his hands down to hide the front of his trousers. He saw Ma looking at them and burst into tears.

'I wet my pants, Ma! I couldn't help it. I didn't mean to. I'm sorry. Don't be angry, Ma.'

Eman reached up to help him down.

'Don't cry, silly,' she said. 'I was so scared I almost wet mine.'

'And I did,' said Musa.

'Me too,' I said.

'Well.' Ma looked resigned. 'We can't change them here and we can't wash them either. You'll just have to let them dry.'

My eyes had got used to the light now. I could see that we'd come to the end of a long track that wound down through fields, some bare and brown, others still green with vegetables. Ahead of it was a road, and the sight of it made us all gasp.

Hundreds of people were walking along it. There were a few men, but most of them were women, with babies in their arms and children trotting along behind them. A few old people struggled along, leaning on sticks, and there was even someone in a rickety wheelchair. They were all loaded down with bags and bundles and jerrycans. Even the smallest children were carrying something, even if it was only an old water bottle filled with olives.

'Who are they?' asked Eman.

'People like us,' Musa answered bitterly. 'Refugees, like us.'

Uncle Mahmud was climbing hastily back into the cab of his truck.

'I'm sorry, Hamid. I can't take you any further,' he said. 'There are soldiers in the village. Fawzia's on her own with Jaber, and God knows he needs protecting too.'

Baba nodded but said nothing. His face looked pinched and thinner than ever.

Ma stepped forward and said quickly, 'You must go, brother. Thank God you came to our rescue.'

'The border's not far,' Uncle Mahmud said, pointing with his chin along the way the people were walking.

He was already climbing back into the driving seat.

Baba suddenly found his tongue.

'*Inshallah*, we shall meet in better times, Abu Jaber,' he said formally. 'You have saved my family. God will reward you.'

The truck roared into life. Uncle Mahmud turned it with a screeching clash of gears and we had to jump out of the way of the spray of stones kicked out from the back wheels as he raced back up the track towards the village and his farm.

It was awful watching Uncle Mahmud go. The last contact with our old life was being snatched away. We stood close together, watching until the truck was out of sight.

Ma looked at Baba and waited. When he didn't move, she said, 'Omar, take the blue bundle and the food bag. Eman, can you manage the blanket roll? Probably easiest to balance it on your head. Fuad, *habibi*, you're a big boy now. Take the jerrycan. Be careful not to drop it.'

She picked up Nadia and looked anxiously at Baba, who was staring silently at the straggling line of moving people. She touched his arm and he looked round and saw Musa struggling with the straps of his small backpack. He went over to help him, then he put one arm round Musa's waist and picked up the black clothes bag with his spare hand.

'It's going to be a long walk,' he said to Musa. 'Lean on me.'

It was a strange and dreadful feeling, joining that endless stream of travellers. One or two people nodded, and someone called out, 'Welcome to nowhere!' but I didn't feel like responding.

We're not like them, I told myself. *We're from a proper family. From Bosra. Baba's got — well, he did have — a job in the government. We're only going away for a bit. Till the trouble dies down. We're real people, not like* them.

Nadia, lying against Ma's shoulder, was nodding off to sleep.

'How old is she?' asked a young woman, who had come up to walk alongside Ma.

'Two and a half,' answered Ma shortly.

The woman didn't seem to notice her cold manner.

'Where are you heading?'

'To Jordan.'

'Of course,' the woman said. 'We all are. Where are you planning to cross the border?'

Baba had been listening.

'At Tel Shihab,' he said.

An older woman, walking ahead, turned round.

'Haven't you heard? Tel Shihab is closed. The army shelled it yesterday. Lots of people were killed. They're trying to stop anyone getting out.'

'I told you, Baba,' muttered Musa.

'Where can we cross then?' asked Ma.

'The big border posts are all being patrolled now,' answered the woman. 'They're shooting people who try to break through. We're going to try to get over the river. There are lots of ways through the border on the other side. The fence is just old barbed wire, so I've heard.'

'You're going to cross the river?' Baba was almost squeaking with shock. 'The Yarmouk? But it's right down at the bottom of a ravine! And what about getting over the river? Are there boats?'

The woman laughed scornfully. It didn't seem to bother her that a man she didn't know was talking to her in front of other people.

'Haven't you realized there's a drought? The river's dry. It's easy to cross on foot. And getting down the side of the ravine and up again is the least of our problems. There are soldiers popping up where you'd least expect them. They open fire on any refugees they see trying to cross. The only safe way is to do it by night.'

'God help us!' Ma cried out, shifting the dead weight of the sleeping Nadia from one shoulder to the other.

From some way back, someone else called out, 'What's God got to do with it? I'm sick of hearing about God. Didn't he abandon Syria a long time ago?'

I've never thought of myself as a sporty type. I like playing football, but who doesn't? To be honest, I'm a bit greedy, and until we left Daraa I'd been on the chubby side, more like Ma, who's round and comfortable, and not at all like Baba, who's short and skinny. But six months of hard work on the farm had toughened me up, burned off the flab and given me muscles.

Poor little Fuad was struggling along with the heavy jerrycan, and Eman's knees were wobbling under the weight on her head. After a few kilometres, I couldn't work out if Baba was helping Musa along or if it was the other way round, because Baba looked ready to drop. Ma was used to carrying Nadia, but even so she kept having to wipe the sweat off her face with the end of her hijab. She'd made us wear our thickest winter clothes, and we were all boiling. Even so, I was managing fine with my two heavy bags. And if I'd had another arm, I'd have helped Fuad out with the water, too.

It's not very nice to admit this, when everyone was so sad and upset (apart from Eman, of course) but a bit of me was enjoying myself. There'd been some good things about life on the farm, but it had been really boring too.

Now we had set off on an adventure. A new start. Travel.

As the hours passed, I let myself dream. Perhaps this would be the first step on my way to Norway, to join Rasoul and . . .

'Omar!'

That was Ma calling. I looked back to see that my family had pulled out of the stream of people and had sat down on the side of the road, only they weren't exactly sitting down. It was more that they had crumpled up. Eman was crouched over her foot, inspecting a blister. Musa was bent double over his knees as if he was in pain. Ma had lain Nadia down on the ground, but she'd woken up and was grizzling. Only Baba was still standing. He was staring along the road with a fierce frown on his face.

'I'm hungry, Ma,' Fuad was saying, his whine about to turn into crying.

'The food bag, Omar,' said Ma, holding out her hand.

I'd forgotten that the heavy bag I'd been carrying was full of food. At the thought of it I realized that I was starving myself. Ma unzipped the bag and pulled out a plastic box. When she unclipped the lid, I saw that it was crammed with sandwich wraps. I picked one out and bit into it. Auntie Fawzia's thick, home-made hummus squirted on to my tongue. I savoured every garlicky moment of it. My last taste of Syria! Then, unable to stop myself, I crammed the rest into my mouth in a few glorious bites, and reached for the next one – crisp farm-grown cucumber and Auntie Fawzia's salty goat's cheese. Ma rummaged about in the bag again and came up with a plastic beaker.

'Trust Fawzia to think of everything!' she said with a shaky laugh.

I discovered that I was terribly thirsty, too. When it was my turn with the beaker, I drank down the water in one long go and held it out for more.

Baba shook his head. He'd sat down to eat, and his angry frown had gone. 'No more now,' he said. 'There's a long way to go. Who knows where we'll find more water, and more food, come to that.'

It was a horrible thought, and I wished I'd made my share last longer.

None of us wanted to get up and start walking again, but as soon as the empty box and beaker were packed away, Ma and Baba were on their feet again. Without a word, we all stood up too.

What happened next was so sudden and shocking that for what seemed like ages we all stood frozen to the spot. Shots cracked out from further up the road, and people began to scream.

'Get down on to the ground, all of you!' shouted Baba.

My instinct was telling me to run, but the rest of the family were flat on their faces, so I dropped down too. After a moment, I lifted my head to see people scrambling past each other to get off the road. Two young men ran past us, into the field behind.

'What's happening?' Baba called out to them.

'Syrian army post,' one of them shouted back. They're shooting at everyone. Trying to turn them back from the border.'

'What should we do?' Baba yelled after them.

'Follow us,' called the other one. 'The river's over this way. Jordan's on the other side.'

More shots and the sound of a heavy vehicle roaring

into life turned my guts to water. We had all jumped up again, and without thinking I grabbed Musa and hoisted him on to my back.

'Take the bags, Baba,' I shouted, and, with Musa cursing me and bouncing around on my back, I lurched as fast as I could after the two young men. They were already way ahead, but one of them turned and called out something to the other. They stopped, and ran back to us.

'We can help you if you'll help us,' one said.

'What do you mean?' panted Baba, coming up behind me.

'The Jordanians don't let in single men unless they're with a family,' the shorter one said. 'Say we're with you, that we're your cousins, and they'll let us in.'

Musa had wriggled off my back, and had rewarded me with a glare.

'Baba, be careful,' he said quietly.

But Baba was already handing our heavy bags over to the stronger of the two men.

Ma came up, carrying Nadia, with Eman behind her. The strangers politely kept their eyes away from them.

'I'm Hassan Mahmoud,' said the taller, older one. 'He's my brother, Yahya.'

I don't know, quite honestly, how we'd have managed without Hassan and Yahya. They just scooped up our bundles and seemed to whisk us over that field. A short time later we had left the screams and shots some way behind us, and I was staring, petrified, down a slope so steep it looked almost like a cliff, while far below a snaking ribbon of pale stones showed the path of the dried-up Yarmouk.

'We'll never get all the way down there before it gets dark,' said Baba, peering anxiously over the edge of the ravine. 'It'll be too dangerous when the light's bad. We'll have to wait here till morning.'

'We can't stop here!' said Ma. 'The wind's getting up already. It'll soon be freezing cold.'

I looked at Ma, shocked. I still wasn't used to the way she'd started contradicting Baba these days. It seemed worse to do it in front of strangers.

Yahya didn't look at her, but he nodded, as if he agreed.

'With respect, sir,' he began, looking at Baba. 'I suggest . . .'

But we never heard what he was going to suggest because the *rat-tat-tat* of shots came again, closer this time, and people still on the road on the far side of the field started yelling in panic.

We all ducked, as if bullets were flying over our heads, and Hassan called out, 'Soldiers! They're coming this way!' So we had no choice. We had to jump over the edge and start to feel our way down, or risk being shot.

If we'd only had more time to find a path leading down to the bottom of that terrible ravine, we might have

made it before nightfall. As it was, we found ourselves
scrambling down falls of big rocks, with thorn bushes
growing between them, and slippery patches of loose
stones running almost vertically downward. I was scared
stiff, but at the same time I felt sort of powerful, too. My
legs were doing things I didn't know they could, jumping
and dodging and swerving. I had to force myself not to
scramble on too far in front of the others.

Hassan and Yahya could have bounded down to the
bottom faster than any of us, but they didn't. In fact, they
couldn't have helped us more if they'd been members
of our own family. Hassan was carrying Eman's huge
bundle and my big bag. Yahya had taken Nadia out of
Ma's arms and was singing funny little songs to her to
stop her crying. Eman and Ma stuck together, helping
each other over the biggest boulders, while Baba stayed
with Musa. Nobody seemed to need me.

'Here, give me the jerrycan,' I said to Fuad. 'I've only
got the food bag now.' But he snatched it away from my
outstretched hand.

'I can manage,' he said seriously.

'Suit yourself,' I muttered in response.

I'd have felt a bit useless if it wasn't for the fact that I was
the one who found the way down. I did it just in time,
too, because the sun had dipped almost to the horizon, the
sky was red, and the ravine looked darker and deeper than
ever. I might have missed the path if it hadn't been for

Musa crying out suddenly. He'd slipped and fallen heavily against a rock. I turned back and that's when I saw the pale scar of beaten earth running diagonally across the steep face of the ravine, down towards the river bed below.

'Over here!' I called up to the others. 'There's a way down!'

We'd only made it about halfway to the bottom when it became too dark to see properly. The only sounds were the clink of stones beneath our shoes, our rasping breaths and the distant bark of a dog. We had to feel our way gingerly with our feet, scared of falling off the edge of the path and tumbling down the steep slope below.

'Stop!' Baba called softly at last. 'This is too dangerous! We must wait here till it's light.'

No one disagreed. There was a sudden burst of brightness as Hassan took out his mobile phone and used it like a torch to light up the path ahead.

'It gets a bit wider down here,' he said. 'There's a place we can sit.'

He was right. A little further on, the path opened out enough to make a sort of landing. We dropped our bags and collapsed against each other, shuffling to get in position side by side, our backs against the rock wall on the higher edge of the path. For a long minute, no one spoke, then Fuad said, 'I'm so hungry, Ma. My tummy's a big zero.'

'Well said, little soldier,' said Hassan.

I didn't like him saying the word 'soldier'. Was he

one himself? Would he and Yahya turn on us when we were all sitting down? Or was he one of the new kind of revolutionary, who were so cruel and violent?

That's just silly, I told myself. *They're nice. I'm sure we can trust them.*

'Omar, the food bag,' said Ma.

There were nine of us now, and there wasn't much to go round. Hassan and Yahya kept trying to refuse the falafels and bread and chickpeas that Baba offered them, but they took some in the end. The worst thing was that once everyone had had a beaker of water, the jerrycan was empty.

A sharp wind was blowing along the ravine, making us all shiver with cold.

'God help us,' Ma said despairingly. 'We can't sit here all night.'

'We won't have to wait here for much longer,' said Musa. 'There's a full moon tonight. It'll be up in an hour or two and we'll be able to see our way down.'

I couldn't see him, but he was sitting right beside me and I could feel him massaging his leg.

'Is that where you hit it when you fell?' I asked him. 'You haven't broken it, have you?'

'Don't be idiotic,' he said sharply. 'I may be Captain Incredible, but even I can't climb down ravines with a broken leg.'

I felt the soft weight of Fuad drooping against me on my other side. He'd fallen asleep. I put my arm round him, leaning my head back against the wall of rock, and shut my eyes. It was freezing cold, I was thirsty, the rock was brutally hard, and there was danger all around, but I was so tired that I fell asleep at once.

A nudge from Musa woke me.

'Look! Up there!' he whispered.

He'd been right about the moon being full. It was well up now, and in the eerie white light I could make out moving shapes coming down the path towards us.

I jumped with fright. The jerk woke Fuad.

'What?' he said loudly. 'Where—'

'Shh,' I whispered. 'Keep still.'

It's the soldiers, I thought. *They're going to shoot us. We're going to die.*

And then I heard a baby cry, and a woman's voice quickly hushed it. I wasn't going to die just yet, after all. The strangers were us, people like us, escaping to the border.

Our whispers had woken the others and a few minutes later we were on the move again. Now, looking back and up in the bright moonlight, I could see a whole long line of people, hundreds perhaps, picking their way down the steep, treacherous path. Nobody shouted, nobody cursed when they slipped. Everyone was creeping as quietly as they could, terrified of attracting the attention of the men with guns above.

I couldn't help myself running on ahead, and I was the first to come off the slope on to the flat beside the river.

My knees were so tired that I kept stumbling, but I felt so triumphant that I didn't care.

'Look! Lights! Up there! They must be in Jordan!' I heard Eman say behind me.

She broke into a run towards the river bed, and I nearly ran with her, but more than anything I wanted to share this moment with Musa. He was still on the slope, limping worse than ever. I ran back to him and waited till he'd reached the flat ground. He staggered, and would have fallen if I hadn't caught him. I could see he was in pain.

'Big moment, eh, little brother?' he said, watching the rest of the family starting to pick their way across the boulders that covered the floor of the dry river bed. 'Shouldn't there be a band? Music?'

'Shut up, you big softie,' I said. 'Now, do you want to be a martyr and stumble on those rocks till you've cracked the other leg and had your head blown off by a sniper, or do you want to get up on my back?'

He pretended to think for a second.

'Hmm. Hard choice. Just this once, I'll let you have the honour of being my beast of burden.'

So Musa rode me across the Yarmouk river towards Jordan as if I was a donkey. And halfway along the easy path that led up the slope on the other side, Jordanian soldiers ran down to us. They picked up Musa and Fuad and carried them up and out of the ravine, leading us all into another world.

PART FOUR

CHAPTER FIFTEEN

Until we arrived in Jordan, I'd always thought of myself as being me: Omar. My father – Hamid. My mother – Leila. My brothers and sisters – well, you know about them. I was Omar Hamid, from Bosra, then from Daraa, then from a village in the country, and my cousin was Rasoul and I was going to be a businessman.

Now, all of a sudden, I was a refugee. And even though my family was still there, nothing felt the same. We were at the bottom of the heap. We had only the clothes we stood up in, a few extra ones and a blanket or two (though Musa had brought his laptop, and Eman had smuggled in a couple of books). Nobody saw us as real people, who had had lives. We were just . . . refugees.

It was only later that all those thoughts came to me. As we came over the top of the ridge and saw the lamps set up under the trees lighting up some big canvas tents and tables with bottles of water on them, I just felt a wild surge of relief. Everyone else, all the people struggling up the path to safety, felt it too. Some were crying and hugging each other, and thanking God in loud voices.

We could still hear the occasional crack of a sniper's rifle on the far side of the ravine. The Jordanian soldiers (and there were quite a lot of them) had guns too, but they were slung across their backs, out of harm's way. And when they turned I could see the little red, green and black flashes of the Jordanian flag stitched on to their sleeves. I knew then that for us, the war was over.

One of the soldiers was talking to Baba, pointing him in the direction of the tents. Another had put his arms out to block Hassan and Yahya's way.

'No, no!' Hassan was protesting. 'That's our uncle, over there. Our family. We've come from Daraa together.'

Baba heard him, turned and nodded, a bit unwillingly, I thought. The soldier hesitated, but then another one nearer the edge of the ravine called out to him, 'Hey, Klef, come and help. There's an old guy with a wheelchair down there.'

Hassan and Yahya saw their chance and hurried over to Baba. They picked up as many of our bags as they could carry and stuck closely behind us as we went towards the tents.

I don't remember much about that night. Someone gave me a bottle of water and a bread roll with some cheese. There was no room under canvas, but we found a place where we could stretch out together under the trees. It was quite noisy. Children were crying, and mothers were shouting at them not to get lost. It was cold too. I was glad then that Ma had made us sweat through the day in our winter clothes. I pulled my jacket over my head and went to sleep.

A kid tripping over my legs woke me up. I scrambled to my feet, fear kicking in my stomach, not knowing where I was. The sun was up and the light was blinding, but I saw the boy who'd woken me, sprawled out on the ground where he'd fallen.

'Oi,' I said. 'You should look where you're going.'

He stuck his tongue out. Then he picked up a stone and threw it at me.

'You little . . .' I began, and lunged for him. He darted out of my way.

'Riad!' a woman's tired voice called out. 'Stop that. Go and fetch water for your sisters.'

The boy took no notice of his mother but ran off to tease a group of younger children. The woman looked at me apologetically.

'I can't do anything with him. He's been out of control since they killed his father right in front of him. They . . .'

I didn't want to hear.

'I'm sorry,' I said hurriedly, and looked round for my family.

Musa was struggling to stand up. His muscles were always stiff first thing in the morning, but I could tell he was having more trouble than usual.

'You all right?' I called across to him.

He scowled at me.

'What does it look like?'

'Like something hurts?'

'My leg. Where I fell on it. Come and help me up.'

He hated asking. Before I could reach him, Hassan was hauling him to his feet. He glanced across to a Jordanian soldier, and I could see he was hoping that his closeness to Musa had been noticed.

Musa grunted something, which might have been 'Thank you', but probably wasn't.

Baba had walked across to join the jostling crowd of people clustering round a group of Jordanian soldiers, who seemed to be checking papers. Beyond them was a line of trucks with canvas roofs as well as a couple of ambulances. Someone with a bloody bandage wrapped round his head was being helped into one of them.

Baba signalled to me. I went over to him.

'Tell everyone to get over here. We've got to stick together now. When they've checked our papers they'll put us on a truck.'

'Where are they going to take us, Baba?'

He turned away without answering, but someone else said, 'To a refugee camp. To a wonderful new life. Five-star accommodation. Top restaurant meals three times a day.'

Amazing visions were sloshing round in my head.

'Really?' I said, my voice coming out all squeaky.

I could feel a stupid grin spreading across my face.

'He's kidding, dumbo,' said Musa.

A soldier started to push at the crowd, herding people into an orderly line. Baba turned and saw me.

'What did I tell you, Omar? Get your mother. Quickly.'

I still get the shakes when I remember how Baba nearly left our papers in his jacket pocket in the stable house. With them, we could at least prove who we were. Without them, we'd have been lost in the desert without any camels.

A couple of soldiers had forced everyone into a sort of line and we shuffled slowly forwards. Hassan and Yahya hovered round us. Hassan tried to play with Fuad, who looked a bit withdrawn, and Yahya flirted with Nadia, in spite of Ma's discouraging looks.

'Overdoing it, aren't they?' Musa muttered to me. He was still suspicious of them.

We were waved through at last. Two of the trucks had already filled up and left and there was a panicky scramble towards the third one. Hassan got there first. He stood on the little flight of steps and blocked anyone else from getting on until our whole family was up inside the truck, sitting by the open back with our bags round us. I smiled at him. He seemed like a nice guy to me. The engine revved up noisily, ready to go, and a soldier lifted the steps into the back on top of our bags.

'Help me, mister!' called a young voice. A boy, who looked about ten years old, was holding up his arms pleadingly to me.

'Me too!' cried the little girl standing beside him.

'Where's your family!' shouted Yahya, above the roar of the engine.

'We're on our own,' the boy said, a desperate look on his face.

I leaned down, grabbed the little girl and hauled her in while Yahya lifted the boy. The truck was already moving. It lurched off with a grinding of gears.

It was strange to be crammed into such a small space with people we didn't know. I was annoyed to see that the boy who'd thrown a stone at me was in the truck, with his mother and three little sisters.

'Stop it, Riad,' his mother kept saying. 'Don't do that.' But it was obvious that she had no hope of being listened to.

Ma kept looking at the two children that Yahya and I had pulled on board.

'Where's your mummy, *habibti?*' she asked the little girl, who stared unsmilingly back at her.

'She's dead,' the boy said in a matter-of-fact voice. 'Everyone's dead. A bomb fell on our house. We got out, just her and me. We ran away.'

'*Wallah!*' Ma's voice was soft with pity. 'Isn't there anyone left? An uncle or an auntie?'

The boy shrugged.

'We don't know where they live.'

He turned to look out of the back of the truck along the way we'd come.

There was no proper road at first, just a bumpy track across the desert. I had to hang on to one of the metal struts that held up the canvas roof and look out of the open back at the horizon to stop myself from feeling sick.

It was better when we turned on to a proper highway. It was silly, I know, but I couldn't help thinking about what the man on the road had said, about lovely restaurant meals.

I'll have the lamb kebabs please, I heard myself saying inside my head. *And some of those stuffed vine leaves. And the bread hot from the oven. With some baklava to follow, dripping with honey.*

I was so caught up in my dream that it was a shock when the truck pulled up with a squeal of brakes. And I was frightened, too, because I was staring out at a tank with a huge gun pointing out from the turret above towards a metal gate.

This is a trick! They're taking us back to Syria! I thought in a panic. *We're going to be in prison. Tortured and shot!*

Then I saw the Jordanian flag flying from a mast nearby, and began to breathe more easily.

Over the loud rumble of our truck's engine, I could hear the driver call out to the soldiers by the gate, 'I've got thirty-five in the back, more or less. Mainly women and children. Couple of young blokes you'll want to check.'

I didn't hear the answer.

I felt shoves from behind and a flurry of arms and legs. Hassan and Yahya were pushing their way to the open end of the truck.

'Thanks for everything, brother,' Hassan said to me quickly. 'We're going our own way now.'

'Where are you going?' Baba called out fretfully.

'Europe!'

Hassan had already jumped down, and Yahya was scrambling out after him. I was sorry then that I'd let Musa's suspicions influence me. I wished I'd been friendlier. They were only doing what Rasoul had done, after all.

'How are you going to get there?' I called out.

'Flight to Turkey. Sea crossing to Greece.'

A couple of Jordanian soldiers were looking at them, and one had started to move forward. Hassan was already walking quickly away, with Yahya almost running after him.

'If you get to Norway, and meet my cousin Rasoul, say hi to him from me!' I called out after them, but neither of them turned round.

There was the sound of a heavy metal gate being drawn back, and then the truck rolled forward. It stopped, and another gate creaked open before we moved on again. A short while later, we stopped for the last time and the engine was switched off. The silence was weird.

I heard the driver's door open. He came round to the

back of the truck and reached in to lift out the steps.

'Where are we?' Riad's mother called out.

'Za'atari. Za'atari refugee camp,' said the driver. 'Come on, get out. This is it. You're here.'

My stupid dream of a nice hotel and a wonderful meal faded away like a light going out as I looked round. The two sets of huge metal gates had shut behind us. They were shutting out the world of war, but they were shutting us in. To what?

I was the first to get out of the truck. Everyone behind me was so impatient I almost fell off the bottom step. I should have helped the others down with the bags and everything, but I couldn't move. I stood in a daze, looking round.

This is what I saw: long rows of dingy white tents, stretching into the distance, set on a flat, gritty, yellow desert, dazzlingly bright in the morning sun. There were European letters in blue writing on every tent. I'm a bit shaky with the English alphabet, and though I tried I couldn't make out a word.

'*Unhcr*,' I muttered under my breath. 'Doesn't make sense.'

'They're initials,' Musa said behind me. 'United Nations High Commission for Refugees.'

'How do you know that?'

He gave me a pitying look and didn't bother to answer.

Everyone was out of the truck now, standing around, not knowing what to do. Suddenly, Musa staggered and half fell against me. I looked round to see that Riad had snatched his bag off his back.

'Hey!' Musa was trying to shout. 'Give that back!'

Riad danced around, waving the bag over his head.

'Cripple! Cripple! Come and get it!'

'My laptop! He'll break it! He'll . . .' Musa was saying desperately.

Um Riad saw what was going on.

'Riad, stop that,' she said weakly. 'Give the boy back his bag.'

Riad took no notice. I lunged for him with murder in my heart. Riad saw me coming, and hurled the bag into the air. I leaped for it and caught it, but landed awkwardly on my ankle, twisting it painfully.

'You little . . .' I began.

Before I could go on, Baba called out, 'Stop dawdling. Get our things together. We're supposed to be following that man.'

Musa had gone white. He held his hands out for his bag.

'I'll look after it,' I said, heaving it on to my back. 'And when I get hold of that imp I'm going to tear him limb from limb.'

It was all a bit of a blur after that. You realize, when you become a refugee, that there's no hurry any more. You might not be about to die from a shell blasting through the walls of your house, or a from barrel bomb falling from the sky, but you might easily die of boredom.

You have to stand about in line, waiting for someone to ask you a million questions and then give you a card which tells you that you're a nobody now. You don't belong anywhere any more. No one wants you. You have to wait in other lines, lots of them, until someone gives you a disgusting meal, which is supposed to be hot but isn't, in a greasy pizza box. And then there are more lines for vouchers that you can swap for a bucket, perhaps, or a thin grey blanket, a jerrycan, a heater.

At last, when we were all getting scratchy with hunger and tiredness, someone took us to our tent. We stood at the entrance looking in.

'Is this it, then?' said Eman disbelievingly.

No one answered her. Sand lay in eddies across the hardboard floor. A pile of grey foam mattresses was stacked up at the far end and the canvas walls billowed in and out in the strong breeze.

Ma said, 'Come on, Eman. Help me sweep out the sand.'

'What with? We haven't got a broom.'

Ma stared at her wildly.

'No broom! No nothing! All gone! Everything's finished!'

It was as if something had cracked inside her.

She ran blindly across to the pile of mattresses and collapsed with her back against them. Then she covered her face with the end of her hijab and burst into tears.

Baba looked at her helplessly. Then he turned on Eman.

'You heard your mother! Sweep the floor! Never mind "no broom". Use anything!'

Eman scowled. She tugged off her hijab and began to swish it across the hardboard, raising clouds of dust.

'Where are Hassan and Yahya?' Fuad said, following the rest of us inside.

'They've gone to Europe,' I said enviously.

Ma lifted her head.

'And those poor little children!' she wailed. 'All their family dead! Where are they?'

'I saw them, Ma,' said Eman. 'A woman came up and took them with her. She looked nice.'

'They'll have special facilities for orphaned children,' Baba said dismissively. 'Omar, come with me, unless you don't want to have anything to eat for the rest of the day. We've got to swap these vouchers for a meal.'

It took ages for Baba and me to find the food place, and then we got lost on our way 'home'. We must have walked for nearly an hour, trudging up and down long straight tracks lined with identical tents, weighed down with a stack of pizza boxes and cartons of juice. I was beginning to panic when I caught sight of Fuad. He was standing out in the road with a look of horrified fascination on his face, watching Riad poking a stick at a little boy to make him cry.

'Baba,' he called out. 'Ma's upset. She thinks you've been arrested. Have you got any food? I'm so hungry!'

As we followed him into our tent I heard a familiar voice. Um Riad was standing in the entrance to the tent next door, calling out, 'Riad! Stop that! Come inside!'

My heart sank. We'd got the neighbours from hell.

While we'd been out, Eman had managed to get some of the sand off the floor, and had arranged the mattresses round the tent's sides. She'd opened the roll that she'd carried all the way from Syria on her head, and had laid a couple of blankets over two of the mattresses. She'd stowed our bags tidily in a corner, too. It didn't look like home, exactly, but my heart lifted a bit.

We sat down and opened the food boxes. We were all starving by now.

'They call this food?' said Ma, poking at a dried-up bit of chicken with a disgusted finger.

I was so hungry by then that I would have eaten a bowlful of mouldy rice. The meal wasn't that bad, but it wasn't nice, either. The rice was soggy, the chicken was as tough as leather, and the vegetables were squashy and tasteless. The best things were the hunks of bread.

I sat back when I'd finished my share, and watched the wind blowing in more sand, making patterns of it across the floor.

Eman whispered something to Ma.

'She needs the toilet,' announced Ma.

Baba wrinkled his nose.

'I've been to the toilets. They're disgusting. She can't go on her own. There are men hanging around.'

I knew what was coming and I didn't even wait to be asked. I needed to go myself, anyway.

'I'll go with you,' I told Eman. 'Musa, Fuad, don't you need to come too?'

Baba had been right about the toilets. They were in a breeze-block building that looked all right from the outside, but inside they were filthy. I'd never seen anything so disgusting in my life. Eman had to manage with her floor-length abaya, too. She looked pale when she came out, as if she was going to be sick.

'You mean we've got to go through that every time?' she said faintly.

I'd made sure to notice exactly where our tent was, but it still wasn't easy to pick it out from all the others.

'Omar, wait for Musa!' Fuad called out, when we were nearly there.

I turned round, and saw that Musa was limping badly.

'It's only a bruise,' I said, sounding unsympathetic even to myself.

'It's not. Hip. Strained it. Coming down the ravine.'

He held out his right arm to me. He didn't need to say anything. I knew what he wanted. I dipped my left shoulder so that he could hook his arm round my neck. We'd often walked like that before, ever since I could remember, in fact. I didn't mind helping him along. I was feeling quite shaky myself, and his touch was comforting.

'Thanks for getting my bag off that little devil.' He was wincing with every step. 'Do you realize they've moved into the tent next to ours?'

'I think he's funny,' said Fuad. 'He's really naughty.'

He looked up, his eyes going from my face to Musa's, reading our furious expressions.

'What are you looking at me like that for? I'm just saying.'

'That poor woman,' said Eman. 'She's got four children and she's completely on her own. Don't you feel sorry for them?'

'No,' I said brutally. 'If Riad's dad was anything like Riad, she's better off on her own.'

CHAPTER SIXTEEN

During those first few weeks in Za'atari camp, our family started falling apart. Ma couldn't stop crying. Baba was silent and tight-faced, then he'd lash out in anger. Musa lay about all day, pale with pain. Fuad was never there. He'd joined a gang of other six-year-olds, and was out roaming round the camp all day long. Nadia and Eman were the only two who were cheerful, Nadia because she didn't know what was going on, and Eman because she was still thrilled to have escaped from Mr Nosy Rat-Face Bilal.

And me? I felt like the dogsbody, fetching and carrying all day long. It was, 'Omar, go and fetch some water . . . Omar, get over to the bread queue before it gets too long . . . Omar, they've given out vouchers for buckets. Go and pick ours up . . .' Omar this, Omar that, Omar the next thing.

It wasn't only our family who used me like a beast of burden. Um Riad appeared outside our tent at least twice a day, making a soft little coughing noise, then calling out, 'Um Musa! Are you there?' Hannan, her eldest daughter, was eight, and she was sent out on errands all the time too. I'd often see her staggering back to the tent with a heavy bucket of water, or a pack of nappies from the distribution centre for the baby. But there were things that were too big for her to carry and Ma would send me off to help. I did it because, in truth, I did feel a bit sorry for them, but then I'd catch sight of Riad, who was running wild with kids older than himself. He'd be throwing stones at the cars of foreign bigwigs, who liked to come and see us in our misery, or stealing a piece of bread out of the bag an old woman was carrying on her back.

Ma was snobbish about Um Riad.

'Her husband was only a labourer, you know. No education at all. People like that—'

'I don't care what her husband did,' I'd say crossly, when I'd dumped some big jerrycans of water outside the tent next door. 'I just want to know why she doesn't get Riad to do her dirty work for her.'

'Shh! She'll hear you!'

Ma was right. You could hear every cough, curse, sneeze, burp and worse from the tent alongside. I'd woken up on our second morning and asked Baba what the time was.

'It's seven o'clock!' Um Riad had helpfully called out from next door.

In Daraa, we'd got used to living without electricity or running water. On the farm, I'd got accustomed to working every day out in the fields. But no one could ever get used to living in a tent in the middle of a desert with the winter coming on. By the end of October, it was so cold at night that we lay shivering under our thin UN blankets, even though we'd piled all our clothes on top of ourselves.

It began to rain, and the desert dust turned to thick smelly mud which was impossible to keep out of the tent. There were floods all over the camp, and you had to watch out for snakes, too, which had been flushed out of their holes. Inside the tent, the damp got into everything and it was impossible to keep our things dry.

Fuad didn't seem to notice how uncomfortable everything had got. He'd become really naughty, copying the hundreds of kids like Riad who were running all over the camp with no dads or big brothers to keep them under control.

'Fuad's so spoiled, he gets away with anything,' I complained to Eman. 'If I'd behaved like that when I was his age, Baba would have gone berserk. Why doesn't he *do* something?'

'Don't ask me,' Eman would reply. 'I mean, look at him.'

And we'd both look at Baba, and see how hopeless and withdrawn he'd become.

'He believed in the government,' Musa joined in, with

more sympathy than either Eman or I felt. 'He can't bear what they're doing to Syria.'

It was Ma who got really angry with Fuad. The third time he came back to the tent filthy from head to foot, after he'd fallen into a greasy puddle, she shouted, 'How do you expect me to wash your clothes? Who's going to fetch the water? Where do you think I can dry them?'

Baba had roused himself at the sound of her angry voice and told Fuad that he wasn't allowed to go out again unless someone went with him.

I knew, of course, who that someone would be. So from then on, every time I squelched off through the mud and puddles to queue for water from the big tank, or fetch our supplies of food, I had to tow Fuad along behind me, while he muttered resentfully all the time.

To be fair to Fuad, though, he didn't stay resentful for long. He never admitted it to me, but I think he'd started to get upset with the things the other kids were doing, the stone-throwing, bullying and stealing. He liked being useful too. The camp authorities had stopped giving us disgusting ready-cooked meals, and instead we had to collect supplies of things like rice and pasta, lentils, oil and sugar, to cook for ourselves. They gave us vouchers, too, which Ma could swap at a supermarket which had opened in the camp. Even though there wasn't enough for fresh vegetables or fruit, Ma and Eman managed to produce meals which we could actually eat without gagging, though there was never enough to make me feel full.

The camp was slowly changing. Every day, huge trucks were bringing in rectangular white cabins, like big caravans, and people were being moved into them out of the tents. Ma kept a watchful eye on what was going on. She had to use the communal kitchen to cook our food and always came back with stories to tell.

'You wouldn't believe what that tall woman told me,' she'd say. 'Those armed thugs, those *shabiha*, they arrested her husband for nothing. Nothing! He'd just picked up a piece of paper off the pavement and was reading it, and they grabbed him and bundled him away. When she got his body back for burial, she could hardly recognize him. His—'

'That's enough, Leila,' Baba would interrupt furiously.

Ma would toss her head rebelliously.

'It's no wonder the kids here have turned into little animals, and Eman and I are scared to go outside the tent. The things they've seen!'

But she'd be talking to empty air. Baba would have already pushed back the flap of the tent and gone out.

It was a sunny day in late November when we finally got our caravan. I was halfway to the water tank with two empty jerrycans when I saw Baba almost running towards me.

'We've got our caravan!' he panted. 'Come with me!'

I lifted the jerrycans to show him what I was carrying.

'Ma sent me for water, Baba. Hadn't I better do it first?'

'Never mind that. Just come. Someone else might sneak in and take it.'

He turned and strode off. I had to hurry to keep up with him.

'Isn't it official, then? Who can take it if it's really ours?'

'I don't trust anyone any more.' His voice was bitter. 'Syrians used to be good people. They're all a bunch of criminals now.'

You have to spend weeks living in a damp cold tent in the middle of a desert to realize how good it is to have four walls and a roof, a window and a door, even if the walls are made of PVC that drips with condensation, and there's only one room to share between seven people.

Baba stayed to guard our new home while I ran back to the tent to tell everyone the good news. I couldn't wait to see Ma's face.

'You've all got to come now!' I said, bursting into the tent. 'Baba's got us a caravan!'

I might as well have said, 'It's Tuesday today and the sun is shining,' because no one took any notice of me. Ma was sitting on one of the mattresses, with Eman on one side of her and Musa on the other. They had their arms round her and were trying to comfort her as she sobbed uncontrollably.

Eman looked up and saw me.

'She met someone at the kitchen from Auntie Fawzia's village. It was bombed last week. Uncle Mahmud's badly hurt. He's lost his left arm. He's in hospital. And Jaber's disappeared.'

Ma struggled to get free of their encircling arms.

'We've got to go back! How can I leave my sister in this trouble? She needs me!'

'Ma, we can't go back,' Musa said. 'Think of Nadia and Fuad. And Baba would be arrested.'

'I don't care! Let them kill us all!' Ma shouted, upsetting Nadia, who had been playing quietly with a couple of spoons and a plate, and who now began to cry. 'Anything's better than living in this misery. I can't bear it!'

'Well,' I said, seizing my chance. 'You won't have to. Baba's got us a caravan. He sent me to tell you. We've got to move into it today.'

If we hadn't got our caravan that day, I do believe that Ma really might have taken us all back to Syria. She would have joined the dozens of desperate people who queued up each morning at the exit, fighting to get on the buses that would take them back home, preferring bombs and probable death to the slow despair of the camp. They were just a fraction, though, of the number of people coming the other way. Thousands were arriving every day, some with bandages round their heads, or arms in slings, some half hysterical, some silent and withdrawn. I kept a sharp lookout as the newcomers came in, wondering if anyone I knew was among them, but they never were.

It took a surprisingly long time to pack up our stuff ready to move. We'd acquired more than I'd thought – buckets and a broom, plates and cups, pots and pans – as well as the things we'd brought with us.

I was shoving my few spare clothes into a plastic carrier bag when I heard a familiar cough outside the tent.

Um Riad didn't bother to be invited in, but lifted the canvas flap and stepped straight inside.

'I couldn't help overhearing,' she said to Ma. 'Have you had bad news from home?'

Ma's lips tightened.

'I won't burden you with our family troubles, Um Riad. I'm sure you've got enough of your own.'

Um Riad wasn't going to be put off.

'And now you're moving!'

'That's right.'

Um Riad's face collapsed into a mask of misery.

'But I'll be alone! How am I going to manage? I'm a widow, with four children! I thought you were my friends!'

'Oh my dear,' said Ma, softening a bit. 'I'm sorry. I really am. But we're not leaving the camp. We'll still be here for you, and your own cabin will come through soon, I'm sure of it.'

Um Riad caught hold of her arm.

'Ask Abu Musa to help me! Ask him to get me a cabin! An educated man like him!'

'I don't think he . . .' Ma was prising Um Riad's fingers off her arm. 'I'm not sure if . . . But I'll ask him. Of course I will.'

'Ma, what about these wet clothes?' Eman called out. 'I don't want to pack them with the dry stuff.'

'Put them in the bucket,' said Ma. 'Fuad can carry them. Nadia, what are you doing, *habibti*? Don't take all those clothes out of the bag again.'

It was wonderful moving from the tent to the cabin. It felt like a step out of misery into . . . well, into something just a bit better. Although we had a heater, which made the evenings more bearable, we still had no electricity. It was now the end of November and getting dark earlier all the time. It was horrible without proper light in the evenings. But we were dry, and warmer, and able to keep reasonably clean.

The best thing was privacy. We could talk in normal voices now, knowing that Um Riad wasn't just on the other side of two thin pieces of canvas.

'You know what this caravan means?' Musa asked me, the day after we moved in.

'Yes, Mr Clever. It means that we're more comfortable, or hadn't you noticed?'

'It means,' Musa said, staring out of the open door, 'that the United Nations people think we're going to be here for a long time. The war in Syria's got years to go. If you were planning to go home, you'd better think again.'

That brought me up short. I suppose I'd assumed that things would soon sort themselves out back home. The rebels would win, or the government would win, and we'd be able to go back to Daraa, or better still, to Bosra, and get the builders in and repair a flat or a house so we could live in it, and life would go back to normal. A horrible thought struck me.

'You don't mean we're going to have to live in this dump forever?'

He shrugged.

'How should I know?' He tapped the lid of his laptop. 'But I can tell you that things in Syria are getting worse, not better.'

I didn't really want to know, if I'm honest. The news from home was so depressing that I could hardly bear to listen to it. I didn't know if Musa was still in touch with Bassem and the others, or even what had happened to them. I was pretty sure, though, that Musa wasn't involved in dodgy stuff any more. Now that we were out of Syria, there wasn't anything he could do, except try to keep up to date with what was happening.

On that terrifying day when we'd dashed away from the farm and made it out of Syria, I'd thought that Musa was daft to load himself down with his laptop, but I'd quickly realized that he'd done the right thing. Information was the most precious thing of all in the camp. Everyone was desperate for news of what was going on in Syria, and to hear from the ones who'd dared to make the risky journey on to Europe and try their chances there.

Musa was super-careful with his laptop. He used it only for a few minutes at a time to save the battery. Even with the spare one that Bassem had given him, the thing had run out of juice completely by the time we moved into the caravan. So who did Musa fix with his big brown eyes to sort the problem out and get his laptop charged? You've got it. My good self.

Ma watched me pack the laptop carefully into a bag to hide it from any chancer who might snatch it off me, then she dug into one of her own bags and brought out her battered old mobile. I looked at it doubtfully.

'Doesn't look as if it will ever work again, Ma.'

'Try, *habibi*. How can I go on without news of my sister? Without this, who can I talk to but Allah?'

Fuad was so used to going with me whenever I went on an errand that he automatically followed me out of the caravan. I stood outside the door uncertainly, not knowing where to go. There was some electricity in the camp, on wires running overhead. They fed the street lamps and the compounds of the aid agencies. I guessed, too, that the enclosures round the edges of the camp, where the aid organizations and Jordanian authorities had their bases, would have good connections.

I set off uncertainly towards the main UN compound. *They'll never let me charge this stuff*, I told myself hopelessly, *but at least I'll be able to tell Musa that I tried.*

Fuad trotted along at my side.

'Where are we going, Omar?'

'To the UN compound,' I said, trying to sound certain and dignified. 'Where else?'

He smirked.

'I know where else. They won't help you. Come with me.'

He darted off so fast, dodging between rows of tents, that I couldn't keep up with him.

'Watch out!' I yelled. 'You'll slip in a puddle! Ma'll go berserk!'

He slowed down at last and I managed to catch up with him. I grabbed his shoulder to stop him running off again.

'So where is this magical recharging place then, or are you having me on?' I panted.

He squirmed out of my grip.

'I'll show you. We're nearly there.'

I'd been so busy up at our end of the camp, going to and from the distribution centre and the water tanks, that I hadn't explored this area. We walked a little further on, then came out from between two tents on to a long, straight track that ran as far as I could see down the middle of the camp. It was as full of people, as bright and colourful, as a busy shopping street in Daraa had always been on a Saturday afternoon. I almost had to rub my eyes. There were shops! Real shops! Some were in tents, with the flaps pulled back to show the goods on tables inside. Others seemed to be made of parts of caravans, their end walls taken off so that they opened on to the street. Quite a few had signboards up on their roofs, each one brightly painted with the name of the shop and advertisements for whatever it was selling. I could see a clothes store, a fruit and vegetable stall, a shoe shop with a display of boots, trainers and sandals, a proper café, with little vases of plastic flowers on the tables, and, best of all, a *shwarma* stall. The revolving spindle of roasting lamb sent out such a wonderful smell that saliva sprouted in my mouth.

'Mind your back!' someone behind me called out. I whipped round and leaped out of the way. Four men were pushing a huge caravan along on a big set of wheels. They edged it into an empty space at the end of the row of shops, then stood in a cluster while a wad of money changed hands.

I realized that Fuad had disappeared. Looking round, I caught sight of him peeping out from behind a toy stall. He came out cautiously.

'Has he gone?'

'Has who gone?'

'There was a policeman over there. Didn't you see?'

He looked anxious and guilty.

'And why, little brother, would you be so scared of a policeman?'

'It wasn't me, Omar, honestly. It was the others. And it was only apples.'

'Fuad,' I said sternly, feeling like a real big brother. 'We're good people in our family. We don't steal. We have . . .' I groped for the right word. 'Respect.'

'I know,' he said in a small voice. 'Don't tell Baba, will you?'

'I won't if . . .' I paused, enjoying the power that the scared look on his face was giving me. Then I relented and put my arm round his shoulders. 'I won't if you show me where I can get Musa's stupid laptop recharged.'

He grinned with relief.

'It's a deal.'

The electrical shop was quite a way down the shopping street. I walked slowly, fascinated by what was going on. It looked as if some places had been open for a while. They had piles of goods and really nice displays – not as brilliant as the ones I'd have made, of course, but not bad.

What interested me most of all were the men standing on the tops of the caravan shops, working on the electric cables that fed the street lamps. There was a forest of wires up there. I could see that the men were attaching more lines to bring the electricity down into their shops.

We reached the electrical store at last. High above it was a hoarding made out of a section of caravan wall, with the word 'Phones' painted on it, and logos for internet and phone connections. Down below, at the front of the shop, was a counter. A man was standing behind it. He had a screwdriver in his hand and was fiddling with an old computer. Behind him was a display of radios, fans, hairdryers and even a couple of TVs. Beside him, on the counter, was a forest of wires running into a jumble of mobile phones.

I felt as if I'd been transported back to Syria, to somewhere normal, somewhere familiar and safe and decent.

The man looked up and caught my eye. I took the bag off my shoulder, lifted out the laptop and mobile and put them down on the counter.

'Please, Uncle,' I said. 'Can you charge them for me?'

He shook his head.

'Too many to do already. Look at all this lot! Bring them back on Friday.'

'On Friday? But my ma, she's so worried about her sister. Her village has been bombed, and . . .'

He shrugged.

'I told you, come on Friday. *Inshallah*, I can do it then.'

Fuad was bobbing up and down beside me.

'Look, Omar. There's a TV on over there. It's got a cartoon on!'

At the sound of my name, the man frowned and looked at me more closely.

'I thought you looked familiar. I know you, don't I?'

'I don't know,' I said, backing away.

Don't trust anyone, Baba had warned me, again and again.

Then the man smiled.

'Don't you remember me? I'm Abu Radwan. I had a shop in Bosra, next to the man you called Uncle Ali. You used to work for him early in the morning, didn't you? He said you were a good kid. Grown a bit, haven't you?'

I relaxed and smiled back at him. I did remember him now. He'd often stopped by to talk to Uncle Ali.

'Is Uncle Ali all right?' I asked him. 'He got scared when that man Bilal came and threatened him.'

'Bilal!' Abu Radwan looked as if he wanted to spit. 'That snake! Yes, your Uncle Ali got out of Bosra. I think he went to Damascus to join his son. I haven't heard anything since. His son was a smart lad. He'll have got his old dad to safety. Uncle Ali won't be going back to Bosra, anyway. Neither will I. All the shops in our row were bombed out. I lost more or less everything.'

He picked up the laptop and Ma's phone. I put out my hands to take them from him, but he put them aside on the counter.

'Don't worry, son. Leave them with me. Priority job. I'll give you a good price, too. Come back tomorrow morning.'

I thanked him, and turned to go.

'And welcome to the Champs Élysées!' he called after me.

'The what?'

But he was already serving his next customer, a woman with a baby in her arms.

'Batteries, *ya* Abu Radwan,' she was saying in a shrill

voice. 'You promised me yesterday! I can't find any in the whole Champs Élysées. How am I going to heat my baby's milk?'

Abu Radwan reached up and took a box down from a shelf.

'How many?'

'Four.'

They settled down to haggle over the price.

'Fuad,' I said as we walked away. 'I owe you one.' We were passing a tent shop with a table outside, covered with a display of sweets. 'How would you like a lollipop?'

He looked up at me, shocked.

'But you *said*, Omar. You *said* we shouldn't steal.'

'Not stealing, silly. I'm going to buy you one.'

I reached into the pocket of my heavy winter jacket. There was a hole in it and through it I could feel inside the lining. I'd hugged the knowledge of my secret hoard of postcard money all this while. I'd have to spend some of it, I knew, on recharging the laptop and phone, but I reckoned that Fuad and I deserved a treat.

'Which colour do you want? Red, yellow or green?' I asked him, feeling grand and generous.

He spent a long time choosing. I didn't want to hurry him.

'Red,' he said at last.

'Two reds,' I said to the sweet seller, handing over a precious note.

It had been such a long time since either of us had

tasted such heavenly sweetness that we didn't talk at all till we were nearly back at the cabin.

'Here, wipe your mouth, it's all sticky,' I told Fuad. 'And don't tell the others, eh? I'm not made of money.'

CHAPTER SEVENTEEN

I went back to the Champs Élysées on my own the next day because Fuad had started school. It was Baba who'd found out about it. In his usual careful way he'd gone off to inspect the place before he'd said anything to Ma. Fuad knew nothing about it until Baba brought home a blue Jordanian school uniform and told him to put it on.

'And if you don't keep it clean . . .' He left the threat hanging in the air.

School for the boys didn't start till the afternoon (the girls had the morning shift). Fuad spent the morning pestering Eman.

'I can't remember reading any more. And tables. Test me, Eman. Please.'

I left them to it and went out.

The Champs Élysées had been love at first sight for me. In the rest of the camp, people were miserable, cold, hungry, and scared of the violent children and young men hanging around. But here people were busy, buying and selling, building up their shops, setting up signs and laying things out on tables. You could almost smell the feeling that there was hope for a normal life here.

A bit of the Champs Élysées spirit had spilt out into the rest of the camp, too. On the way there I passed three men sitting on stools, selling cigarettes, sweets, biscuits and tissues out of packing cases on the ground.

It wasn't until I was past them that I had my Big Idea. I stopped dead, letting it blossom in my mind, then I walked on slowly, planning how to go about it.

I reached Abu Radwan's shop sooner than I'd expected. No one else was there, and I was scared that someone would come up and interrupt me, so I launched into talking at once.

'Abu Radwan, there's something I want to ask you.' That wasn't what I'd planned to say at all. I took a deep breath and tried again. 'I've got a – a business proposition for you.'

Abu Radwan had been examining the insides of a TV set. He looked up at last.

'Oh, it's you. What was that? A business proposition? Well, well.'

I had to press on now I'd started.

'That lady, the one who said she couldn't find batteries anywhere, she wasn't the only one. Round our caravan, people are desperate for them.'

'And where is your caravan?'

'Near the distribution centre.'

'Lucky you.'

'Yes, but it's a long way from here and there are loads of women with little kids who don't want to come all this way on their own.'

He leaned his elbows on the counter and looked at me properly, not laughing now.

'So?'

'So I thought – well, if you'd sell me a whole box of batteries, at a really good price, I could sell them up there, and make a bit of profit for both of us.'

'*Ya* Abu Radwan!' someone behind me called out. A big man was elbowing me away from the counter. I glared at him, but he didn't take any notice.

'That phone you sold me yesterday,' he went on. 'It doesn't work.'

He slapped a small black phone down on the counter. Abu Radwan picked it up and fiddled with it.

'Nothing wrong with it. You're not getting a signal, that's all. It's never good round here.'

I saw my chance.

'Excuse me, sir. The signal's better up near the main UN compound. You have to walk round to find the right spot. The best place is to the left of the big metal gates.'

Both men looked at me.

'All right, I'll try it,' the big man said. 'But if I can't get it to work I'll want my money back.'

When he'd gone, Abu Radwan said, 'And will it work?'

'Should do. There's always loads of people shouting down their mobiles up there.'

He nodded.

'Uncle Ali was right about you, Omar. You are a sharp lad. I'll give you a chance. Can't spare any batteries today, but I'll order an extra box for next week. Come back on Sunday and we'll see how it goes.'

I turned to go, trying not to show him the massive grin on my face.

'Hey, aren't you forgetting something?' he called after me.

He pulled Musa's laptop and Ma's phone out from under the counter. I stowed them carefully in my bag.

'How much do I owe you, Abu Radwan?'

'Got money then, have you?'

'I earned it,' I said proudly. 'Back in Bosra. I used to sell postcards at the ruins for my cousin Rasoul.'

'Rasoul? I remember that rascal. Handsome lad. Came through the shelling all right, did he?'

'He wasn't there. He's in Norway now. We're going to start a business together one day. That's what I was saving my money for.'

'Then you'd better go on saving it. There'll be no charge this time, since we're going to be business partners.'

It wasn't until I was halfway back to the cabin that the Big Flaw in my Big Idea hit me. It was hard enough to keep

off the gangs of kids from me and Baba on our way back
from the distribution centre with the family's supplies.
But if I was out somewhere alone, sitting in one place,
with valuable batteries, I'd be asking for trouble. And
then there was Baba. I wasn't sure what his reaction
would be. He'd be quite likely to forbid my new career
or, even worse, take my stock off me.

I won't tell them yet, I thought, opening the door of the
caravan. *I'll have to think things out.*

There was no problem keeping my secret. No one
would have listened to me, anyway. Ma almost snatched
her mobile out of my hand. Musa grunted with pleasure
and turned his laptop on, his eyes fixed to the screen.

'"Thank you, Omar. How wonderful you are",' I said,
aggrieved. 'Aren't you even going to ask me how I did
it?'

Ma was too busy punching the keys on her mobile to
listen but Musa looked up and grinned.

'No need. You're amazing. We all know that.' Then
his eyes narrowed. 'You're up to something, Omar.
What is it?'

I gave my head a tiny shake by way of warning.

'Later,' I mouthed.

Ma held out her phone to me. There were tears of
disappointment in her eyes.

'It doesn't work!'

'You have to go outside to get a signal, Ma,' I told
her,' I told her. 'Up past the kitchens.'

And if anyone else in this family needs me to tell them what to do, I said to myself, *they only have to ask.*

She hurried out of the caravan at once, the phone clutched in her hand.

'So go on then,' Musa said. 'How did you get them charged? You're dying to tell me.'

'Went up the Champs Élysées, didn't I?'

'The what?'

'The Champs Élysées.'

Eman, who had been washing Nadia's clothes in a bucket of cold water by the door, snorted with laughter.

'Stop being an idiot, Omar. The Champs Élysées's in Paris. It's a big grand street with lots of posh shops.'

'No it isn't. It's a souk, right here in Za'atari camp. It's brilliant, Eman. You can buy anything there. I couldn't believe it.'

She made a face.

'Buy? What with?'

I hesitated. I'd never told Eman and Musa about my secret store of money. I didn't really want to now, but the temptation to impress them was irresistible.

'Well . . .' I began, but I saw that I'd lost their attention. Nadia was shoving at the tub full of water, threatening to push it over, and Musa's eyes had gone back to his laptop. He was breathing heavily and clenching his fists.

'Look what they're doing now! Bombing civilian areas! Hundreds dying!'

I didn't want to hear any more. I retreated to another corner of the cabin to think out my business plan.

Ma came back. Her face was screwed up with anxiety. She kicked her shoes off by the door, picked up Nadia and began to cuddle her fiercely.

'Any news, Ma?' asked Eman.

'The line's so bad! But I heard her voice. She's alive, thank God. And your uncle's still in hospital.'

She buried her head deeper into Nadia's neck and began to rock backwards and forwards.

The next day was Friday. Baba went out early and came back looking unusually energetic.

'Musa, Omar, Fuad,' he said. 'Smarten yourselves up. We're going to Friday prayers.'

This was new. It had been ages since we'd been to Friday prayers. I think, out of all of us, Musa was the happiest to go out. His hip had mended enough for him to walk again, but he was scared of going outside alone and facing the bullying children, even though he'd never have admitted it.

I'd noticed the new mosque a few days earlier, one of many that were opening in the camp. It was in a caravan, not far from ours. It didn't have electricity, of course, so there was no loudspeaker to broadcast the call to prayer, but once or twice I'd caught the sound of a strong voice singing it out. It had made me feel homesick, actually, not for Bosra, or even for Daraa, but for the village, for

Auntie Fawzia and Uncle Mahmud and even a bit for Jaber too.

I realized, looking round, why Baba had chosen this mosque. There were faces I recognized from Daraa. They looked as if they'd been government people, like Baba.

It felt good, standing and kneeling in rhythm with the others on the carpets spread out on the floor. I even liked the imam, although I didn't bother to listen to his sermon. I was too busy thinking about how I was going to manage my battery project.

Afterwards, it was just like the old days. Baba stayed behind to talk to the other men. Fuad and Musa went on back to the cabin, while I hung back, looking around in case Abu Radwan was there, but he wasn't.

A gang of ten- and eleven-year-old wannabe criminals were standing a few metres away from the mosque when I came out. Beside me, Musa stiffened. They'd shouted insults at him and tried to knock him over last time he'd left the caravan.

'Let's go the other way,' Fuad whispered, pulling at my sleeve.

But I could see that the boys weren't interested in us. They had made a tight knot around two little toughs who were in the middle of a furious argument. One suddenly sprang at the other and they began to fight. It was hard to make out what was going on, but then I saw that one of the fighters was Riad. He was losing. With one vicious kick, the other boy felled him to the ground. And then, like a pack of dogs, the others piled in, yelling, kicking and stamping.

I don't like watching anyone get hurt, not even a little toad like Riad. I was half blinded by fury and before I knew what I was doing I'd launched myself into the fight.

I was few years older than those kids, and bigger, of course, but even so they could have had me down on the ground and kicked me to bits if they'd had the sense to act together.

They had no sense at all, of course. A few minutes later, I'd scattered the lot of them and was picking Riad up from the ground. He was shaken and bruised and one eye was already swelling up. He was crying, too, with big gulping sobs and he suddenly looked much younger.

The other kids were circling round me again, but shouts from the men coming out of the mosque sent them scampering off. I grabbed Riad by the arm and dragged him away down the main 'street' towards our caravan. It wasn't easy to keep hold of him. He was small but wiry, and was desperately trying to wriggle out of my grasp. He'd stopped crying now.

'Let go! You're hurting me!'

'I'll let go when you say thank you. Properly.'

'Thank you for what?'

I wanted to kick him.

'I've just saved your life, or didn't you notice?'

His eyes flickered up to mine and down again.

'Thanks, Omar.'

'What was all that about, anyway?'

'Nothing.'

'What do you mean, nothing?'

He tried to wrench himself loose. I grabbed his other arm and twisted him round to face me.

'I'm not going to let you go till you tell me.'

He was sniffing and looking sorry for himself again. I waited.

'I don't care how long this takes. What were you fighting about?'

For a minute I thought he was going to kick my shins, but the brief spurt of anger had died out of his eyes.

'Those boys, they're not from my gang. The big one, Mustapha, he took my money off me.'

'What money? You haven't got any money.'

He said nothing.

'Where did you get it from? Go on. Tell me or I'll march you back and throw you to that bunch of mini-murderers.'

He sniffed again.

'Stole it,' he said, and his voice was so quiet that I could hardly hear. 'Ma told me to. She says she needs money for the baby.'

I was so stunned that I let go his arm. He didn't try to run away.

'Your ma sends you out to steal?'

He flushed.

'She says I've got to. We need food.'

'You've got ration cards, haven't you? Why don't you take them to the distribution centre? They'll give you stuff.'

He shrugged.

'Ma lost the ration cards. She didn't understand them. Can't read. She didn't know what to do.'

I looked down into his dirty, pinched little face and felt an annoying stir of pity.

'I don't owe you anything, you little horror. You've done nothing but aggravate me, *and* you and your mates have bullied Musa.'

He looked surprised, as if it had never occurred to him that anyone would notice or mind.

'Yeah, but he's just a . . .'

'He's a genius,' I said sternly. 'Worth a million times any of you lot.'

We stood there, Riad looking down at his feet, bare and blue with cold in their mud-caked plastic flip-flops, and me trying not to listen to the voice of my conscience.

At last I sighed. I had just been to Friday prayers, after all.

'I suppose I'll have to sort you out,' I said. 'You'd better come back with me.'

He backed away.

'You'll get me into trouble. You'll have me arrested.'

'I was planning,' I said stiffly, 'to help you with your ma's ration cards and show you how to get her supplies.

But if you want to go back to stealing . . .'

'I don't. I get scared.'

'Come with me then. Or don't. Your choice.' I started to walk away, half hoping that he wouldn't follow me.

He did.

As we turned out from between two lines of caravans, a boy ran up to us.

'Hey, Riad, you got caught by Mustapha's lot?'

Riad put on his usual careless swagger.

'Yeah. Saw them off though, didn't I?'

'With a lot of help from me,' I said crossly.

'Who's this?' the boy asked.

'My big cousin,' lied Riad, without a blink.

'Oh.' The boy looked at me curiously. 'Anyway, I just came to tell you, we chased Mustapha's gang off our patch. We're going down the Champs Élysées. You coming?'

'Nah.' Riad shot a glance at me. 'Got business. With my cousin.'

It was the word 'business' that did it – a new Big Idea to overcome the Big Flaw in my business plan. I waited till the other boy had gone, then spun Riad round to face me again.

'I'm going to do a deal with you. I'll help you, but you've got to help me, too.'

He looked back at me warily.

'Help you? Doing what?'

'I'm starting a business. Selling batteries.' It sounded

grand when I said it loud. 'And I don't want any hassle from you kids. No harassing my customers, no stealing, no snatching, no name-calling.'

His eyes narrowed to crafty slits.

'What do I get?'

I shook my head, exasperated.

'You get your life, which I've just saved. And I'm going to get proper help sorted out for your ma and the kids.'

We walked on while he thought about it. Our caravan was now in view.

'All right,' he said. 'It's a deal.'

For the first time I saw that he could smile.

Musa and Fuad were waiting for me at the door of the caravan.

'That wasn't Riad you were talking to, was it?' asked Musa. 'I thought you couldn't stand that kid.'

'I had my reasons. He won't be bothering us any more.' I pushed past them into the caravan. 'That can't be meat I can smell? Are we really going to have a proper Friday lunch for once?'

If only it had been a proper Friday lunch, or even an ordinary lunch, Friday or no Friday.

Actually, it was a disaster.

Baba took much longer than usual to come back from the mosque.

'Go and find him, Omar,' Ma said at last. 'Something's happened. I can feel it.'

I'd been looking over Musa's shoulder at a news broadcast on his laptop, trying to keep my mind off the longing to eat that was gnawing at my insides. I jumped up, but before I could reach the caravan door, Baba burst in.

He was pale with fury, his eyes burning in his thin face. He strode across the caravan, hauled Musa to his feet and slapped him hard across the face. Musa lost his balance and fell against me. Baba lifted his hand to hit him again.

'Hamid! What are you doing? Stop!' screamed Ma.

I put my arms out in front of Musa to fend Baba off.

'Get out of my way!' he hissed, his face screwed up with anger. 'I'll kill him, the snake! This is all his doing!'

He was clawing at my arm.

'What's he done?' Ma sounded hysterical. 'Hamid! Have you gone mad?'

'I'll tell you what he's done! Betrayed us, betrayed *me*! *He's* the reason why we're living in this hell!'

I knew then what had happened and I could tell that Musa knew too. I think I realized, at that moment, that nothing in our family would ever be the same again.

Baba was in such a rage that it took a while to sort out what had happened. Among all the thousands of new arrivals flooding into the camp every day, there'd been the man from the Ministry of Agriculture in Daraa who'd phoned Baba and tipped him off to leave Syria. It seemed there'd been some kind of mistake. Perhaps the man had been too scared to make himself clear, or maybe in his panic Baba hadn't understood. Anyway, that Friday morning they'd greeted each other cautiously after prayers, not knowing who, even here in Jordan, might be listening. It hadn't taken Baba long to realize that it was Musa who had been under suspicion, not himself.

If Ma and I hadn't held him off, I really think that Baba would have beaten Musa half to death. He gave up trying at last, and collapsed on to a mattress, looking exhausted.

'Baba . . .' Musa began tentatively.

Baba lifted his arm and pointed a shaky finger at him.

'Never speak to me again. You're not my son. I disown you, you useless crippled imbecile!'

Musa flinched as if he'd been stabbed.

'Baba!' I was so shocked I spoke louder than I'd meant to. 'How can you—'

He turned his red eyes on me.

'You were in it too, weren't you? Scheming against your own country! See what you've brought on this family? Hell and disaster!'

'That's not fair!' I could hardly believe that I was daring to speak so angrily to him. 'If we'd stayed in the village we'd have been bombed, like Uncle—'

He stared at me, as if he couldn't see me. 'You know nothing, you stupid, ignorant lump of a boy.'

So that's what he thinks of me, I told myself. Something shrivelled inside.

'Baba, please,' Eman said gently. 'Omar is only—'

He turned on her. 'And you! Disobedient! Rejecting the husband I found for you!'

He struggled to his feet. 'I'm not staying here in this nest of snakes. I'm going back to Daraa. I'll clear my name, root out Musa's network of traitors, find Bilal and get the marriage properly fixed up. You'll see. You'll see!'

Could we have stopped Baba going back to Syria if we'd tried harder? I don't know, but I wish we had.

The rest of that day was awful. Baba was in such a rage that he seemed half crazy. Ma cried all the time. Musa was as touchy as a wounded dog, Eman was pale with worry at the thought of Bilal, and even Nadia grizzled and whined. As for me, I felt almost winded with the hurt of Baba's words.

'Stupid', he'd called me. An 'ignorant lump'.

The rest of the day was a dreadful blur of anger and guilt. Ma was frantic, pleading and sobbing, clutching at Baba and calling on God to stop him going. Baba shouted at her to be quiet, then stormed off to 'make arrangements' to leave the camp.

I don't think any of us believed he was really going back into the hurricane of war until, two days later, Ma and I were standing by the bus that would take him home. Eman, Musa and Fuad had wanted to come, but he'd told them curtly to stay in the caravan. As the moment neared for the bus to leave, though, his anger seemed to die away. He looked almost happy.

'It's for the best, Leila,' he said to Ma. 'I can't support you or the children here. I'll get my salary reinstated, at the very least, and I'll settle things with Bilal. I can't protect Eman any longer. This marriage is the only possible thing for her. She'll come round to it soon enough. *Inshallah*, the war will soon be over and I'll come and fetch you and take you home.'

People were crowding round us, saying anxious goodbyes to other people who couldn't stand life in the camp any longer. Ma said nothing. She was staring at Baba with big, hopeless eyes, tears trickling down her cheeks.

Baba turned to me.

'I'm relying on you, Omar. Support your mother. Look after Eman and the little ones.'

'Baba,' I blurted out. 'Don't blame Musa. He—'

Baba was already being swept away towards the bus.

'He was led astray,' he called back. 'I'm going to find whoever it was who corrupted him and—'

'Hamid!' Ma called out suddenly. 'God protect you!'

'And you!' he called back.

And then he was being thrust up the steps of the bus by the crowd behind him, and had disappeared inside.

PART FIVE

CHAPTER EIGHTEEN

I thought it would be a relief without Baba's heavy, stern presence in the caravan, but in the first few days after he'd gone I realized how much he'd done. It was up to me now to deal with the camp authorities, queue for everything on distribution days, make sure Fuad got to school on time and worry about Ma and Eman if they were out of the caravan on their own. I knew I couldn't rely on Musa. He was trapped inside by the violent gangs of children as much as Eman was, and anyway, Baba's anger and cruel words had made him almost ill.

Winter was really on us now. Some mornings there was a layer of ice on the puddles and the stony ground outside the caravan glittered with frost. I felt weighed down by my new responsibilities. I wanted Ma to tell me what to do, but she seemed to expect me to know. In any case, she was fretting over Nadia, who was unwell again.

'Look,' she kept saying to Eman. 'See how tired she is?

So pale, and hardly eating. Feel her little hands. They're blocks of ice!'

It wasn't only our family I had to support. I'd almost forgotten my promise to Riad, but the day after Baba left I came out of the caravan to find him standing waiting for me, his gang in a threatening bunch behind him.

'Later,' I said, resisting the temptation to turn round and go back inside. 'I've got to get Fuad to school.'

Riad crossed his arms and the other kids took a step closer.

'Not later,' said Riad. 'Now. Our food's run out.'

I may be a stupid, ignorant lump, but I can think like a prize-winning rocket scientist when I have to.

'All right,' I said, and pointed to the two biggest boys in Riad's group. 'You, and you. Come here. What are your names? No, I don't want to know. I'm calling you "Tiger" and "Eagle".'

The boys looked at each other, and I saw the biggest one mouth 'Tiger' experimentally.

'Musa, can you come out?' I called over my shoulder. 'Have you got time to take Fuad to school today?'

Musa appeared at the door of the caravan. He took in the scene with one sweep of his eyes.

'I suppose so,' he said casually. He was scared stiff but nothing would have made him show it in front of the kids who'd tormented him ever since we'd arrived in the camp.

I hauled Tiger and Eagle forward and made them stand in front of Musa.

'These two are your protection,' I said to Musa, ignoring the shocked glances of the boys. 'Any trouble from them, any *hint* of disrespect, a single word out of place, and I will personally deal with them. It won't be pleasant.'

It might not have worked. For a long moment I was afraid it hadn't. Tiger smirked. Eagle waggled his head mockingly. Then Riad said sharply, 'You heard my cousin. Musa and Fuad are family now.'

I bit my lip as I watched Musa limp off with Fuad holding tightly to his hand. What had I let my brothers in for?

I didn't have time to worry. The other boys were crowding round me.

'What's my name?' said a little guy, whose bare feet, blue with cold, were curled away from the icy ground.

'Um . . . you look pretty dangerous to me. Scorpion.'

'And me?'

'And me?'

'And me?'

'Wolf. Lion. And, er, Antelope.'

'I don't like Antelope.'

'Cobra then. Happy now? Happy, all you animals?'

'Don't call us animals!' objected Wolf.

'All right then.' I scratched my head. 'Tell you what. From now on you're the Hooligans. OK?'

'Yay, we're the Hooligans!' little Cobra shouted. 'The Hooligans are the best!'

Riad batted them away.

'Omar – my ma.'

'OK. Let's go.'

And that was how, without me ever meaning to, I became the big daddy of the Hooligans, a bunch of fatherless brats.

It was a cold winter. Cold and mean and hungry. New people were arriving from Syria every day, pouring off buses and trucks from the border only a few kilometres away. The camp was growing further and further out across the desert, new caravan cabins arriving every hour. They were stretching in lines, kilometres long, into the distance.

Most people in the camp seemed to be bored to death, but I was busy all day long. This may sound wicked, and perhaps it is, but to be honest, after the first week without Baba, I didn't miss him much. Every now and then a text would come to Ma, so that we knew he was all right. I stopped thinking about him. I was getting used to taking decisions and sorting things out on my own.

I would have got a bit cocky, I suppose, if it hadn't been for Musa. I don't know how he did it, but after that first day he had the Hooligans under his thumb. The daily walk to take Fuad to school soon involved all of them, while Riad followed me around like a faithful dog.

The kids quickly learned to understand Musa's mangled speech, and he started to tell them stories, using the silly names I'd given them. They hung around him and begged for more.

I was a bit put out, actually. I was the one who'd tamed them, and who was getting the benefit? Mr Charming, of course. Not that I really minded. With his protection in place, Musa was free at last to go out. Ma even let Eman go with them sometimes. She loved going to the school, talking to the teachers and watching them in class. The children were hard to control. Some had never been to school before, and all them had been off classes for months. They'd seen awful things, too, and were really naughty all the time.

What with Baba going, and me having to sort out Um Riad's lost ration card, as well as all the extra fetching and carrying I had to do, it was five whole days before I had time to go back to the Champs Élysées to see Abu Radwan. And he wasn't at all pleased to see me. He looked up briefly, recognized me, then went on studying the wires he was untangling on his counter.

'Where have you been? Thought we had a deal. I sold all the batteries I got for you.'

My heart sank with a thump.

'Oh please, Abu Radwan. I couldn't come. My baba, he . . . well, there was a row at home and he went back to Syria.'

That shook him. He looked up at me at last.

'He did what?'

'He went back to Daraa. He works – *worked* for the government.'

'So I've heard,' Abu Radwan said drily.

'He said he was going to try to clear his name.'

I stopped, aware that I was saying far too much.

Abu Radwan said nothing.

'And there's this kid,' I went on desperately. 'His dad's dead and his ma's on her own. She lost her ration card. I had to help her get a new one.'

'Did you now?'

'And I've got to do stuff for my ma. My older sister helps her in the caravan, with my little sister who's not very well, but she can't go out, and my older brother can't do much either. He's disabled.'

'Any more excuses, or have you run out?'

I felt my cheeks flame with indignation.

'They're not excuses! I'm telling you the truth!'

He smiled at last.

'Calm down, Omar. Stop snarling at me like an angry dog. I believe you.' He reached under the counter and pulled out a box of batteries. 'I did sell the ones I bought for you, but I got another box just in case. So, are you going to go out there and get selling?'

My sigh of relief practically blew a bunch of papers off his counter. I reached out to take the box. He snatched it back.

'Hey, not so fast. We haven't sorted out the deal yet.'

*

I was lucky with Abu Radwan. He gave me a really good deal. I felt like the conqueror of the world as I pranced back to our caravan with my box of batteries tucked into my bag. I'd been right about the demand, too. My first load of batteries melted out of my hands like frost under the midday sun. When I pressed the profits into Ma's hands, with a casual, 'Got something here for you, Ma,' my grin was so wide I thought it would crack my cheeks.

'Where did you get this money from?' she asked, looking up with a suspicious frown.

'Earned it, didn't I?' I said proudly. 'Got my own business now.'

And it was great, because once I'd explained, she was so pleased with me her eyes actually filled with tears.

'You're a wonderful son, Omar! A gift from Allah!' Then she spoilt it by adding with a sigh, 'What have we come to, when my boy is nothing but a street hawker? You should be in school!'

Eman saw the look on my face and said quickly, 'One day he will be, Ma. Look, we can get some fresh vegetables. Maybe even a few apples! You're a marvel, Omar, you really are.'

I'll show her, I thought as I strode back to the Champs Élysées for another box of batteries. *I don't need school any more.*

*

For two or three weeks, I was the king of batteries round our part of the camp. The Hooligans were doing their job just fine, keeping an eye out for me, and making sure I was OK. They started melting away after a while, but I'd got confident by then, and I reckoned I'd got things sorted.

It was a freezing Monday morning when the good times ended. I was doing my usual rounds, going between the caravans calling out, 'Battery! Battery! Buy five, get one free!' when I heard what, for a second, I took to be an echo.

'Battery! Battery!'

I looked round, shocked. This was no echo. This was a threat.

I marched round the corner. Mustapha, the snotty kid from the rival gang, the one who had tried to beat Riad to a pulp, was in the very act of selling two batteries to one of my regular customs.

I let out a roar and charged. He dodged out of my way and yelled, 'Come and get me, *Cousin* Omar!'

Then he disappeared between two caravans.

The woman who'd bought his batteries wagged her finger at me.

'No need for fighting. You don't own the place, you know.'

And where were the Hooligans all this time? Where was my protection? I'll tell you where. My precious brother Musa, aided and abetted by my treacherous sister

Eman, had started to lure them off to school. One by one, they'd persuaded the little monsters to get themselves enrolled. Instead of protecting my business, they were either sitting in the classroom chanting, 'What is your name? My name is Ali/Maher/Ahmed,' in appalling English, or hanging round Musa begging him to tell them another stupid story.

I sold less than half my usual quota of batteries that morning, and by the time I went back to the Champs Élysées for a refill, my feet were sore with the furious kickings I'd given the stones along the way. To make matters worse, Abu Radwan only laughed when I told him what had happened.

'Stop scowling, Omar,' he said. 'That's just business. And no, before you ask, it wasn't me who sold him his batteries. What you've got to do is have another bright idea.'

I gaped at him, my mind whirring round like an electric fan.

'SIM cards?' I said wildly. 'Torches? Um, er . . .'

Abu Radwan didn't answer. He was looking at me thoughtfully.

'I have a better idea,' he said at last. 'Come back later this afternoon. I may have something for you.'

And that was how I moved up in the world, from being a street hawker, flogging batteries from a cardboard box, to being a sort of trainee electrician.

Abu Radwan gave me a chance any boy in the camp would have jumped at. But I had to work hard for it. He had me running round like a sheepdog at first, taking equipment out to people setting up generators or tapping into the power lines, delivering orders when he'd managed to get items into the camp, and then running the stall whenever he went off.

I worried at first about how Ma would manage without me, but it was more or less all right. It was just as well that Musa and Eman had the Hooligans to rely on. In the mornings they went in a gaggle with Musa and Eman to get their families' supplies from the distribution centre, and Musa helped them to sort out the muddles when the camp administrators got things wrong.

None of us needed quite so much protection now, anyway. As the winter ground on, Jordanian policemen were beginning to show up round the camp. Hundreds of people were still pouring in from Syria every day, but things weren't as wild as they had been at first. The gangs of kids and half-crazed teenagers were slowly being brought under control.

Being an electrician is really fiddly work. You have to be careful and neat, because if you get things wrong you can cause blow-outs and breakdowns, and even give yourself a horrible shock.

At first, when I was at the back of the shop, trying to remember Abu Radwan's instructions for mending a broken heater, or fixing a light fitting, I had to concentrate totally, but after a while I started to take part in the conversations that were always going on at the counter.

People usually talked about Syria, of course, and the news was always bad. I hated hearing it. The thing I worried about most was hearing Baba's name and finding out that something awful had happened to him.

'We thought it would all be over in a month or two!' I heard a man say. 'It'll be another year at least, I reckon.'

'Two years,' said another.

'Two? Five!' someone else chipped in. 'Let's face it, we're not going back to Syria, not soon, and maybe not ever. I'd get my family out to Europe if I had the money. I've got a cousin in Germany. There are jobs there. There's nothing for us here. Nothing.'

It was the mention of Europe that made me prick up my ears. Europe meant Norway to me, and Norway meant Rasoul. But Rasoul hadn't texted me for months. He still sent messages to Ma from time to time. The last one had said:

Got a job in a café in Oslo. Prices here so high you wouldn't believe it. Say hello to the kids.

There'd been no message for me. No mention of a shop. I'd been mending a switch on a heater, but my hands stopped working as for the first time I faced up to a reality that I'd known in my heart for a long time.

My dream of opening a shop with Rasoul was just that – a dream. It was never going to happen.

He was only being kind to me when he said all that stuff to me in Bosra, I told myself. *Why would he want to be saddled with a kid like me? I can't even speak English, never mind Noray-ish, or whatever they call their language.*

I'd tried to keep my dream alive, but now I had to let it go.

I went back to sorting out that stupid switch, but my eyes were blurred with tears and I did it all wrong.

Back in the caravan, the gloomy talk was just as bad. While Baba had been around, we'd kept our thoughts to ourselves, but now he was gone, Eman and Musa moaned all the time. Eman was spending longer and longer at the school after she'd dropped Fuad off, helping with whatever the teachers would let her do.

'Another kid dropped out of school today,' she told Ma one evening, as we sat around our supper. (It was lamb stew with carrots, bought, I'm proud to say, with *my* wages from Abu Radwan.)

'What a shame,' Ma said absently. She was trying to spoon another mouthful into Nadia, who had closed her lips tight and turned her head away.

'Do you mean Maher?' asked Fuad. 'I didn't like him anyway.'

'Don't talk with your mouth full,' said Ma automatically.

'The family managed to get out of the camp. They've gone to live on the farms,' said Eman enviously.

'All very well for ones with a father to look after them,' Ma said bitterly.

'They can earn money, that's why they've gone,' Eman went on. 'They're sending the kids to work in the fields.'

I felt Fuad stiffen beside me, and looked down to see the anxious look on his face.

'At starvation wages,' scoffed Musa. 'It's illegal, anyway. If the Jordanians catch them they'll send them back to Syria.'

Eman shrugged. 'So what? Anything's better than living in limbo here! What have we got to look forward to? Nothing. There's no school for Musa and me, no work . . .'

'Hey!' I objected.

Eman dismissed me with a wave of her hand.

'You've been lucky.'

'Lucky?' I nearly choked on a mouthful of stew. '*Lucky?* So it was just luck that made me think of batteries, and luck when I impressed Abu Radwan so much he gave me a job?'

'Shut up, Omar,' growled Musa. 'Go on, Eman.'

Eman sighed. 'I just feel hopeless, that's all. We're in a sort of prison. We're nowhere. And we might be here forever.'

Her voice shook and she turned her head away.

'You'd better keep on working, then, Omar,' Musa said, trying to lighten the mood. 'Earn enough for us to get a smuggler to take us all to Europe.'

Ma never knew when Musa was joking.

'Don't be silly, *habibi*. It would cost thousands and thousands to get us to Europe. You want us all to drown in the sea? Suffocate in the back of a lorry? Anyway, there's no need for that. Your baba will be back soon. He'll know what to do for the best.'

Musa and I looked at each other.

He's not being silly, I thought. *He really is thinking about Europe.*

My dream of working in Norway with Rasoul had been one thing. But the thought of our whole family going to Europe was cold and scary.

Good thing it can't happen, I told myself with a shudder, and pushed Fuad out of the way to help myself to another spoonful of lamb stew.

CHAPTER NINETEEN

At first, when Ma started panicking about Baba, I didn't listen. A week passed without a text from him. Two weeks went by. Then three.

'I'm sure it's all right, Ma,' Eman kept saying. 'You know what it's like in Daraa. No electricity. All the phone masts will be down. He just hasn't been able to get through, that's all.'

'He's in trouble!' Ma snapped back at her. She pressed a hand to her chest. 'I feel it *here*.'

'We'd have heard if anything was wrong,' Musa chipped in. 'Someone would have let us know.'

Musa's probably right, I thought, but after a month had passed, I was worried too. It was Baba who had always made the decisions, down to the smallest things, like the colour of Eman's hijab. It was Baba who had earned the money to feed us, who had dealt with our papers, got our ration cards, permits and vouchers. I'd managed all right since he'd gone, but I couldn't imagine being without him forever.

There were worrying changes at work, too. Abu Radwan was spending more and more time away from the shop. There were frequent visits from the same tall, heavy-looking man, who didn't buy anything but leaned over the counter, talking quietly. The strangest thing was that deliveries had stopped arriving at the shop and the stock was running low.

'We need more mobiles,' I said to Abu Radwan one morning, after I'd had to turn away a couple of customers. 'When are the new ones coming in?'

He didn't answer. I looked up at him, and something in his face made my heart miss a beat.

'Look, Omar,' he said at last. 'There aren't going to be any more deliveries. I'm selling up. My cousin in Dubai is setting up an electrical goods store and he's asked me to join him.'

I stared at him, speechless.

'Abu Maher's buying me out,' Abu Radwan went on, not meeting my eyes. 'That big fellow in the brown jacket. I asked him to take you on, but he's got sons of his own. There's not enough work for another boy.'

'You mean,' I managed to say, 'that I'm fired?'

He tutted at the word.

'I haven't got a choice, Omar. I'm not going till the end of the month. You can stay on till then. You're a smart kid. Someone else might give you a job. I'll ask around for you. Hey, no need to look like that.

The world hasn't come to an end.'

I could hardly keep myself from bursting into tears as I stumbled 'home'. Only that morning, I'd had dreams of running an electric cable off the street light into our caravan. I'd imagined the look on Ma's face when I'd switched on a light. I'd even decided to ask Abu Radwan to give me an old TV, and thought how brilliant it would be for Fuad (and, let's face it, for me) to watch cartoons again.

All that was over now.

Why does everything always go wrong? I thought miserably. *Why does it always happen to me?*

That evening, I could hardly eat a mouthful of supper. Musa was ranting on about another battle in Syria, Eman had more silly gossip from the school, and Fuad was moaning about his homework. Only Nadia was quiet, but she usually was these days.

I can't tell them, I told myself, pushing my plate away. *They'll think I'm a loser.*

Ma's voice broke through the thoughts grinding round in my head.

'Omar, dear,' she said. 'Why don't you ask Abu Radwan for a pay rise? Nadia needs a new coat. In this weather—'

'A rise? Ma, I've been sacked!' The words were out of my mouth before I knew it. 'It's all over! I'm not going to earn any more money. I'm just a useless, stupid, ignorant lump.'

Ma put her hand up to her cheek. '*Ya haram!* Omar, what did you do? He can't just—'

'I didn't do *anything*!' I shouted. 'Abu Radwan's selling his business! He's moving to Dubai! Why do you always blame me?'

'Oh, *habibi*!' Ma came over and sat down beside me. 'I'm sorry. I didn't think.'

Her arm was round me. I wanted to push her away, but she felt warm and soft, and her old, familiar smell was too much for me. I leaned against her and awful, gulping sobs broke out of me.

After a while I felt Nadia's hand on my leg.

'Why are you crying, Omar?'

'He's crying because he's a useless, stupid, brilliant, idiotic, ignorant lump of genius,' said Musa.

'No he isn't!' Nadia was indignantly shaking her head. 'He's Omar. He's my brother.'

'And mine,' said Fuad loudly.

'Mine, too,' added Eman.

'I suppose he's mine as well, now I come to think of it,' said Musa, 'though as we all know, I'm a million times better looking. And now that we've sorted that out, why don't we tell him about that chunk of cake Eman brought back from school today, and a give him the biggest slice?'

I was glad when I woke up the next morning and realized that it was Friday. It was my day off, and I'd have a bit of time to calm down before going back to the Champs Élysées on Saturday.

Since Baba had left, we had stopped going to Friday prayers, but that morning Musa was chivvying Fuad into washing his face and combing his hair before I'd even finished breakfast. He looked across at me.

'You coming, Omar?'

I nearly said, 'What's the point? Prayers don't help,' but then I thought of the long day ahead with nothing to do. At least going to the mosque would get me out of the caravan.

It took ages to get ready, and we didn't get to the mosque until after the prayers had started. Baba had always helped Musa with the movements – standing, bowing and kneeling – and I had to do it now. I was glad we were at the back, where most people couldn't see us.

What was it that made me fearful? Perhaps it was the concerned look I caught on a couple of the men's faces, as they glanced towards us and looked away again. Or perhaps it was some sixth sense that gave me a few minutes' warning.

We had stepped out of the mosque caravan and I was helping Musa to put on his shoes when the imam called us back inside.

'It's Omar, isn't it?' he said, smiling down at me with a sorrowful face. 'And Musa. And is this Fuad?'

'That's right, sir,' I said cautiously.

Here it comes, whatever it is, I thought.

'Leave your shoes,' the imam went on. 'Come in and sit with us.'

A group of three other men were sitting cross-legged on the carpet. I recognized two of them. They were from Daraa. We sat down awkwardly. We weren't used to being included in discussions with grown-up men. My skin was prickling with nervous dread.

'I don't think you know Abu Bashir? He escaped from Syria only last night.' The imam put his hand out towards the third man, who nodded towards us without smiling. 'Abu Bashir has some news for you. It will make you sad, but remember, we are all in the hands of Allah. Whatever happens is His will.'

Abu Bashir shuffled his shoulders awkwardly. He looked down at his hands, which were resting on his knees.

'I'm so sorry, boys. There's no easy way to tell you this. Your father – has passed away.'

There was a kind of buzzing in my ears. Beside me, Musa's arm jerked violently. He tried to speak, but his tongue seemed stuck to the roof of his mouth.

They don't know really, I thought. *It's just a rumour.*

Musa spoke again. The men looked at me. They hadn't understood.

'He wants to know how you know,' I said.

My hands were clenched so tightly that my nails were digging into my palms.

'This gentleman used to work with your father at the

Ministry,' the imam said gently. 'He was there when they came to arrest Abu Musa.'

Musa was trembling violently now. His arm shot out again, out of control.

'My fault!' he tried to say. 'Because of me!'

Luckily, none of them understood.

'That can't be right,' I said. 'Baba never did anything against the government. It must have been someone else.'

'Things are bad now in Daraa,' one of the other men said. 'A lot of innocent people have been arrested.'

'It seems he was talking to a colleague, and this other man was a suspect,' Abu Bashir said. 'The police swept them up together and took them to prison.'

'Did they hurt him?' Musa asked hoarsely.

'Did they torture him?' I translated.

Fuad tugged at my sleeve.

'What's it about, Omar? Did someone hurt Baba?'

'Later, *habibi*. Wait now,' I said.

Abu Bashir was shaking his head.

'He never even reached the police station. A shell fell on the van before it got there. There were no survivors.'

'You can't be sure!' I burst out. 'He might be in hospital! Perhaps . . .'

Abu Bashir shook his head.

'I'm so sorry, Omar. I saw his – I saw him with my own eyes. We buried him, me and our friends.'

'What is it, Omar?' Fuad was shaking my arm violently. 'Is it Baba? Did he die?'

I felt as if my strength had gone. I leaned over and shut my eyes, blocking out the ring of concerned faces.

'Yes, Fuad,' said Musa. 'Baba died.'

Fuad broke into loud wails.

'Don't cry, little man,' I heard the imam say. 'It's the will of Allah. He spared your father from suffering. You have to be strong now.'

Musa coughed and swallowed, preparing to speak as clearly as he could. 'What about the death certificate? Our papers? The camp authorities?'

'Did he say "camp authorities"?' asked the imam.

When I didn't answer, he went on, 'Who's the head of your family now? It's you, Omar, I suppose.'

I looked up. Musa was frowning at me.

'Musa's older than me,' I mumbled. 'It's him.'

The imam looked doubtful, and went on talking to me, as if Musa wasn't there.

'And your mother, she's here in the camp?'

'Yes,' said Musa. 'With our two sisters.'

'Two sisters,' I repeated automatically.

One of the other men had reached into an inner pocket and brought out a sweet. Fuad put it in his mouth, and his crying turned to huge, shuddering hiccups.

Abu Bashir cleared his throat.

'I have some good news for you too,' he said. 'Before he passed away, your father managed to contact your brother-in-law.'

My head jerked round to face him.

'My what?'

'Your sister's husband. Bilal.'

'My sister isn't married.'

'As good as, your father said. Bilal knows you're here. He's coming as soon as he can to take her.'

The men were nodding and making encouraging noises.

'God is indeed merciful,' the imam said. 'You'll have someone, a good man, to help you.'

'But . . .' I began.

Fuad had finished his sweet. He was tugging my sleeve again.

'Omar, does Ma know about Baba?'

The thought of telling Ma was so painful that I couldn't answer. Musa spoke for me.

'No, we'll tell her. We'll go home and tell her now.'

I helped him to his feet. The men stood up too. I could tell they were relieved that their duty was done.

The imam patted my shoulder.

'My wife will come this afternoon and visit your mother. What's the number of your caravan? She'll let me know if there's anything I can do to help.'

If Baba had died in Syria, we'd have known what to do. There would have been ceremonies and prayers. Musa and I would have gone with him to the burial place and visitors would have streamed through our house. Later, Ma and Eman would have laid flowers on his grave.

Here, in this strange, prison-like place, none of that could happen. People barely had time to comment before the next person lost a husband or father, mother or sister.

A few people came to the caravan to offer sympathy. Um Riad was the first. She could barely hide her satisfaction at the thought that Ma was now a widow too.

Ma's face had drained of colour when Musa had gently told her, and she'd sunk down on a mattress. I'd expected her to break down into hysterical wails. Instead, streams of tears flowed silently down her cheeks.

'I knew it!' she said. 'Didn't I tell you? When I saw him step on to that bus, I knew I would never see him again!'

Her comfort was the messages she was receiving from Auntie Fawzia. Uncle Mahmud was out of hospital. Jaber had sneaked back home from wherever he'd been hiding and was doing most of the farm work. Prayers and blessings pinged down the airwaves into Ma's phone, and she read them out to us, her voice choked with tears.

Musa and I had agreed not to mention Bilal to Eman until we had to, but we'd forgotten to warn Fuad.

'Why can't I go to school?' he whined, when that long, strange weekend was over.

'Because we're in mourning,' Eman told him. 'We've got to show respect.'

'But I *want* to go to school. We're going to draw rainbows today.'

'Well, you can't.' Eman had run out of patience.

'I hate you!' Fuad shouted at her. 'I'm glad you're going away!'

'I'm not going anywhere.' Eman was folding up a pile of clothes that had taken days to dry on the line strung across the caravan. 'Don't be so rude, and stop pulling at the washing line.'

Fuad was red in the face with anger.

'You *are* going away. Mr Rat-Face Nosy's coming to get you.'

I gave Fuad a warning look, and Musa tried to grab his arm.

'It's true!' Fuad went on. 'The man at the mosque told Musa and Omar. Rat Face knows where you are. You've got to marry him now. He'll be here soon.'

Eman's face had gone white. 'Is this true? Musa? Omar?'

I nodded.

'We didn't want to worry you. He mightn't be able to get out of Syria. No need to . . .'

Eman was looking furious now. 'You had no right to keep this from me! It's *my* future you're talking about! I'm not going to marry him, and that's final!'

'No need to yell at me,' I said, offended. 'Musa's the head of the family now. You'd better thrash it out with him.'

Eman locked her eyes on to Musa's. She looked shocked now, as much as angry. The younger brother, whom she'd scolded and cosseted throughout his difficult childhood, was now in charge of her. He would make every decision about her life from now on.

I remembered, with a sinking heart, that Musa hadn't opposed the marriage when we were at the farm. 'Don't make her, Musa,' I said. 'You can't.'

Musa shook his head.

'The truth is, we don't know how things stand. We don't know what Baba did or didn't do. We may not be able to get out of it.' To my relief he shot Eman one of his rare, glowing smiles. 'I'll do my best for you, I promise.'

Life went back to normal in a weird kind of way after a few days, if anything in Za'atari camp could be called normal. After all, Baba had been gone for a while already, so we were used to his absence. Fuad went back to school, and I went to Abu Radwan's shop, though there was less and less for me to do. Eman barely left the caravan, as if she was afraid that Bilal would snatch her away the minute she showed her face outside. Ma seemed frozen in misery.

Musa spent more time than ever on his laptop, leaving me to do all the fetching and carrying.

'Who's going to charge that thing for you when I've finally lost my job?' I said nastily to him, resenting the fact that I'd had to bring Fuad back from school. 'What are you doing, anyway?'

Musa didn't lift his eyes from the screen.

'You'll find out.'

Later that day he clapped his hands in the air and

whooped triumphantly, 'Gotcha!'

'What? Got who?' I said.

He didn't answer.

None of us noticed how quiet Nadia had become. She no longer bounced on the mattress or tried to catch bits of fluff floating in the air. She lay still, sucking her thumb.

'What a good girl,' Ma would say, stroking her head as she passed. 'No trouble to anyone.'

The thought that Bilal might turn up at any moment obsessed me. Hundreds of people were still pouring into the camp from Syria every day. They were mostly women with children, but there were men, too, and I scanned every one of their faces. Once or twice I thought I saw Mr Nosy's long ratty nose and close-set eyes, but it was always a false alarm.

And then, one day, it wasn't.

I was on my way back from the Champs Élysées, worries churning round in my head as usual. How would we manage without the money from my job? How could I find another one? Were we doomed to live in the camp forever?

Suddenly a hand gripped my elbow, painfully hard. I spun round.

'Hello, Omar.' Bilal's wide smile showed his small, uneven teeth. 'On your way home, are you? I'll come with you.'

'N-no,' I stammered. 'I'm fetching . . . um . . . bread from the distribution centre.'

'I've only been here a couple of days,' said Bilal, 'but aren't you going in the wrong direction? Never mind. I know where your caravan is.'

I couldn't hide my dismay.

'How did you find out?'

'Oh, that was easy.' He was walking on fast and I had trouble keeping up with him. 'You only have to ask around here. A big village, isn't it?'

'Not really.'

He ignored that.

'I was sorry to hear about your father. We understood each other so well. And now we're to be brothers! Your sister, is she well?'

'I – yes, I suppose . . .'

'We never expected to hold a wedding in a refugee camp, did we?' He laughed. 'But we'll manage. This way, isn't it? Don't worry, I can find it. Your mother needs the bread, I'm sure.'

'I'll get it later,' I said hastily, trying desperately to think of a way to head him off, but we were almost at the back at the cabin and there was nothing I could do.

To my surprise, Musa looked almost pleased to see Bilal. He came out of the cabin to greet him, then sent Fuad back inside to fetch the two little stools that Ma and Eman used when they were preparing our food.

'He's here!' I heard Fuad say, as he bounced back into the cabin. 'Mr N— I mean, Bilal.'

There was a horrified gasp from Eman and a pleased

one from Ma, who appeared at the door a moment later, a rare smile on her face. They talked for a moment or two, but I didn't listen. I was too busy watching Musa. He was standing as tall as he could, and there was an expression on his face that I'd never seen before: a serious, heavy look.

He looks like Baba, I thought, surprised. *He's grown up.*

'I'll get coffee,' Ma said at last, hurrying back inside.

Musa waited till she'd gone and pointed to one of the stools. Musa sat down, and Bilal sat opposite him, a patronizing and contemptuous look on his face.

'Your father and I sorted everything out,' he said bossily, looking over Musa's head at me. 'I'm going to fix the wedding for next—'

'You – are – not – going – to – marry – my – sister.'

Musa spoke loudly and slowly so that Bilal could understand, but even so, for a moment I thought I must have heard him wrong. I hadn't, and felt a shock of joy. Bilal started with surprise, then smiled at Musa pityingly.

'My dear boy—'

'I'm – not – your – dear – boy.' Musa's voice was harsh and grating.

'This is ridiculous. You have no right—'

Musa turned to me.

'Omar, fetch my laptop.'

I'd never seen Musa like this, so sharp and commanding. I obeyed automatically. Eman was standing behind the caravan door, her face tight with anxiety. Ma had heard nothing. She was fussing with the coffee things in her little kitchen area at the back of the caravan. I grabbed the laptop and hurried out again.

'Your full name, it's Bilal Maher, isn't it?' Musa was saying.

'You know it is.' Bilal was getting angry.

'And you lived in Duma, near Damascus, six years ago? You were working in a bicycle store?'

'Look here, what is all this?' blustered Bilal.

Musa took the laptop from me and flicked open the lid.

'I've downloaded the bit we need to look at.' He was speaking too fast, but Bilal seemed to have no difficulty understanding him. He was shifting his weight awkwardly on his stool.

'The crime is detailed here.' Musa jabbed a finger at the screen. 'Rape. A nasty case. You nearly killed the poor girl.'

I saw a flash of panic in Bilal's eyes, but he quickly controlled it.

'This is ridiculous! There must be hundreds of people called Bilal Maher. How dare you—'

'It is you.' Musa was scrolling down the screen. 'There's a photograph of you. Look, it's quite clear.'

Bilal jumped to his feet, knocking over the stool. Behind the door I heard a muffled shriek of delight from Eman. Ma appeared, a little tray of coffee glasses in her hands.

'We won't need that, Ma.' Musa struggled to his feet. 'This man has to go.'

'What? But the wedding! You can't have fixed everything already?' said Ma, looking bewildered.

Bilal was stepping away from us.

'It's all a lie! Blackmail! There was never . . . I didn't . . .'

'I wondered why a man of your wealth had never found a wife,' Musa said coolly. 'After all, who would give their daughter to a rapist?'

Ma gave a little scream and dropped the tray. The tiny glasses shattered on the ground and black coffee splashed up her robe. Bilal advanced on Musa, a threatening fist held up.

'You can't do this, you pathetic little cripple. I gave your sister a fortune in dowry. That necklace . . .'

The door of the caravan was wrenched open. A flash of gold flew through the air and landed at Bilal's feet.

'Take your necklace!' Eman shouted, and slammed the caravan door shut again.

Bilal was red in the face and breathing heavily now. He took another step towards Musa. Behind him a little crowd had gathered, attracted by the raised voices. A few of the Hooligans were watching, ready to protect Musa.

'It's all right, boys,' I called across to them. 'This guy's on his way.'

But Bilal wasn't finished. He lunged, his fist ready to strike. I jumped in front of Musa, and took the punch in my stomach. I doubled over, winded.

'It's all right, Omar! We've got him!' I heard Tiger shout out as I gasped for breath. 'What do you want us to do?'

'Get him out of here,' Musa said, turning to go back into the caravan. 'And make sure he doesn't show his face round here again.'

I still couldn't breathe properly, but I looked up to see Bilal bend down to try and scoop the necklace off the ground. Before he could reach it, the Hooligans had dragged him away. He looked at me with poison in his eyes, but he was beaten and we both knew it.

Lion picked up the necklace and handed it with a flourish to Musa.

'Here you are, Boss,' he said, and scampered away.

'Boss' is it now? I thought. *Who does Musa think he is?*

'It's all very well driving him off like that,' Ma said later, as we sat around our evening meal. 'But I can't believe Bilal ever did such a terrible thing. It's impossible! And say what you like, he was generous. He'd have looked after us all.

Eman flushed.

'I'd never have married him. Never! I was planning to throw his necklace in his face if it came to an actual wedding.'

Ma looked shocked.

'Wherever did you get such an idea from? What a

scandal you'd have brought down on the family!'

'Would you rather I'd married a rapist?' Eman said passionately. 'I knew he was evil the moment I saw him.'

Ma hadn't finished. She turned to Musa.

'How did you find all that out, anyway? You can't be sure that person was him. Perhaps—'

'It was him,' Musa said with a frown. 'Let it go, Ma. We won't talk about that disgusting man any more.'

All through her life, Ma had obeyed the men of her family without complaint: first her father, then her husband. And now Musa was taking on the role. I could see a struggle in Ma's face as she heard the new authority in his voice. I waited for her to say something, but Musa spoke first.

'Eman, make some tea for Ma. She's had a shock. We're on our own, Ma, and we'll manage on our own. We won't be in this camp forever. We'll find a way to get out, I know we will.'

Ma's mouth fell open, then she shut it again. At that moment, I had blinding revelation. Musa hadn't really been Ma's favourite son. He'd been her baby. She hadn't noticed that he didn't need her fussing over him any longer. I could almost watch the revolution happening in her head.

One was happening in mine, too. I suddenly realized that I didn't have to jealous of Musa any more.

CHAPTER TWENTY

It was March by now, and the days were warming up. The nights were still cold, but the rain, which had bucketed out of the sky all through the winter, had stopped. The ground was still flooded, though. Some of the puddles had turned into mini-lakes, with water that came halfway up your thighs if you accidentally stepped in them.

It was six o'clock on one chilly, damp evening. I had plodded back from the Champs Élysées feeling hopeless and miserable. There were only three days to go before Abu Radwan left the camp, and although I'd asked every shopkeeper up and down the whole souk, no one had a job to offer me. Even Abu Radwan had nothing much for me to do. He was only keeping me to the end out of kindness.

It was my fault that I slipped in the mud and went sprawling. I'd been lost in my thoughts and hadn't looked where I was going. It wasn't easy to get up as my feet kept sliding out from under me.

I looked down at myself with disgust. My legs, right up to my knees, were slimy with mud and my hands were filthy, too. I washed them off in a dirty puddle, hunched my shoulders against the evening chill, and went on.

Eman pulled a face when she saw me.

'You might try to be a bit more careful, Omar,' she said bossily. 'Those jeans will take days to dry out.'

Shut up! I shouted in my head. *Just shut up and leave me alone!*

'Supper's ready!' Ma called out. 'Set out the plates, Fuad.'

'Where's Nadia?' Musa said suddenly.

Ma's hands were full of dishes. She pointed with her chin towards a corner of the caravan.

'Asleep, over . . . Oh! She's not there!'

For a long moment, we all stood in horrified silence. There was nowhere to hide in the cabin. Nadia had gone. I had been struggling to take off my muddy trousers. I yanked them back on again, ignoring the clammy cold around my legs.

'She must have gone outside,' I said. 'I'll go and look.'

'But it's nearly dark!' Ma's voice was sharp with panic. 'She's been stolen! Someone's taken her! She—'

'Ma, no one could have stolen her.' Musa had struggled to his feet. 'No one's been in the caravan except for us all day.'

Eman clapped a palm to her forehead.

'She was sitting on the doorstep earlier. There were

some children playing with a kitten. She was watching them.'

'How long ago?' rapped out Musa.

'I – I don't know. Two hours? Longer, maybe.'

'You know how much she loves cats,' I said. 'She must have gone out to play, too. She can't have gone far.'

I was trying to sound calm but inside I was shivering with fear. The light was really bad now, and it was too late and cold for small children to be outside.

And the puddles! I thought with new horror. *Some are so deep she could easily drown!*

I forced my feet into my filthy shoes and stepped outside. Musa followed me.

'I'll call up the Hooligans,' he said.

The next half-hour was one of the most horrible of my life. I ran from caravan to caravan, shouting, 'Nadia! Nadia! It's me, Omar, *habibti*! Come home!'

At door after door, the answer was the same. No one had seen a little girl out on her own.

It was impossible to go too fast, for fear of slipping in the mud. I felt as if I was in a nightmare, and my legs had somehow been tied up to prevent me running. Several men had joined in the search now, bringing solar lamps out to help them. From some way away, I could hear Musa calling, and the high-pitched cries of the Hooligans.

At last there were shouts in the distance.

'We've found her! Omar, where are you!'

'Here! Here!' I yelled hoarsely, stumbling towards the voices.

Short, shadowy figures were appearing, edging round a large pool of water towards me. Musa was limping behind them, struggling to keep up. Now I could see that the boy in front was Wolf, and he was carrying a large, still bundle in his arms.

Cobra ran up to me.

'I was the one who found her, Omar. She's all cold and wet. She was hiding under a tent flap.'

She's dead, I thought, rushing forward.

Wolf slid her into my arms. I turned to carry her back to our cabin, but then I stopped, confused. The tall street lamps were shooting bright reflections off the puddles, making everything look different, and the rows of white cabins seemed to stretch on forever, one exactly the same as the next. I looked down at the bundle in my arms. Nadia looked horribly pale. Her eyes were closed, but her lids were fluttering. I could hear her breathing, too: fast and rasping.

Musa was beside me now.

'Come on! What are you waiting for?'

He limped off and I stumbled after him. He turned, and called out over his shoulder, 'Thanks, boys. And Cobra, you did brilliantly!'

Ma and Eman were outside the caravan, a knot of neighbouring women round them. Ma saw us coming and let out a shriek. She dashed forward, took Nadia out of my arms and darted inside. We followed her.

'Thank God!' the women called out after us. 'Thank God, she's safe!'

They moved slowly away.

Ma had lain Nadia down on a mattress and was rubbing her limp hands.

'Open your eyes, *habibti*! Nadia, look at Mama!'

'Is she going to die, like Baba did?' Fuad asked loudly.

'Don't say such a thing!' Eman told him sharply. Fuad shrank into himself and went to sit on one of the mattresses, hugging his knees.

As the evening went on, his question was soon in all our minds. Nadia, who had been shaking with cold, was soon burning up with heat. Her breathing was worse and her eyes stayed half shut.

'She needs a doctor, Ma!' Musa said at last.

'You think I don't know that?' Ma almost screamed at him. 'You think we're at home in Bosra, with the clinic just down the street?'

The tap on the door was so gentle that I was the only one to hear it. I opened it cautiously. One of the women who had been waiting outside with Ma was standing there.

'How is the little girl?' she asked. 'Would you like me to examine her? I am – *was* – a nurse back home.'

I stood back to let her in. Ma looked up with a distracted frown.

'I haven't come to disturb you,' the neighbour said

quickly. 'You might not know that a hospital for children opened in the camp last week. Over on the far side. And when I heard the little girl's breathing . . . If she's got pneumonia—'

'Pneumonia!' Ma reared back with fright. 'Oh God, help us!' She stopped, trying to pull herself together. 'Is there really? A children's hospital?

Um Ali nodded. 'I'd go along with you, but I can't leave my baby.'

'No need,' said Ma. She'd been kneeling over the mattress on which Nadia was lying, but now she scrambled to her feet. 'Um Ali, you're a true friend. Omar, come with me. Eman, find her winter coat. We'll keep her wrapped up in the blanket.'

I was already shrugging my outside jacket back on and was making for the door to find my shoes, but my mind was racing. What if I got lost again? The camp was huge now. What if I couldn't find the hospital? If Nadia was so sick, by the time Ma and I had gone stumbling round all over the place, she might be . . .

'Please, Um Ali, where is it exactly?' I asked.

She had been feeling Nadia's forehead with the back of her hand, but looked up to give me directions.

'There are children's drawings all along the outside walls,' she said. 'And Omar, I think you'd better hurry.'

The hunt for Nadia had been nightmarish, but that dash through the dark and the mud to the children's hospital was worse. I knew which puddles were deep, and instinctively avoided them, but Ma needed guiding every step of the way. Several times she skidded on the mud and nearly fell. We were going horribly slowly.

'Here, Ma, let me take Nadia,' I kept saying.

She wouldn't answer, but clutched Nadia even more tightly to her shoulder.

I knew she'd go down, and when we were only halfway to the hospital, she did. I just managed to grab Nadia before she splashed down into a huge puddle. She floundered around in the water, trying to get up. With Nadia in my arms, there was nothing I could do to help.

Then I made a dreadful discovery.

'Ma,' I said hoarsely. 'I don't think Nadia's breathing any more.'

'No! No!' Ma was on her feet at last. 'Take her, Omar! Run!'

I stood still for an agonizing moment. How could I leave Ma alone, lost in the camp, in the dark?

'Just go!' she screamed at me. 'Run!'

Panic seized me and I took off. Words tumbled round in my head.

Nadia, little sister, don't die! Don't die!

All that came out of my mouth was dry, heaving sobs.

The hospital was there in front of me at last. Light shone from the windows. I stumbled towards the door, and gave it a kick.

'Help!' I shouted. 'Please, someone, come!'

The door opened. A woman in a blue tunic stood there.

'It's my sister,' I tried to say, though my throat was almost too tight to speak.

She reached out and took Nadia out of my arms. The blanket fell away, and I saw my sister's face, pale and still.

'What's her name?' the woman asked.

'Nadia,' I managed to say. 'Nadia Hussein. She's dead, isn't she?'

The woman didn't answer. She turned and ran off through a door at the back of the room calling out, 'Dr Jean! Emergency! Room Three!'

She shut the door behind her, leaving me alone.

I stood, frozen, staring at the closed door. Behind it I could hear hurried footsteps and urgent commands in a foreign language. Was it too late? How could a child get sick so quickly, and die within a couple of hours? It was impossible. It *must* be impossible!

Then I remembered Ma. I stepped back through the outside door. My eyes were still used to the bright lights in the hospital, and the darkness seemed murkier than ever.

It took no more than a few minutes to reach Ma. She had hardly moved from where I'd left her. She was standing still, looking round helplessly, completely lost.

'Omar!' she gasped when she saw me. 'Is she . . . Did you get her there?'

I took hold of her arm.

'The doctor's seeing her now. Come with me.'

There was someone else in the little room just inside the hospital: a young man, who was sitting at a desk tapping things into a computer. He frowned when he saw us.

'This is a children's hospital. We don't treat adults here.'

He spoke Arabic with an Egyptian accent.

'Please,' Ma said, hurrying up to the desk. 'My little girl, Nadia Hussein? My son brought her in a few minutes ago. How is she? Will she be all right?'

The man's face softened.

'*Inshallah*. They're working with her now.'

'Can I see her? I must see her!' Ma put a pleading hand down on the desk. 'She'll be frightened. She . . .'

The young man looked disapprovingly at Ma's muddy hand, which was leaving a dirty mark on the desk.

'You'll have to wait,' he said. 'In any case you need to clean yourself up. We don't want infections in the hospital.'

Ma snatched her hand off the desk.

'Of course? Where?'

He pointed to a pair of washrooms.

'I'll tell you as soon as I hear anything. Come back here and wait.'

*

Why do some hours pass quickly and others creep by as slowly as water evaporating from a puddle? As the minutes crawled past, I had nothing to do but stare at the white walls and the coloured pins on the crowded noticeboards in front of me.

Occasionally, a door would open and someone would come into the reception area. Ma would be on her feet at once.

'My daughter! Nadia Hussein! What's happening? Tell me, please!'

The answer was always the same.

'She's in good hands. Wait here.'

At last, when it felt as if we'd been there for a week, a tall European woman, who wore a stethoscope dangling round her neck, came into the room.

'I'm Dr Jean,' she said, holding out her hand to Ma. 'Are you Nadia's mother? And who's this?'

'Omar,' I said out loud, but inside I was yelling at her, *Get on with it! Tell us about Nadia!*

'Let's go into my consulting room,' she said.

My heart sank. Why couldn't she just tell us quickly that Nadia was all right?

Ma and I sat perched on two plastic chairs facing Dr Jean in the little room.

'There's good news,' the doctor began. 'Nadia is responding well. She's a very sick little girl, but she'll recover.'

Ma turned a beaming face to me.

'Did you hear that, Omar? Thank God!'

But I was still looking at Dr Jean, wondering why she wasn't smiling.

'But,' Dr Jean went on, 'I'm afraid there's another problem. Have you noticed anything about Nadia that might have worried you?'

'Never!' Ma was still smiling. 'She's such a quiet child, no trouble at all. She wandered out of the caravan today, but only because of a kitten, and—'

Dr Jean coughed to stop Ma's flow.

'The thing is, Um Omar . . .' she began.

'She's Um Musa,' I mumbled, embarrassed at having to interrupt her.

'Thank you. The thing is that Nadia has a problem with her heart.'

My own heart missed a beat, and Ma's hand flew to her cheek.

'She's had it since she was born. Has a doctor never examined her before?'

'A doctor? Why? She's never been ill!' Ma was looking defensive. 'I told you, she's just a normal little girl.'

'Not quite normal, I'm afraid,' Dr Jean said gently. 'I'm afraid that Nadia is going to need an operation. Quite a big one.'

We both sat and stared at her, speechless with horror.

'A heart operation?' whispered Ma. 'But we don't have any money! How much do you charge?'

Dr Jean shook her head.

'Our health care here is free, but we can't operate on Nadia in this hospital. She needs a specialist surgeon. An intensive care unit.'

I couldn't hold back any longer.

'What will happen if she doesn't have the operation?' I blurted out.

Dr Jean looked grave.

'The outcome won't be good.'

There was panic in Ma's eyes.

'What can we do? Where can we go? We're stuck here, in this camp. If you can't help us, who can?'

'I think I may know the answer.' Dr Jean leaned forward across the table. 'Um Musa, how many people are in your family?'

Ma was looking dazed. She shook her head mutely.

'There are six of us,' I said. 'My sister, Eman, she's eighteen. Musa's sixteen. He's got cerebral palsy. There's me. I'm fifteen, and Fuad's eight. With Ma and Nadia, that makes six altogether.'

Dr Jean nodded.

'Your brother has cerebral palsy?' She made a note on the pad on her desk. 'Can he walk without help?'

'Yes, but he needs help doing stuff. He's really clever, though. Much cleverer than me.'

'I'm sure he is.' She paused, her eyes on my face. 'Omar, there's a hospital in London that could help Nadia. They have specialist surgeons there for her kind of heart condition.'

'London?' I said stupidly. 'In England? Nadia can't go all the way to London. She's only four.'

'She wouldn't go alone.' Dr Jean was watching Ma now. 'You would all go. I can make an application for visas for you all. In the circumstances, an asylum claim would be likely to succeed.'

I could barely take in what she was saying.

'Asylum? You mean we'd stay there? Permanently?'

There was a knock on the door. A nurse put her head into the room and nodded. Dr Jean stood up.

'Um Musa, you can see Nadia now. Omar, you should go home. Your brothers and sister will want to know what's happening. Come back in the morning. Bring your family's papers and we'll get things under way. Don't look so shocked. London's not a bad place, you know, in spite of the weather.'

CHAPTER TWENTY-ONE

The camp was silent and deserted as I stumbled back to our cabin. The full moon was casting eerie shadows over the glistening mud. I'd left my phone behind in the mad scramble to get Nadia to the hospital, so I had no idea what the time was. It felt like the middle of the night.

The dim light of a solar lamp shone out from the mass of cabins. It could only come from ours.

Eman must have been straining her ears to hear me coming, because she opened the door before I had time to knock.

'What's happening? Why did you take so long?'

'She's going to be all right. Sort of.'

I was struggling to take off my filthy shoes.

'What do you mean, sort of? Where's Ma?'

'Give me a chance. Just let me get cleaned up.'

Eman ran to the little kitchen area while I struggled out of my mud-caked clothes and hauled on my pyjamas. Fuad was lying in a tumble on a mattress, fast asleep, but

Musa had been waiting up with Eman. He was watching me impatiently.

'Are you going to take all night?' he said crossly.

I flopped down beside him. A wave of exhaustion was swamping me.

'Tell you everything in the morning,' I said sleepily, sliding sideways so that I could lie down.

Musa prodded me up again. 'No you don't. Talk now.'

It felt as if hours had passed before they let me go to sleep, and even when at last my eyes were closing I could hear their urgent voices, talking on and on.

I woke much later than usual. Eman was already dressed in her outdoor clothes, and was standing in front of the broken piece of mirror I'd found behind a stall in the Champs Élysées, fixing her hijab in place. I sat up groggily.

'Where's Musa? And how come Fuad's sleeping so late?'

'He was out for ages trying to get a message to the Hooligans so they can show me the way to the hospital. He crashed out again when he got back. Musa's gone to the mosque. He says the imam knows someone whose sister's a cardiologist in Damascus. He's going to find out more about what's wrong with Nadia.'

I struggled to my feet, yawning and stretching.

'Why doesn't he just go to the hospital and ask Dr Jean?'

'He doesn't see why he should trust a foreign woman. She's a children's doctor, isn't she? What if she doesn't know much about hearts?'

She was halfway to the door, a couple of bulging plastic bags in her hands.

'Hang on a minute,' I said, ferreting around to find Baba's old trousers. 'I'll come with you. What's in all those bags, anyway?'

'Clean clothes for Ma, washing things, her phone. Don't come, Omar. Stay here and keep an eye on Fuad. He's really upset. I'd text you but my battery's dead.' There was a knock on the door. 'That'll be one of the boys. Tiger, probably. There's a bit of breakfast for you and the tea's still warm. See you later.'

And she was gone.

There wasn't much for breakfast, just a few flaps of stale bread. I took them and went to sit down again, moving quietly so as not to wake Fuad.

I looked round the cabin. I wasn't used to being in it without either Ma or Eman. It was almost as if I was seeing it for the first time. We'd done our best with it. We'd managed to acquire some cardboard boxes to use as rickety tables, the piece of mirror, and a broken chair that Eman had found at the school, which I'd patched up with a splint. The colourful blankets we'd brought with us from Syria, which we'd laid out on the mattresses, were the only cheerful things, but they, like everything else, were hard to keep clean and dry. I could never call the cabin 'home'. It was a cramped, mean sort of place and the only good thing about it was that there were no lunatics outside with their fingers on triggers, sitting in tanks or flying around in helicopters getting ready to blast us into bits of nothing.

'England,' Dr Jean had said. 'London.'

I tried to imagine it. I wasn't the same silly kid who'd dreamed of Norway with Rasoul. England was something that might actually happen. The thought of it was exciting, but scary, too.

They'll make me go back to school in England, I thought. *I'll be the stupid one again, the thicko, the ignorant lump.*

It would be even worse than any school I'd been to before because I wouldn't understand a word of English.

I tried out in my head the few words I knew.

Hello, my name is Omar. I am fifteen years old. Manchester United. What is your name?

I tried to remember my old selling rhymes.

'Antiques, nice and cheap . . .' I muttered.

It was no good. I'd forgotten the rest.

It won't happen, anyway, I told myself. *No one gets out of the camp and goes to Europe, bang, just like that.*

Fuad stirred and opened his eyes. He looked unseeingly at me for a moment, then sat up with a jerk.

'I fell asleep, Omar. Where's Ma?'

'At the hospital. With Nadia.'

'Did she die?'

'No. The doctor says she should get better, but she's

got something wrong with her heart. She's got to have an operation.'

I realized guiltily that I hadn't thought about Nadia much since I'd woken up.

Fuad nodded.

'I know about operations. Scorpion's ma had one in Daraa. It made her better. When's Ma coming back?'

'I don't know. Musa and Eman have gone to find out. We've got to wait for them.'

'Is there any breakfast?'

'A bit, I think. Go and look.'

He came back with some bread in his hand and sat down beside me.

'When will the operation be finished, Omar? Is Nadia coming home today?'

'No. The doctor says she has to get better first, and then go and have the operation in England. We're all going there too.'

His mouth flew open.

'You mean leave the camp?' There was panic in his eyes. 'We can't! It's safe here! No one's trying to kill us!'

'I don't think anyone's going to try and kill us in London.'

'How do you know? There might be a war going on there too. We can't leave here. Baba did, and he died.' Tears were spilling out of his eyes. 'I *like* it here, Omar! The Hooligans are here. And we're doing stories at school.'

I was shocked.

'You can't like it here, Fuad! It's awful! Think of how nice it was in our old house in Bosra.'

'I can't remember Bosra!' he screamed. 'You can't make me go! You'll all have to leave without me.'

I gave up.

'Don't worry about it,' I told him. 'I bet it doesn't happen after all.'

Musa and Eman came back together. He had gone to the hospital after the mosque. I'd been fretting with impatience. Was Nadia really going to be all right? Had I imagined the whole thing about going to England? Why were they taking so long?

When at last they came back I could see by their faces that the news wasn't good.

'She's holding her own,' Eman said, unbuttoning her coat, 'but she's not out of danger.'

My heart kicked with fright. I'd thought the worst was over.

'That English doctor, I don't know if she's any good,' Musa said. 'What does she know? She's not a heart specialist.'

I wasn't sure what to think. I'd trusted Dr Jean, but maybe Musa was right to be suspicious.

'Ma's feeling terribly guilty,' said Eman. 'She keeps saying she should have noticed that something was wrong. She doesn't want to leave Nadia, but I persuaded her to come home this evening. I'm going to cook her a proper meal, then I'll go to the hospital for the night, so she can come back here and get some sleep.'

'Did you see her? Nadia, I mean?' I asked.

'Only through the door. They wouldn't let us go near. She looked so tiny, Omar, with tubes sticking out of her little arm and . . .'

She broke off and wiped her eyes. I suddenly couldn't bear to stay in the cabin any longer.

'I'll fetch the bread ration,' I said. 'Come on, Fuad. I'll drop you off at school.'

The day passed horribly slowly. I did my usual chores, filling the jerrycans with water, queuing up for bread, and fetching our weekly ration of lentils, rice and pasta from the distribution centre.

I came back to the cabin at last, loaded down with bags, to find that Ma had come in before me. She and Musa were standing face-to-face in the middle of the cabin and I could tell that I'd burst right into the middle of a furious row.

'It's not right for us to run away to England like a bunch of cowards,' Musa was shouting. 'We ought to be helping the revolution in Syria! We should be trying to get home!'

'What home?' snapped Ma. 'There *is* no home! Haven't you seen what they've done to Daraa? And Bosra? Don't you *want* Nadia to have a life-saving operation? Don't you *care* about your sister?'

A red flush spread over Musa's cheeks.

'Of course I do! But what do you know about this English woman doctor? If she's so good at her job, what's she doing here in Za'atari? I don't trust her.'

'So what do you propose to do?' Ma's hands were on her hips and her head was thrust forward. 'Plunge straight back into the war and travel all the way up to the children's hospital in Damascus? We'd never get that far alive.'

'We should wait here,' Musa said. 'We ought to get a second opinion anyway. I'll see what I can find out on the internet. Nadia can't travel until she's well enough. It gives us time to think out other options. We've still got Eman's necklace, don't forget. It should be enough to pay for a surgeon. Don't worry, Ma. I'll decide what to do.'

'No!' exploded Ma. 'You won't decide anything! I've had enough – do you hear? – of the men in this family making decisions to suit themselves. If Dr Jean can get us to London, one of the best children's surgeons in the world will have the chance to save your little sister's life. And your other sister! Have you thought about her? *We* haven't got her necklace. It belongs to Eman. *She's* the one who'll decide what to do with it.'

I was standing stock-still with one shoe off and one shoe on, too stunned to move. I could see that Musa was shocked, too.

'Of course I want what's best for the girls,' he began. 'But in England we'd just be a bunch of refugees, living on charity. You know what the British say about Arabs and Muslims? They think we're all crazy terrorists. Think about it, Ma! We're Syrians! We need to stay close to our country. We should be too proud to—'

'Proud?' Ma interrupted furiously. 'You think being here should make us proud? Where do you think this cabin came from? Charity! Where did Omar get today's bread ration from?'

They both swivelled round to face me. I put my hands up and stepped back, nearly tripping over my discarded shoe.

'Charity!' Ma almost shouted. 'Anyway, it's too late, Musa. I've asked Dr Jean to go ahead. She's contacted UNHCR. They're asking for asylum seekers' visas for us. She's told them it's urgent. And before you say any more rude things about foreign women doctors, one of the nurses told me more about Dr Jean. She's a famous children's specialist who's working in this camp for *charity*.'

She stopped.

Musa said nothing. At last he shrugged and turned away.

Ma breathed out. She had won. I could see her deflating slowly, like a balloon when the air comes out of it. And I realized that I'd just witnessed a massive turning point in our family. Musa had been toppled off the throne he'd only just inherited, and Ma had taken control.

*

The weeks that followed were the strangest of all our time in Jordan. Eman and Ma took turns to be with Nadia in the hospital. She was getting better, but too slowly to travel for a while yet. I felt nervous every time I went to see her. I couldn't play with her, like I usually did, because she was too weak, and if I pulled faces to make her laugh, she started coughing and I felt bad. Musa was better with her. He sat by her bed for hours and told her stories, not minding if she fell asleep in the middle.

Dr Jean had started a process that sometimes scared me stiff, and sometimes filled me with excitement. Sometimes we thought we'd be on a plane to London in a couple of days' time, and the next day there'd be a hitch and it looked as if we'd be stuck in Za'atari forever.

The day Nadia came out of hospital was the best we'd ever had in Za'atari. We all went to fetch her. Ma held her as carefully as if she was made of china. Eman and I walked on each side, carrying Ma's bag and Nadia's clothes, with Musa and Fuad following on behind. It hadn't rained for a while and the mud had started to harden. The weather was warming up. Soon the floods and slime would be gone, and clouds of dust would swirl about the blistering desert.

The nurses and Dr Jean all came out to say goodbye to Nadia. They'd become fond of her while she'd been in the hospital. Musa stepped forward when we were ready to go. He swallowed hard, and said as clearly as he could, 'On behalf of my mother and my family, I want to thank you all very much for taking such good care of my sister . . .'

Before he'd quite finished, Ma dashed forward and flung her arms round Dr Jean's neck, and they stood there laughing and crying together.

When we got back to the cabin, our neighbours were waiting for us, along with Um Ali, who'd somehow managed to get hold of a cake. They crowded round Nadia, petting her, and for a moment I actually felt sorry that we were going to leave Za'atari camp. I actually felt as if we belonged.

Our visas came through the next day, and then our air tickets came too. There were seven days until our departure, then six, then five. There was no need to worry about packing. We had almost nothing to take with us. But there were still things I needed to think about, and top of the list was Riad.

He'd burst into tears when I'd told him I was leaving.

'You can't go! You can't leave me!' he gasped out, between heaving sobs.

He took to following me round like a dog. It was exasperating, but sort of touching, too. I kept trying to think of how I could help him, but I couldn't come up with a single idea. But the day before we were due to leave, Riad found a way to help himself.

I was on my way down the Champs Élysées to see if I could persuade the new owner of Abu Radwan's shop to charge our mobiles along with Musa's laptop. Riad, as usual, was sticking to me as close as a shadow. But suddenly he darted off round a corner. I grabbed his collar just in time before he disappeared into the maze of cabins.

'Where do you think you're going?'

'I'm hiding! I can't go past that shop. The man – he'll see me.'

'So?'

'So I don't want him to.'

He was looking guilty. I frowned.

'You stole from him, didn't you?'

He nodded reluctantly.

I gave him a shake. 'Riad, you've got to stop being scared. You're a reformed character now, remember? You've turned over a new leaf. Made a fresh start.'

'Yes, but Omar – he doesn't know that, does he?'

'How many shops along here have you got to avoid?'

'One or two. Three or four. Quite a lot, actually. Most of them never caught me. He did, though.'

'You can't go on hiding from people forever. You'll have to sort it out.'

'How can I? If he catches me, he'll beat me up.'

'No he won't. Not if you do it right.'

'What do you want me to do, then?'

I looked down into his thin, anxious face and wanted to kick myself. Why had I saddled myself with this dreadful child? Now he was looking at me like a hopeful dog.

'OK, Riad. Listen. Here are two things I'm going to say to you that you're never going to forget.'

He nodded, his face serious.

'Honesty is the best policy. That's number one. It means you don't lie or steal or cheat. Especially if you're a businessman. Say it after me: "Honesty is the best . . ." Go on.'

'Honesty is the best pol- pol— what?'

'Policy. It means the best way of doing things.'

'All right. What's the other thing?'

'If you've done something wrong, or made a mistake, you have to put it right.'

He took a step backwards.

'You mean . . . ?'

'Yes, I do mean. You've got to go and say sorry to that man.'

He was poised to bolt. I took a firm grip on his arm.

'I can't, Omar! He'll kill me!'

I put on my sternest look.

'What did you steal?'

'Hair slides for my sisters. And a couple of other things.'

I shook my head sorrowfully.

'You really are an idiot, Riad. You committed a crime for the sake of a few cheap hair slides?'

He looked indignant.

'It wasn't a *crime*, Omar. And they were nice.'

'Stealing *is* a crime. People who steal are thieves. You

were a thief. Right. We start from here.' I fished into my pocket, brought out a few of my precious coins, and put them into Riad's grubby hand. Then I gave him a little push.

'Go on.'

'Go on and what?'

'Go and confess what you did to that man and say sorry and give him the money.'

I had to grab him again or he'd have been off and away.

'No!' he squealed. 'You go and talk to him!'

I let him go and held my hands up.

'I'm not going to do that, Riad. And I can't make you. If you want to grow up to be a good person, you've got to do it yourself.'

He was looking down at his filthy bare toes as they squirmed around in his plastic flip-flops.

'What do I have to say?'

'Work it out for yourself! Go on. I'll be right behind you.'

I had to admire Riad at that point, I must admit. He squared his shoulders, puffed out his thin chest and trod resolutely up to the front of the shop. The owner turned round, and I saw his face for the first time. He was big and ugly and looked terrifying. He was setting out some bottles of nail varnish among the combs and lotions and fancy hijab pins on his counter.

'Please, sir,' Riad began nervously.

The man looked down at him.

'You!' he barked furiously. 'Back again, you little thief? You touch one thing in this shop and I'll tear your head off!'

Riad flinched, but held his ground.

'Please sir, I've – I've come to say sorry and – and pay for what I took.'

The man snorted.

'This is a trick, isn't it? How can you pay me for all the cream and shampoos and lipsticks—'

'Those weren't me,' said Riad. 'It was the others in the Hooligans.'

'The who?'

'I only took three hair slides, for my little sisters, and a nail file and a plastic rose for my ma.' He held my coins out with a trembling hand. The man took them reluctantly, checked them over and put them in his pocket.

'Enough . . . just,' he said grudgingly. 'Why are you doing this, anyway?'

'I'm doing it,' Riad said carefully, 'because honesty is the best pol- pol—'

'Policy,' I prompted him.

The man turned his glare on me.

'Don't I know you?'

'I've been working with Abu Radwan,' I said. 'He's been training me to be an electrician.'

He nodded, and I could see that his glare wasn't as frightening as I'd thought.

'Abu Radwan's a good man. I hear he's leaving.'

'Yes,' I said. 'And so am I. With my family. Any day now.'

He looked puzzled.

'What's this boy to you, then?'

'He's my cousin,' Riad said proudly, before I could answer.

I nudged him.

'Honesty, Riad, remember?'

'I know you're not really my cousin, Omar, but I wish you were. I really, really wish you weren't going away.'

The shopkeeper was losing interest in us.

'I'm helping him,' I said hastily, 'because he's a good lad at heart, and his dad's dead, and his ma can't cope, and he's got three little sisters.'

'Same as thousands of others in this camp,' the man said, unimpressed.

He was tearing open a box of children's jewellery and was starting to set the pieces out on the counter.

Riad watched with a critical eye.

'If you put those little pink bracelets in the front,' he said, 'the smallest girls will be able to see, and pester their mums to buy them.'

The man gave him a sharp look.

'You like these sorts of thing, do you?'

Riad looked wistful.

'Yes. I love pretty things. You've got some nice stuff here.'

The man scowled again.

'Can't sell it though, can I? No one's got any money.'

I could almost read the thoughts revolving round in Riad's head.

'It's not just the money, sir,' he said. 'Women like my mum, with little kids, they can't easily get to the Champs Élysées. But if you'll let me make up a box with a few nice things in it, and sell them to me for a really good price, I'll go round the cabins up our way and . . . and there'll be a bit of profit for you and me as well.'

I could hardly stop myself from bursting out laughing.

'Riad, where on earth will you get the money from to buy a box of stuff? You haven't got a cent.'

'He'll steal it,' growled the shopkeeper. 'Once a thief . . .'

'I won't,' Riad said earnestly. 'I'm a reformed character. I've turned over a new leaf and I'm making a fresh start.'

A muscle twitched in the man's cheek.

'And did you hear what your *not*-cousin said? If you don't steal the money, where will you get it from?'

Riad turned a blazing smile on me.

'I'm going to borrow it from Omar.'

I'd seen that one coming.

'And when do you propose to pay me back?' I asked.

'Not yet. I can't yet. But I will one day, Omar, I swear it. I'm going to save and save what I don't have to give to Ma, and when we go home to Syria I'm going to have a shop full of beautiful ladies' things like this one, and I'll be able to buy a house and look after Ma always.'

The breath caught in my throat. I recognized the dream in his eyes. I was looking at my younger self, the boy who had built castles in the air on packs of flimsy postcards. Riad would never make more than a few cents from his sales round the cabins, but who was I to stop him trying?

'All right,' I said gruffly. 'I'll do it on one condition. You've got to go to school and learn how to read and write and do your sums. Now, how much do you reckon you'll need?'

When I got back to the cabin, I found Musa there on his own.

'Ma's taken Nadia to the mosque,' he said. 'Eman's gone to pick Fuad up from school. Did you get my laptop charged?'

'Yes. Cost me a fortune. Everyone round here seems to think I'm a millionaire. When are you going to pay me back?'

He flashed me a smile.

'When I'm a professor of political science at Oxford University.'

'In your dreams, loser.'

He shrugged.

'It's all we've got now, isn't it? Dreams.'

There were voices outside. Eman was back.

'Musa!' she called out. 'Come outside. The Hooligans want to talk to you.'

Fuad came into the cabin, clutching a bunch of papers.

'Miss gave me all my drawings to take to England,' he said proudly. 'Look, Omar.'

I picked up the first one. It showed a tank with a streak of yellow light coming out of the barrel and people lying in front of it in pools of red.

'When did you do this?' I asked him.

'When we first came, I think. Look, I did this one yesterday. Miss said it was really good.'

I held his picture out, trying to make sense of it.

'That's an aeroplane, is it?'

'Of course it is! Can't you see the wings?'

'And those people inside the windows? Are they us?'

'Yes, silly.'

'And what's that horse doing in the corner?'

'It's because I like horses. And cats. And rabbits.'

I handed it back to him.

'They're very good, Fuad.'

'Do you think children are allowed to draw pictures in school in England?' he asked, looking anxious.

Why does everyone keep asking me questions I can't answer? I thought.

Aloud, I said, 'You bet, Fuad. With felt tip pens and everything.'

Outside, I could hear Cobra's high-pitched voice shouting, 'Tell us a story, Musa!'

Fuad dropped his pictures and ran to the door. He left it open. I could see Musa settling himself on the step outside, and the Hooligans squatting in a ring round him. Fuad squirmed in between Lion and Scorpion.

'Once upon a time,' began Musa, 'there was this incredibly handsome prince who had cerebral palsy, and who spoke in a kind of interesting way that only special people could understand.'

'That's not a story!' called out Wolf. 'That's you. Tell us a proper one.'

'All right. Once upon a time there was a group of extremely fierce and dangerous Hooligans who decided to do great deeds in the world. There was a Tiger, a Wolf, a Lion—'

'A Cobra!' piped up Cobra.

Musa wagged a finger at him.

'Don't interrupt.'

The boys wriggled happily, then settled down with their mouths open, as the story got under way.

We had a strange last meal in an almost empty cabin. Ma had given away all our remaining supplies of food to Um Riad, along with the pans, plates, cutlery, bucket, water cans, heater and stove the UN had supplied us with. But our neighbours had brought in so many dishes for us that our supper that night was the best we'd had since we'd arrived in the camp.

We had to be at the main gate by five o'clock in the morning to be on the transport to the airport in Amman before half past seven. Our few bags were packed, and our clothes, which were as clean as Ma and Eman could make them, were ready to put on.

'Best try to get some sleep,' yawned Ma, settling down with Nadia in the crook of her arm. 'I've set the alarm on my phone for four.'

I lay down and pulled a blanket over me. I couldn't sleep but lay watching, through the cabin's small high window, the clouds that were drifting across the face of the moon. On the next mattress Musa was tossing and turning.

'Are you awake?' I whispered, when I'd given up all hope of going to sleep.

'Of course I am.'

'How long does the flight to London take? Do you know?'

'About five hours.'

'So that means – let me see – in eleven hours we'll be in London?'

'Well done, genius.'

We were silent for a while.

'Musa,' I said at last, 'do you still think that we're running away from our duty by going to Britain?'

'Of course we're running away. But it's too late now. We've got to go for Nadia's sake, anyway. I see that now.'

There was a rustle from the far side of the cabin. In the faint moonlight, I could see Eman sitting up.

'What are you two whispering about?'

I sat up too.

'We can't sleep.'

'Neither can I.'

'Come over here, then.'

I made room for her and Musa on my mattress, and we sat side-by-side, hugging our knees.

'Musa, I'd have sold my necklace if we'd had to get an operation for Nadia here. You know that, don't you?' said Eman.

'Of course I do. But Ma was right. It's yours.'

'And don't think, brother dear, that you and Ma are going to marry me off to the first Syrian man you meet in London.'

'How did you guess?' said Musa. 'It's my sole purpose in life to get rid of you.'

She gave him a nudge that nearly toppled him over. I had to haul him up again.

'At least there'll be boys queuing up to marry you,' he said. 'Let's face it, I'll never find a girl who'll look at me.'

'Don't you believe it,' I said, a bit too heartily. 'Clever guy like you. They'll—'

'Shut up, Omar,' he said bitterly.

Nadia coughed. Ma half woke, murmured something and pulled her closer.

'Are you scared?' whispered Eman. 'I am.'

'Terrified,' said Musa.

'I feel as if I'm looking over the edge of a cliff,'

I said, 'and I can't see the bottom.'

The dark cloud that had been covering the sky moved away and moonlight flooded into the cabin.

'What's the time?' I asked.

Eman angled her wrist to the light to look.

'Five to four. Time to get up. This is it.'

She reached out and grasped my hand. I put out my other one to take hold of Musa's.

'Do you think we'll be all right in Britain?' I whispered. 'Do you think they'll like us?'

They didn't answer.

ACKNOWLEDGEMENTS

I couldn't have begun to write this book without the encouragement and support of many people in Jordan, both in Amman and in the refugee camps at Za'atari and Azraq on the Syrian border. Many people in Britain have helped me along the way too.

In Jordan: Abu Ibrahim, Um Ibrahim and their lively family, especially Hannan, Ibrahim and Mohammed; Georgie Hett, who introduced me to the Abu Ibrahim family and answered many of my questions; Maher Alatef, who told me about his early life as a schoolboy postcard seller in Palmyra; Ahmed the taxi driver, who let me into the secrets of his rhyming sales techniques; Laura Marshall, who facilitated my workshops in Za'atari and Azraq refugee camps; John Cutliffe, who looked after me all the way to Azraq, where we visited a desert school; Muna Abdul Quran, who answered so many of my questions and translated for me during my workshops in the camps; and the many courageous teachers and youth leaders that I met in the camps, who are working hard, against severe odds, to try to create a future for their families and the school children in their care.

In Britain: Dr Marwa Mouazzen, who gave me many tips and pointers on life in Syria; Peter Coleridge, an expert in disability and the Middle East; Dr Jean Bowyer, who has worked with sick children in many parts of the Middle East; David McDowall, a historian with a wide knowledge of Middle Eastern history and politics, and, as always, Jane Fior, for her wise advice and friendship.

A LETTER FROM THE AUTHOR

Welcome to Nowhere is a story about a boy and his family living through the devastating war in Syria. Like all wars, it has brought about terrible suffering and the massive destruction of towns and cities, and it has caused millions of people to flee their homes and find safety in other countries. It's the cruellest kind of conflict too – a civil war, which means that people in the same country are fighting each other, neighbour against neighbour, the government against some of its own people.

Some years ago, I lived in Lebanon during another shattering civil war in which many parts of the cities were destroyed and many people died. I saw at first hand how lives were disrupted and families lived in fear.

As the situation became worse and worse in Syria, and desperate refugees risked their lives crossing the sea to find safety in Europe, I felt, like so many other people, that I had to do something. The numbers of people seemed overwhelming, and their suffering too much to take in. I wanted to look beyond the long lines of refugees into the faces of individuals, to begin to understand how it was for them.

So when I was invited to Jordan to run some writing workshops with teachers and youth trainers in two Syrian refugee camps, Za'atari and Azraq, I accepted at once. The participants, who had all had to leave their homes in Syria, welcomed me warmly and I was deeply touched by their courage and endurance. As I talked to them, and met other people from Syria living in circumstances of great difficulty outside the camps, I asked what I could do to help. They encouraged me to write their story, and Omar and his family began to crystallize in my mind. Soon they became real people to me and I began to care deeply about them.

If you have read to the end of the story you might be wondering what will happen next to Omar, Musa and Eman. How will they get on in their new life in Britain? Will people welcome them? Will they be accepted in their new schools? Will they be helped to settle in and follow their dreams?

The answer to those questions lies with you.

With best wishes

Elizabeth Laird

WHAT CAN YOU DO TO HELP?

While I was in Jordan, I saw at first hand the work of the big aid agencies. They do a great job, and are well worth supporting. But I also met an inspiring group of people who work with a network of small local charities called *Helping Refugees in Jordan*. They can plug the gaps and respond quickly and effectively to the needs of Syrian refugees as they arise.

This initiative has been working to set up a school for refugee children who have no other chance of education. It's called the **Hope School**. So far, seventy-five children are getting the chance of a lifetime at the school. As you can imagine, they need all the things that you have in your school: books, desks, paper and pencils, pictures, whiteboards and equipment of all kinds, not to mention money to pay the teachers, who are all refugees themselves. They are supported in the UK by the Mandala Trust [Registered Charity No. 1096861]. To assist in their work with the Hope School, and other educational projects, Pan Macmillan will be making a donation of fifty pence for every hardback copy of *Welcome to Nowhere* sold in the UK, ahead of the paperback publication in July 2017.

If you would like know more, look at my website,

www.elizabethlaird.co.uk, and follow the link to the Hope School. You'll find the latest news of how the children are getting on and what their needs are. You'll also find suggestions for how you could raise money for the school yourselves, and where to send it to, so that you can directly help some of those children like Omar, Musa, Eman and Fuad whose lives have been so changed by the war.

ABOUT THE AUTHOR

Elizabeth Laird is the multi-award-winning author of several much-loved children's books, including *The Garbage King*, *Red Sky in the Morning*, *The Prince Who Walked with Lions* and *The Fastest Boy in the World*. She has been shortlisted for the prestigious CILIP Carnegie Medal six times. Having lived all over the world, Elizabeth lives in Britain now, but still likes to travel as much as she can.

In November 2015, Elizabeth visited and volunteered in two Syrian refugee camps in Jordan. The people she met there inspired her to write Omar's story in *Welcome to Nowhere*.

Oranges in No Man's Land

Elizabeth Laird

This was my chance. I slipped under the chain and bolted, running into no man's land as fast as my flip-flops would let me.

Ayesha lives in a battle-scarred building with her granny and her little brothers. Outside, a war is tearing the city apart – but Ayesha doesn't even know why the two sides are fighting.

Life gets even scarier when Granny falls ill, and Ayesha has no choice but bravely to embark on the dangerous journey across no man's land for medicine. Will she be able to find a doctor and make it back before it's too late?

'A tribute to the human spirit' TES